shades of style: book 3

Praise for Marilynn Griffith's writing:

"Marilynn Griffith is a fresh voice in Christian fiction. Her funny, breezy style is sure to take the market by storm!"

Tracey Bateman, author, *Leave It to Claire*
and the Mahoney Sisters suspense series

"From beginning to end, you can't help but see the hand of God ministering through Marilynn Griffith's work."

Vanessa Davis Griggs, author, *Promises Beyond Jordan*
and *Wings of Grace*

"Marilynn Griffith digs deep inside to write a novel about everyday people who love the Lord."

LaShaunda C. Hoffman, editor, *Shades of Romance* magazine

"With poetic description and compelling storytelling, Marilynn Griffith delights readers with every sentence."

Stephanie Perry Moore, author, *A Lova' Like No Otha'*,
Payton Sky series, and Carmen Browne series

"Looking for a sassy, engaging read that keeps you turning pages and recalling your faith? Look no further. Marilynn Griffith won't disappoint."

Stacy Hawkins Adams, author, *Speak to My Heart*

"Marilynn Griffith's writing makes the five senses come alive. Her writing makes you taste color, smell love, hear hearts, see purpose, and touch God's truth in every word and phrase. She is a master storyteller!"

Gail M. Hayes, author, *Daughters of the King*

Tangerine

Books by Marilynn Griffith

SHADES OF STYLE
Pink
Jade
Tangerine

Tangerine

Marilynn Griffith

Revell
Grand Rapids, Michigan

Published by Fleming H. Revell
a division of Baker Publishing Group
P.O. Box 6287, Grand Rapids, MI 49516-6287
www.revellbooks.com

Printed in the United States of America

            Library of Congress Cataloging-in-Publication Data
Griffith, Marilynn.
    Tangerine / Marilynn Griffith.
        p.   cm. — (Shades of style ; bk. 3)
    ISBN 10: 0-8007-3042-9 (pbk.)
    ISBN 978-0-8007-3042-0 (pbk.)
    1. Women fashion designers—Fiction. I. Title.
    PS3607.R54885T36 2006
    813′.6—dc22   2006029439

Scripture quotations are taken from the Third Millennium Bible, New Authorized
Version, copyright 1998. Used by permission of Deuel Enterprises, Inc., Gary,
SD 57237. All rights reserved.

For Shayla,
I miss you. I'll see you some day.
You made this book better. And me better too.

A Woman of Strength

A strong woman works out every day to keep her
body in shape . . .
A woman of strength kneels in prayer to keep her
soul in shape.
A strong woman isn't afraid of anything . . .
A woman of strength shows courage in the midst
of fear.
A strong woman won't let anyone get the best of
her . . .
A woman of strength gives her best to everyone.
A strong woman walks sure-footedly . . .
A woman of strength knows God will catch her
when she falls.
A strong woman wears the look of confidence on
her face . . .
A woman of strength wears grace from head to toe.
A strong woman has faith that she is strong enough
for the journey . . .
A woman of strength has faith that it is in the jour-
ney she will become strong.

Author Unknown

Prologue

"We're at a dead end." The lawyer leaned back in his chair and clicked his briefcase shut. To Jean Guerra, the plastic case looked like a piece of luggage, stuffed with her hopes and dreams. To this man, it meant something else—closing a case he'd probably given up on a long time ago. And there was nothing Jean could do about it. This man, the best in the business, everyone said, held her husband's future in his hands. After all the money and time she'd invested in gaining her husband's freedom, was this the end of the line? It couldn't be.

She smoothed her hands across a place mat at her kitchen table where they were sitting. Her nail traced the edge of a peach on the place mat. Jean's eyes followed her hand, but all she could see in her mind was her husband's face. "So, it's over? Just like that?"

The man shrugged his shoulders. As he'd said many times, he thought Jean should keep her money and move on with her life. He'd never come out and said he thought her husband Nigel was guilty of armed robbery as he'd been accused, but lately it certainly seemed as though he thought the verdict was deserved. "I suppose we could appeal again, to a different judge. I could file the paperwork on Monday to get things started but—"

"How much?" Jean wiped her hands across the mat in front of her. Then she grabbed the edges of the table, as much to brace herself for the reply, as to pull herself to her feet. The beautiful men's suits Jean had cut today, the beautiful people she'd been with, blurred across her mind. At work, she was part of that world. Untouchable. At home, there were lawyer bills and prison calls. Need.

"Five hundred would get things rolling," the man said, averting his eyes.

Jean fixed her weary gaze on him. If she was going through this again, he could at least look at her. For the five years Nigel had been in prison, Jean had gone from shock to advocacy. Fierce advocacy. Her husband hadn't robbed the liquor store. He never went near the place except to talk to some vets he knew from the war. When they'd returned from Saigon, people weren't proud. They were angry. Many of the vets got angry too and stayed that way. Nigel, who came back to his tailor shop job to find his services not needed, did odd jobs, sold fruit, and sought out the men who'd served in Vietnam.

Jean told her husband to stay away from the places where the vets hung out. "Go to the tailor shop. Let them see that you're okay. That you're ready to work anytime." Nigel only kissed her and shook his head, saying that he wasn't okay, that he couldn't be okay with so many men who'd served their country disappearing into the streets. So Nigel sought out the men he'd served with, praying with them, listening to their stories and telling his. What hurt Jean most was that he never asked what had happened to *her* in the army hospital where they'd met. Did her silence make him think that she wasn't hurting too? And now this, five hundred more dollars. Her daughter's birthday money.

The briefcase snapped a second time as the lawyer flipped the metal tabs closed. "Well, I'd better be going. You seem preoccupied. Give me a call when you decide."

Jean held up a hand for the lawyer to wait. Her husband's words during their last conversation replayed in her mind. "My time will come. God will get me out of here, just like he did for Joseph. Trust me. Trust God," he had said. She'd tried to trust her husband, but he seemed more concerned with converting the entire prison than getting home to his family. As for God, well, while she didn't begrudge her husband's belief, her own bullet-riddled faith wasn't going to just come together now even if she did say a prayer for her husband each night. No, trusting God—and man—had gotten Jean nothing but a cold bed and a bunch of bills. She was going to have to handle this herself.

"I have the money," Jean said.

The lawyer fumbled in his pockets, again not wanting to watch as Jean pulled her last dime from the jar on the counter. The money he required was almost exactly the amount she'd set aside for her daughter's *quinceañera*, the fifteenth birthday celebration traditional to their community. The amount was a pittance compared to what the other girls' families would spend, but after the household bills, the phone calls, Nigel's canteen, the bus trips and hotel stays upstate to visit him, the lawyers . . . There just wasn't much money left after all that. Jean's savings seemed to slip through her fingers. Like now.

She walked to the cabinet and dumped out a mug that read "#1 Dad." Had Jean subconsciously been planning to spend the money on her husband all along? The half-finished birthday gown she'd been going to work early and staying late to work on for her daughter said something different. For once, she'd wanted for something to be just about her daughter Monica. She extended the wad of bills to the lawyer. Maybe next time. "Here. Go ahead and start the appeal. Thanks for coming and explaining what's going on."

The lawyer paused, then closed his hand around the money. "No problem. I'll be in touch."

Jean sank back into the chair, overcome by weariness.

The man prepared to leave, then stopped and spoke again. "Look, you seem like a nice lady and you've paid me a lot of money. The years are passing. Maybe it's best if you just let your husband do his time. Maybe you need to think about moving on. I know that everyone wants to think the best of the people they love, but—"

Jean shot to her feet, sucking back her fury. "Nigel didn't do it." This wasn't the first time she'd heard this. Friends, neighbors, even family had said as much. Jean refused to believe it. "He couldn't have. He doesn't even drink. The only time he ever went to that liquor store was to be with his friends, VA vets who hung around there."

The man cleared his throat. "Exactly my point. Many of those men have been convicted of crimes since. A few days before, your husband was seen near—"

"Can you help us or not? If you can't, maybe I should take my money back." Her voice sounded steady, but inside, Jean's heart was quivering. Was the issue really Nigel's innocence? Or was it Nigel's faith that was on trial? She'd seen many men with crosses on their necks and Bibles in their pockets changed by the guns in their hands. She'd seen a side of herself during the war she hadn't thought existed. But Nigel had found something else. Someone else. Jesus. Had Jesus been bigger than that gun they said had Nigel's fingerprints

12

on it? She didn't know anymore. "Maybe we should forget the whole thing."

The man crossed his arms. It was obvious he knew Jean wouldn't make good on the threat. It'd be even harder to pull a new lawyer into Nigel's case now. He was the best and he knew it. "I'm going to go now. I'll file the paperwork. I'm sorry if I upset you. It's just that I've worked cases of inmates who were wrongly accused. Your husband doesn't fit the profile. He's too . . ."

"Joyful?" Jean said before turning her back to wipe a tear. Why did all of this have to hurt so much? Why did it have to be so hard? Five years and it hurt like yesterday. She turned back to face the lawyer. "What you see in my husband isn't guilt, sir. It's faith. Something you will probably never understand."

Jean spoke the words with conviction that she herself lacked. Despite the accusation in the man's tone, she knew her husband's Christianity was no jailhouse conversion. Nigel had found Jesus on a bloody battlefield in Saigon. A few miles away, Jean's faith had buckled under the weight of dead teenage boys and living needy men. Though she might not be found in church every week, she still believed in something. Her family. And she'd do whatever it took to keep it together.

"I'll be in touch." The lawyer headed for the door.

Jean's daughter entered as the man left, giving her mother a questioning look about the lawyer's presence before mumbling hello. Jean swallowed hard at the sight of Monica—red-rimmed eyes and dark curls tumbling into her face. Now she had to do this too, to tell her daughter there would be no big fancy birthday party for her, no big white dress. Tell her that, like always, Daddy needed their support.

Monica would pretend to understand, though she'd long since stopped trying to. The girl had done well with Nigel's incarceration the first few years, but once the teen years hit, she drifted a little farther away each day. Now Jean had to disappoint her . . . again. She opened her arms to her daughter. They both needed a hug. "Come here. I need to tell you something."

Her daughter's back straightened. Her curly hair fell forward into her eyes. Eyes so much like her father's. She was the best of both of them, this girl. Now her chest heaved with anger, her fists clenched in disappointment. She was the worst of both of them too.

"You don't need to tell me anything." Her eyes flashed. "I know what it means when that lawyer comes. Beans and rice. Always beans and rice, just like you like it."

Jean's arms dropped to her sides. Her daughter could be a little saucy at times, but not like this. This wasn't about money or Nigel. Monica was covering something. Something big. It would be a long night if she didn't get to the real problem.

"So, you in trouble too?"

Monica paused before answering. She stuffed her fists into the pockets of her jeans. "Not really. I just need for you to give me my birthday money. All that womanhood stuff is stupid anyway. If Daddy was here maybe . . . Anyway, can you just give me the money?" She leaned back on the door now, her elbows pressed against the dark wood.

Jean took a step back to the kitchen table and pulled out a chair to sit down. Suddenly, her husband, the lawyer, the money . . . none of it seemed important. Another question flashed in her brain like a neon light. What would her daughter need with half a grand? The truth came to her in images of long shirts and loose pants. It came and sucked her breath away.

"Oh," Jean said to no one in particular. She folded her hands in her lap.

Her daughter raked her hair back from her eyes, revealing a worried look. "Why did you say 'oh' like that? Just give me the money. I'm fine."

14

Jean let herself fall forward a little. "How far along are you, and why didn't you tell me?"

The girl went limp. She slid down to the floor and hugged her knees. "Miguel said it's not too late, that I can still get rid of it. But I don't know. Will God forgive me if I do that? It's a baby, right? That's what Daddy told me when Tanisha said she gave her baby up for abortion. He said that meant she killed it."

Jean was on her feet now, then on the floor beside her daughter. Guilt washed over her, the kind only mothers know. She'd been so worried about her daughter's grades, about making sure Monica spent time with her father so she wouldn't get into trouble like the other girls. She'd done all she could, but here they were. In a mess.

Tears wet through Jean's blouse. Her one goal had been to keep her family together. Somehow she'd torn it apart. "Monica, forget about the money and the boy. We can get through this, but we'll have to stick together."

"Okay." Her daughter sobbed into her neck. "But I'm scared."

Jean nodded but didn't answer out loud.

Me too, she thought, not wanting to add to her daughter's fear.

The ring of the phone broke their embrace. Jean reached for the receiver out of habit, always wanting to be there in case her husband called. Until now, anyway. Now everything had shifted. Changed. "Hello?"

After a short silence, an automated voice responded. "You are receiving a call from an inmate at—"

Jean hung up the phone and turned back to her daughter.

The girl wiped her eyes. "Who was that?"

"A wrong number," Jean said, staring straight ahead, bracing herself against the uncertainty of the choice she had just made. Numbing herself to the sacrifice of the love of her life.

15

1

Fifteen years later . . .

Fall came to New York like a Good Samaritan, blanketing the city with a generous wind. Clouds floated tall and wide, majestic like a grown man in a good suit. Jean Guerra lent her short hair to the cold, giving the wind a place to leave some of its goodness. Instead, the air blew past her face and brushed her lips like a kiss from God.

Hands buried in her coat pockets, Jean smiled at the thought of God's mouth upon hers. She cherished it like the memory of long-ago love and last night's dream of her husband's fingers lingering on her skin. Those days were gone, but these God-caresses came often now, reminding her to live. To love.

Jean had no problem with the living part, but the love thing slid sideways in her mind and escaped before she could grasp it. Even now, as November air fogged from her mouth, she remembered how good her

16

husband had always looked in a suit. Even at his trial, he'd looked regal, staring into her eyes as the judgment on their life came down. She could still hear the judge's words sometimes, at the edge of her mind when she least expected it—"Nigel Salvador, I now pronounce you guilty . . ." Nigel made the sign of the cross before they handcuffed him. He'd done the same thing when they came into their home and pulled him out of bed in the middle of the night. "Don't worry, Peach," he'd said, feigning a smile. "God willing, it will be all right."

God willing. Those words had rankled Jean then. They comforted her now. Nigel's prayers for her had finally come true this past year when Jean returned to the faith she'd once embraced. His hopes for their marriage had not. In those years, she'd spent her weekends upstate, her weekdays in red tape. Another lawyer. Another appeal. She was always the one fighting while he prayed, assuring Jean that freedom in Christ was enough. It wasn't enough then. Not for Jean and not for their daughter Monica.

When Monica spent her fifteenth birthday at a prenatal appointment instead of at the big party she'd planned, Jean had truly given up on God . . . and her husband. Now, looking up at the clouds forming a heavenly dress coat, Jean knew that neither of them had given up on her. In the past few months, she'd made a shaky peace with what had happened. Jean was thankful that she hadn't taken the advice of so many people and divorced her husband, but she accepted, even embraced, spending the rest of her life alone. It was just too late to get back what she'd lost. What they'd all lost.

He lost everything too. You abandoned him.

Such thoughts erected what remained of Jean's defenses. True enough, she'd left Nigel when he needed her most, and without meaning to, he'd done the same to her. She'd told him not to go out that night, and all the nights before, when he sat with the other vets and listened to their stories. He went anyway, forgetting that she'd been in Saigon with him too, that she'd also heard things, seen things, felt things . . . that she too needed his prayers, his touches. She sniffed away the cold. What did it matter now?

I will give back all that the locusts have eaten. ALL.

Jean pulled her coat tighter at her neck, looking from left to right. The women she worked with talked of this, of God speaking to them, but she wasn't so sure about it. What the clouds and the wind spoke were enough for her. And locusts? What did that have to do with anything? She pumped her arms, taut from incessant exercise and frequent dashes for the train, and ran away from the charitable fall and the suit made of clouds.

Away from the voice of God.

She slipped into work and ran down the hall, grateful to have avoided any co-workers. Was her mascara running? She could always blame the wind. She turned the knob and stepped into her office, only to be ambushed by her boss, Chenille.

"I have a surprise for you!" Chenille shouted, her outfit blurring like a blue watercolor painting in Jean's teary eyes.

Jean wiped her face quickly and assessed her friend and employer, with her curls piled atop her head and nacho cheese powder on her fingertips. Jean ground her teeth as she pulled off her coat. She hated surprises more than anything. Everyone she worked with knew this, but they were convinced she'd change her mind if they pulled off one great surprise. They were wrong. If she hadn't sent in her friend Lily Chau's clothes to *The Next Design Diva* show, Lily might still be around, instead of in her own home office designing clothes for her new line. If her old friend were still in the office, things like this "surprise" wouldn't happen. Lily knew Jean well enough to talk the others out of their crazy ideas.

She stared at her smiling employer and stifled a laugh of her own. The woman really meant well, she just didn't know Jean as well as she thought she did. *Does anybody really know me?* Jean wondered. She'd spent the last few years listening to the problems of her friends and co-workers, but there were many things about her life that she had never shared with them. Even Lily, whom she'd talked to daily when they worked together, had no clue that Jean was still married. More and more, Jean tried to bring it up when they talked, but Lily's juggling a grueling production schedule, coordinating care for her mother's Alzheimer's, and being a newlywed took up all her friend's time. Instead, Jean spent more and more time talking with Chenille, though sometimes, like now, she wondered if the woman heard a word she said.

"No surprises, please. Really," Jean said in a tone lower than her usual work voice. Though she'd been a tough cookie for the past several years, today she felt tired. Fragile. Jean's growing belief in Christ and the thoughts of her husband that followed had sapped some of her strength. Add to that, dealing with Chenille's husband's recurring cancer, trying to help with Lily's old workload, and keeping an eye on a boy-crazy granddaughter, and Jean was worn out. She'd even started catching naps during the daily creative hour prescribed by her employer.

People said that fifty was the new thirty, and in some ways Jean agreed, but at other times it was just plain fifty, and she felt it. Today was one of those days, despite the glorious cloud cover she'd viewed on her way in. And now Chenille had a surprise. Jean shook her head. "What is it? Just spit it out so I can hurry up and get over it. We've got a lot of work to do today."

Chenille stepped toward her with another one of those grins Jean had once hated. It was still a silly expression, but it'd sort of grown on her. She tried to fight back the smile forming on her own face, this time to no avail. Jean shook her head. "Oh boy. This is going to be a doozy."

Her boss nodded, looking like she knew the best-kept secret in New York. "You know how you've been talking about going back into menswear design?"

Jean covered her mouth. Had she made her intentions that evident? Had a comment here and there been so obvious? Or was it inquiries Chenille had received about her from Yves Saint Laurent? At first, Jean had flatly refused to even consider another job, but during the past year, she'd seen how God had used her time at Garments of Praise. Her job had been a time of healing and maybe even a place of hiding, if she was honest. It wasn't until Jean had appeared on Lily's winning episode of *The Next Design Diva* that word had gotten out where she was working. Everyone had contacted her, it seemed.

Everyone but Nigel.

"I do miss menswear, Chenille, but don't worry. I'm not leaving you hanging. I know things are tight with Lily gone. I'm not worrying about that right now. Maybe I'd do a side project if I found the right one, but—"

"How does designing a business casual collection for Reebok sound?" Chenille said, then shrugged apologetically. "That didn't come out quite right. I meant to drag that out some more. Create more suspense. I just couldn't hold it in anymore."

Jean couldn't hold it in either. The information went straight to her brain. Only one word came to mind.

Perfect.

Too perfect. There had to be a catch. She leaned against her desk, thankful that Chenille had been waiting in her office instead of at the reception desk. She needed some energy to process this. She scanned the exercise equipment lining the far wall of her office and kicked off her pumps. A few push-ups would do nicely.

Chenille rolled her eyes. "Can you stop with the exercise already? Someone's coming from Reebok, and you're going to be all sweaty."

She stopped all right, dropping flat on her belly. "Who?"

"I don't have a name yet. This all happened pretty fast. I've been getting emails and faxes all weekend."

Jean took a deep breath. This was the kind of stuff she hoped would happen to the younger women around the place, that they'd have a chance to expand their skills, to try new things. In her mind, Jean had seen everything in fashion design. Nothing seemed fresh anymore. Except this. It seemed too good. Too much. "How did this happen?"

Chenille reached down to pull her up, supplying the details in a stream of speech only she could provide so quickly. "Remember the suits you sketched for the Knicks when they wanted a team suit? I still can't believe how well those turned out. I'm still getting thank-you notes from the team owners. I'd heard you were great with menswear, but to see it—"

"Thanks." Jean nodded in agreement, not about her own ability, but about how well the suits had turned out. That project had been what whetted her appetite for menswear design again. On short notice, the management of the New York Knicks had chosen to have all the players have a team suit to comply with the NBA dress code. Others had bid on the account, but Jean's designs had blown the competition out of the water.

"Reebok had already worked with us on Raya's Flexability sportswear line, so they were happy to work with us again on

21

a retail line. We got blessed, woman. It's that simple." Chenille crossed her arms, satisfied with her pronouncement.

Far from satisfied, Jean flung her arms wide. This was crazy. "Okay, boss lady. Slow down. Give me details. Who's coming from Reebok? The lady we worked with on the Flexability line? She's good, but all sportswear. I'd need someone with menswear experience."

Chenille held a finger up to her lips. "Shhh. As I was trying to explain, Reebok has found someone new. He tailors for some of the guys in the NBA and outfits professional soccer teams in Mexico and LA. No design house experience, but they say the guy's a natural."

Goose bumps pimpled Jean's flesh. She'd heard that one before. "He's probably a natural-born fool. No matter. I'll do a consult with them later. This is a retail collection, though? No uniforms?"

Chenille laughed. To stay afloat at the beginning, Garments of Praise had made everything from track suits to choir robes. Even a wedding dress. Now they were starting to become known for sportswear. "This is definitely a retail line. Coordinates. Shirts. Ties. Jackets. It's called Suiting Up. There will be a blazer for each NBA team. Like throwback jerseys but dressed up. You get it?"

She did. Jean shooed her boss away from her desk. She grabbed her sketchbook and began scribbling notes. Maybe perfect existed after all. She couldn't have thought up a better angle if she'd done it herself. Pages flipped as she scribbled furiously with Chenille leaning over her, trying to see. Jean kept going, too taken in to worry about her boss looking on. "This is brilliant, Chenille. Truly. Who came up with this idea anyway?"

"I did." A man's voice, one Jean heard in her dreams, sounded at the door.

Both women turned to the doorway, where a man wearing a winter white wool suit rested his head against the door's frame. His long, brown fingers rested on the doorknob. Time swept against his temples in tiny streaks of gray. Dimples set off both cheeks as if holding his handsome face in place.

Nigel's face.

Jean felt the drawing pad drop from her fingers. Her drawing pencil fell too and jabbed into her suede boot as it landed.

It can't be . . .

Chenille found her voice. "You must be from Reebok. So sorry we weren't at the desk to meet you. We lost track of the time."

In what seemed like one stride, the man entered the room and knelt in front of Jean, gathering her pad and pencil. "No problem. It happens," he said softly in a forgiving voice.

Jean's boss extended her hand. "I'm Chenille Rizzo, the owner of Garments of Praise. And this is Jean. She's the one who'll be working with you on the—" At the sight of Jean's mascara-veined face, she stopped short, looking confused and a little frustrated.

I should explain, Jean thought. But she didn't. She couldn't. All she could do was look at him. Although she was already crying, Jean closed her eyes anyway, knowing that if she didn't, she might lean down and dig her fingers into Nigel's hair, and . . .

Somehow the thought filtered through that Chenille must be terribly confused, like someone watching a foreign film with no subtexts. Jean didn't even try to clue her in. No words that made sense came to mind.

Nigel rose slowly, moving so close that the fabric of his suit brushed against Jean's hands. "It's good to meet you, Chenille. I'm glad to be here. As for Ms. *Jean*, she and I have met before." Nigel paused and took a long look at his wife. "Hello,

23

Peach. It's good to see you again," he said before leaning in and kissing her on the mouth as though he'd just come home from an errand. As though he'd never been gone.

Still unable to speak or think, Jean managed to kiss him back. When she reached out to smooth the gray at his temples, he pulled away.

"My apologies," he said, turning to Chenille. "Like I said, we know each other."

Both shocked and amused, Chenille cleared her throat. "So I see," she said, more question than statement. Usually Jean teased each of the women on staff about their relationships. This time, the joke seemed to fall squarely on Jean and roll her right over.

Nigel smiled. "Forgive me. It's just been a long time since I've seen Mrs. . . ."

"Guerra," Jean answered softly.

A dark cloud of hurt seemed to pass through his eyes. Or had Jean imagined it? His quick and sincere smile made her wonder. "Yes, Ms. Guerra. Anyway, I didn't mean to be so forward. Please do forgive me." He extended a hand to Chenille, who shook it quickly.

Jean swallowed hard, watching as they shook hands. She wondered if her breathing sounded as loud to them as it did in her head. Right now, breathing in and out seemed a big job. As her eyes snagged on Nigel's ring finger, for a moment she forgot to exhale. Her throat tightened at the sight of the gold band on his finger. It was the one they'd bought from a pawn shop before taking part in a group ceremony on the base where they landed after the war. He was still wearing his ring, after all this time. The mate to that ring hung on a chain inside Jean's blouse.

As he released her boss's hand, Nigel eyed Jean carefully. His mouth was smiling, but a deep crimson spread across the tops of his ears, giving him away. Their daughter Monica did the same thing when she was angry. Was he mad because Jean hadn't introduced him to Chenille as her husband? Because she went by her maiden name? Or was he simply as overwhelmed as she was by their reunion? Nigel was still hard to read. Some things never changed.

The sound of the door clanging against the wall cut through Jean's thoughts as a woman in a red suit and matching glasses tumbled into the room. "There you are, Nigel!" she half screamed, moving toward them like a bright column of hips and hair. She looked eerily similar to what Jean had looked like before she'd started her workout program. Though she'd worked hard to lose her hips, seeing them on someone else didn't sit too well with her.

Nigel cleared his throat. "Hey, Carmen. I didn't hear from you last night, so I just came on down myself—"

"No problem." The woman adjusted the Reebok folder she was holding and extended her hand. "You must be Chenille."

Jean shook her head before taking the woman's hand, careful to avoid the tips of her ruby-colored acrylic nails. "No, I'm Jean. This is Chenille."

The woman covered quickly. "Of course. I think I've even seen you in *W*. Didn't someone from here win that reality show? Yes, I remember. Nigel was looking at you though, Jean, so I thought you must have been the boss." Carmen released Jean's hand and grasped Nigel's.

Jean wondered if the woman could see the blood draining from her face. She certainly felt it. "Nice . . . nice to meet you anyway. I'm Jean Guerra, and I'll be working with Nigel on the project. Will you be working with us too?"

The woman froze, then looked at Nigel. "Jean Guerra?" She said the name slowly, in disbelief. She turned to Nigel. "Is this her? Your wife?"

His gaze dropped to the floor, but not before he nodded.

Carmen lunged toward Jean and swallowed her in a hug. "I'm so glad to meet you. He's been looking all over for you. I told him you'd probably gone back to your maiden name, but you know men . . . Anyway, this is great. Once you finally sign those divorce papers, maybe I can get this guy to accept my marriage proposal."

Jean tried to breathe, to scream, but the woman's cologne and sea of hair seemed to smother her. She stood still, wondering how long it would take her to suffocate. Just as quickly as she'd come, the woman moved away, leaving Jean to take a deep breath and say a quick prayer. *Nothing has changed*, she'd thought when Nigel kissed her, and yet, everything had changed too. Divorce papers? In all their time apart, she'd never filed any. Now looking at this curvy, crazy woman, she wondered if what she and Nigel had was really a marriage. Or was it just a legal fact? Her heart said it was more, but her head knew better. He had someone new.

Lord, sometimes there's just no going back.

Though obviously shocked herself, Chenille held Jean upright as she started to lean. The smile she painted on indicated an upcoming attempt at humor.

Jean braced herself for what her boss would say . . . and for what Nigel would leave unsaid.

Chenille put an arm around Jean. "Well, it's nice to meet both of you. You can head down to the conference room and wait for us. I think you've accomplished what we've been trying to do around here for years. You've finally surprised Miss Jean."

You can say that again.

Jean closed her eyes, not wanting to see Nigel's reaction and glad she couldn't see her own. If she looked anything like she felt, it wasn't good.

2

"It's so good to see you." Nigel hugged his old friend Doug LaCroix and took a long look at the doctor he remembered from Vietnam. The man who'd been engaged to Jean when Nigel met her.

Doug laughed. The lines at the corners of his eyes streaked outward like a sunburst. "It's great to see you too, man. I'm sorry I lost track of you. I should have come up and visited you more—"

Nigel shook his head. "Don't worry about it. It's over."

"Is it?" Doug asked, his voice resonating with concern. "From what I hear about this Carmen woman trying to marry you—"

"I didn't know that Carmen was coming. Or that Jean would be there. Carmen shouldn't have said what she said. I don't even know if Jean wants me anyway. I prayed so long to find her, and now . . . well, it's a mess."

A waitress interrupted and motioned them to a table. Both men sat quietly, thinking through the last words spoken as she rattled off the daily specials. Nigel squeezed lemon into the glass of water in front of him and ordered a Cobb salad. His friend ordered the same.

"I shouldn't have said that thing about upstate. That wasn't funny," Doug said as soon as the waitress retreated.

"It's okay. You should have said it. Hey, time is short. We're old. No use beating around the bush."

"Speak for yourself, guy. I'm a newlywed," Doug countered with a smile, adding lemon to his water also.

"So I see." Nigel leaned over and turned down his friend's collar to reveal a patch of red skin. "What did they call those things in the army? Passion marks?"

Embarrassment colored Doug's face. He burst out laughing. "I knew I'd planned to wear a turtleneck this morning for a reason. I couldn't remember why for the life of me, though, when I was getting dressed." He pulled his collar back up and looked toward the waitress, probably wondering if she'd seen it too. "I went to Nigeria for a few weeks to help with the new clinic, and let's just say that my wife and I had a very happy reunion."

Nigel forced a smile, trying not to envy the joy in his friend's voice. A happy reunion. It must be nice. "Well, I wish I could say the same. Peach and I didn't get off to such a good start. I had no idea she was the one on the project. Shouldn't she have known I'd be the one working with her? She didn't look too happy when I came in this morning. I wonder if I should leave."

Doug leaned back so that the waitress could set down his salad. "Jean didn't know you were coming." He took a sip of water. "But I did—"

"What?" Nigel stared at his old friend. When they'd met, Nigel was a new convert to Christ and Doug an angry missionary-kid-gone-astray. They agreed to disagree and in the end became friends despite Nigel breaking up Doug's future with Jean. After seeing the connection between Jean and Nigel, both men had been gentlemen enough to discuss where things were going. All three had come out friends. Nigel and Doug had hooked up again a few months ago by email, with Doug giving him referrals and advice about corporate fashion design.

A shock of silver hair, the longest lock on Doug's cropped head, fell forward as he perched his chin on both fists. "I'm not proud of this, and if you don't trust me anymore, I'll understand." He leaned in closer. "I got an email from Reebok a few weeks ago. I put in a call to recommend you. I had no idea you'd end up working with Jean and Chenille. I thought you'd be working with me. I guess Lily and I have done all women's designs, so they didn't feel comfortable going that way."

Nigel took a sip of water. "Hey, that's just business. Nothing to be ashamed of. I really do appreciate the recommendation. I wondered who'd dropped my name in their ear."

Doug took a long blink. "Don't let me off the hook just yet, man. Let me finish."

"All right." Nigel's jaw tensed.

"Though Jean didn't know you were coming, when Lily told me about the emails from Reebok about menswear, I figured they might send you. I thought about calling you or calling her, but I didn't know what to do. Jean and I only discussed you once. She asked if I'd heard from you, and at the time, I hadn't. She said that she couldn't find you, that she hadn't heard from you. That she didn't want to, that she was finally over it. When you started emailing me, I started praying about it, but I kept feeling like I needed to stay out of it and let things play out. Sorry I let you walk into a minefield on that one."

Nigel squeezed his fork tighter, stabbing at his salad, though his appetite had fled with each of Doug's words. Five years into Nigel's sentence, Jean had stopped taking his phone calls, but he'd continued to write. When his name was read during roll call one morning, he couldn't believe it. The envelope contained a photo of a baby girl and a short note. At first, he'd thought it was Jean's child and felt his heart rip in two. Then he read the short note. *This is your granddaughter. She has your eyes.* It was impossible, but true.

From then on, he'd sent only Christmas cards and what little money he'd made at his job in the prison laundry. Now and then, money would show up in his canteen, but he always sent it back to the last address he had for Jean. Eventually, the letters came back, saying no one by this name lived at this address any longer.

Those had been dark days in his faith . . . in his life. Then one day, one of the vets he'd befriended in the streets showed up in Nigel's cell. When the guy learned of Nigel's charges, he wept. Nigel had tried to get the man to get rid of his gun days before the robbery. Nigel's concern had landed his fingerprints on a weapon used in a robbery. "You didn't rob that store. I did," the man said, both to Nigel and to the many lawyers involved in the case. It took months, but eventually Nigel was pardoned and released. But it was too late. Everyone he contacted to find his family said the same thing—"They're gone." What they didn't say, but implied—that his family was better off without him—hurt just as much.

Though Nigel still sent Christmas cards to all Jean's last-known addresses, at some point, he'd realized those people might be right. After years of praying and searching, Nigel decided that God could do what he wanted with his marriage, just like he'd done with his life. His only consolation had been finding his granddaughter through her online journal. Some of the things the girl wrote about troubled him, but at least she never mentioned her family or whereabouts directly. Nigel was still learning about the Internet, but he knew it could be a dangerous place for kids. Not daring to chance scaring her off, he left comments under an online name and savored every mention of her "pretty *abuela*."

Seeing Jean today though, he knew that "pretty" could never describe her. Nothing could have prepared him for the joy of seeing her again and the pain of hearing that, if she'd had it her way, Jean would have never seen him again.

Perhaps it's just as well. Closure. Isn't that what you prayed for?

It was certainly what Carmen wanted. They'd been friends since back in LA, a few years after he got out of prison. He'd been hurting then and done some things he now regretted, most of them with Carmen. Though it didn't mean much to him then but something to dull his pain, the voluptuous sportswear designer took their time together to heart. She'd pursued him the past few years as relentlessly as he'd sought after God for forgiveness and after that, sought after Jean for reconciliation, something he knew now probably wouldn't happen. Nigel stood and took out his wallet. He had to get out of here, clear his head before facing his wife again.

Doug shook his head. "Oh, come on. Sit. I'm already going to be in hot water once my wife finds out I even thought you were coming. I won't be getting any hickies for a long time after this, buddy. Humor me. As for the money, don't worry about it. Lily and I have an account at this restaurant for the business."

The business. In prison, no one would have believed that Nigel was friends with Doug LaCroix, the famous designer, so Nigel didn't bother to tell them. He merely smiled whenever commercials for his friend's clothes came on TV. When Doug had disappeared from the fashion scene in 2001 and some people had presumed him dead, Nigel had prayed for the man daily. Seeing him now was bittersweet. He'd almost thought Doug was kidding when his friend explained in his first email how he and his wife had met as part of a fashion designer reality show. When he saw a billboard in California for Worlds Apart Fashions with Doug's face and the face of a beautiful Asian woman, Nigel knew it had to be true. Little did he know that Doug's wife had worked with Jean and been her close friend. The world suddenly seemed a little too small for his liking.

"Thanks for the lunch, Doug, but I need to sort through some things before I go back to the office. And no, I'm not upset with you about this. In fact, I appreciate you. You may have saved me from doing something else stupid." He put a bill on the table for the tip. Though the waitress hid it well, Nigel could tell by the sway of her back and the way she held one hand on her stomach while taking their orders that she was pregnant. Her ring finger bore no wedding band.

His friend stood to join him, then paused. He grabbed Nigel's arm. "Something else stupid? Oh boy. What did you do? I lost my cell phone in the airport, and I haven't checked email since I heard from you. Lily told me about the other woman and everything, but that was all I could make out with her talking so fast. What else did you do, call her Peach?"

Nigel chuckled. If only that was all he'd done. "I did that too, but that wasn't what I meant. I kissed her. I didn't know what to do, what to say, when I saw her. All I could think of was that the night before they took me, I'd forgotten to kiss her good night. For all those years in prison, I never got over that, not kissing her. So when I saw her there, so beautiful, looking just like when I left her . . . I just wanted to kiss her good night." He swallowed. "Now I'll just have to figure out a way to keep from making a fool of myself again."

Doug stepped around the table and grabbed his old friend by the shoulder. "Good luck with that. The women who work at that place have a good track record of driving men crazy. Wait until you meet the rest of the guys. You'll see."

The two men walked silently between the tables. Violins played softly in the distance. A woman squealed with delight as they passed a young man kneeling on one knee. An old pain rose in Nigel's chest as he considered his friend's words.

Luck had nothing to do with it. The next few weeks were going to require the kind of faith Nigel had been seeking since begging for forgiveness on a Vietnamese battlefield. The kind of faith that had once seemed close enough for him to touch. The kind of faith he'd almost wrecked with Carmen before explaining to her that he couldn't ignore his wedding vows any longer, no matter what the circumstances. Reebok had assured him that his part of the job would be over by the first of the year. He hoped they were right, for everyone's sake.

Nigel walked ahead of Doug, striding through the café and toward the door. A few years ago, he'd been living on prayers, making clothes in a storage unit in LA. Then came the store, the contracts, the clothes. Now he was back in New York, and all the old hurts . . . the old yearnings to be with a woman . . . hit him hard. He turned to wave good-bye to Doug before pushing through the door and onto the sidewalk. He let the cold air cut into him as he ran for a cab. Carmen had promised not to show up at his place tonight as she had the night before. He hoped she meant it.

As he went, he could think only one thing: *I'm just a man, Lord. Just a man.*

"Your husband? The girlfriend? He kissed you? I can't believe this stuff happens after I stop working here." Lily Chau,

Doug's wife and Jean's former co-worker, shook her head. Jean was glad to see her but wished it'd been under different circumstances. "Now, we've been taking your advice for a long time, Jean. Do we get some input on this one?"

Jean buried her head in her hands, unable to face her friends. They were all there: her boss, Chenille Rizzo, and her friends Lily Chau and Raya Dunham, the head designer at Garments of Praise. These women knew Jean well. A little too well. Jean wondered how much Chenille had told them. By now, everyone in the building probably knew Nigel was her husband.

After almost a minute of Jean's silence, it was Raya who finally spoke as she put her arms around Jean, tickling the woman with the pink boas from her sweater. "I never thought I'd see you speechless. This must be some serious business with a serious man. I'm going to have to stick around for an introduction. I have to see this one for myself. I don't think fine even begins to explain what this guy has to be."

"Oh, he's fine. I'll tell you that much." Jean lifted her head just enough to get out the words. Though she'd spent time with her share of men, none of them came close to her husband, in looks or character. The problem was that her husband hadn't come close . . . to her. Not until now, anyway. And now that he was here, she had no idea how to make things right, if they'd ever been right at all. And that was without factoring in the hippy vixen who wanted to marry him.

Lily pulled up a chair next to Jean. She folded her cashmere kimono, probably the piece she'd been working on when Chenille called, into her lap. "I can't stay for an introduction. Mother is having a consult today to see if she's a candidate for a new medication. All I can say is that I love you and that any time you want to talk about this, you know where to find me." Hurt swelled in the pauses between her words, but Lily wouldn't push for more answers. Not yet. As for the other two women? Well . . .

Jean squeezed her friend's hand. It was Jean who usually said these words, who worried over them and their relationships. Being on the receiving end of one of these little girlfriend interventions was a lot less fun. "It's not that I don't want to share with you, all of you. It's just that I don't quite know what to say. I thought . . . I thought that part of my life was over. I abandoned Nigel. Then I tried to find him and couldn't. It's been a hard kind of love. I'm sorry I never told you all about him."

"Uh-huh. I always knew you had some skeletons in your closet along with all those St. John suits. I just never knew that one of them was a husband. Let me just see if he's in the hall . . ." Raya's thigh-high boots clicked against the floor as she inched toward the door and peeked into the hall. The scent of bay rum cologne whispered into the room. "Well, if he looks half as good as he smells, I know we're in for a tripped-out Christmas," Raya said, closing the door again gently.

Christmas. It had been Nigel's favorite holiday and the one time she went all out with food and decorations. Her granddaughter's birthday fell on Christmas too. Her fifteenth. Jean had planned to throw her a big party, but the girl had asked her not to. Now she had Nigel to deal with too. Jean felt as though her heart might burst. Instead, she exploded in laughter. "He smells good, huh?"

Before the other women could nod, there was a knock at the door. Nigel stuck his head in. "Sorry to interrupt, ladies. I just wanted to let Jean know that I'm back from lunch and going down to start on some sketches."

Jean shook her head as Raya and even Lily dropped their jaws at the sight of her husband. "We're almost finished here," she said softly. "I'll be down in a minute."

35

He nodded and closed the door. Jean watched to see if Carmen appeared behind him. She'd trailed him all morning, but it seemed that she'd finally left. Now she could be alone with him, once she got through with the nuts. From the looks on their faces, she'd have to kick them out or leave them there.

Raya brushed some imaginary lint off her sweater once the door clicked shut. "Well, Miss Jean, you might not know what to say, but we do, and we'll say it again—"

"That is one fine man!" All three women joined together before dissolving into laughter.

Lily held her stomach from laughing so hard. "Oh, how I miss all of you. You're still crazy. Working with Doug is great, but there's nothing like these girl moments. I never thought there'd be any more fine-man humor, though, with Raya and me married off. Who knew that you'd be the next one to have man face . . ."

Jean threw her head back and groaned. *Man face*, the silly name that Chenille had coined for each of their gaga looks when talking about their husbands.

Lily gave Jean a quick hug before waving good-bye and disappearing into the hall. Instead of turning left out of Jean's office like she should have, she turned right, no doubt going by the conference room, where Nigel was setting up. So much for her not having time for an introduction. Jean tried not to imagine what her friend might say.

Raya grabbed her purse and made for the door next. "I've got to go too. You know nothing brings me here on my off day, but this was a must-see. I wish I could have seen the heifer who wants to marry him too, but if she never shows up again, it'll be fine with me." She took her camera phone from her purse and flipped it open toward Jean. "See you tomorrow, mystery woman. What are you going to tell us next, that you're undercover for the CIA?"

Jean rolled her eyes. "Will you hush? And put down that phone. Don't even think about taking his picture—"

Raya swung the door open with a smile, waving her phone. "You know I have to get a picture of that man! Flex is standing by for the photo. My poor husband thought I made it all up. When I finally convinced him, he said he had to see the man who'd managed to marry you. Besides, you know we're going to be in warfare prayer mode for your marriage."

Jean's shoulders slumped. Oh, man. Warfare mode? When they prayed like that, all kinds of crazy stuff started to happen. The past two days had been enough. She'd barely slept last night as it was. This morning, she would've been almost glad to see Carmen sashaying down the hall behind Nigel. Now, they'd be alone . . . and her friends would be praying. She suddenly felt tired.

"Maybe another time, huh, Ray?" Chenille had laughed at the teasing, but now concern showed on her face, along with a stifled giggle. "Mr. Salvador really is here to work despite the unexpected circumstances. Let's be as professional as possible. No pictures."

Raya raised an eyebrow at her boss and friend. "Are you for real?"

Chenille nodded. "I am, and besides, I've already emailed you a picture of him. And the hippy heifer. Now get. I need to talk to Jean before she goes back to work with Señor Fineness."

"Hmmm . . . Señor Fineness. I like. Very fitting. Okay, I'll go." She kissed Jean's cheek. "See you later, hot mama." Satisfied, Raya stepped into the hall, turning the correct way to get out of the building.

Jean rested back against her office chair, both relieved and uneasy to be alone with Chenille—and then Nigel. "Everyone will be talking about this for weeks, huh?"

Her boss snorted with laughter. "Weeks? Try years."

I have tried years. Too many years, in fact. It didn't quite work out, but I've been loving him anyway.

"I know you need to get in there, but first I need to know if you're up for this. It doesn't seem that you and Mr. Salvador are unfriendly toward one another, but things are definitely awkward. I know it's been a long time since you've seen each other. I don't need details necessarily, but are you going to be able—"

"He is the only man I've ever truly loved besides my father. He's the only man I ever gave up on besides my father."

Jean had two rules: Don't Complain and Don't Explain. She was breaking the second one. Again. "Over twenty years ago, he went to prison. I haven't seen him in almost that long. How's that for details?"

Chenille sat down on the corner of Jean's desk. She wrung her hands. "I am so, so sorry. You don't have to do this. If you can't, I mean, I understand."

Jean surveyed her reflection in the computer monitor. "That's where you're wrong, Chenille. I do have to do this. Everything I think about God, about love, has something to do with Nigel. It's good to know that he's well. I have to get through this, to say good-bye."

Chenille gave Jean a sad look, almost a look of pity. She shook her head. "This might not be good-bye. God delights in resurrecting dead things. I know it's been a long time and lots of things have happened, including that Carmen woman, but don't close the door on the possibilities."

Jean clenched her fists. "See, this is why you never knew about him. I knew that's what you'd say, what you'd think. You don't understand. I can't be that woman again, I can't be weak. My granddaughter needs me. If I let myself love him, I'll be like . . . like . . ."

"Me? Lily? Raya?" Jean's boss stood slowly. She crossed her arms and held them close to her body. "I know that you think you're a strong woman, Jean. But that can only get you so far. Trust God to be strong in your weakness. Let him make you into a woman of strength."

Without answering, Jean straightened her skirt and grabbed her sketch pad and a folder full of her favorite menswear designs. Her Bible notes were in the folder too, scribbled on the backs of her sketches.

Some of Jean's best ideas now came to her during the Sunday sermons she'd once tried so hard to avoid. The small church she'd been attending had been studying the rebuilding of the temple on Sunday and the miracles of Jesus on Wednesday nights. She still went to mass at the Catholic church most Saturdays, or to a Spanish language Eucharist at Lily's church when they both had the time.

Trusting God had become easier. She prayed for her granddaughter and daughter daily, her co-workers and friends, family scattered far and near. It was Nigel whom she prayed for most often lately. She prayed that God would bless him and keep him safe. Instead, God had brought him to her. And Chenille was right, no matter how many push-ups Jean could do, she wasn't strong enough for this.

Fewer steps than she'd liked brought Jean to the conference room door, brought her to Nigel. His blazer hung neatly over one of the chairs. He sketched furiously at an easel only inches away and with more skill and passion than she'd remembered. Though his back was to her, he nodded slightly at her entrance. His muscled back flexed against his shirt, making a greeting of its own.

The warmth that flushed through Jean was not from one of her usual hot flashes—or "power surges," as Chenille liked to call them. At a conference they'd attended at Chenille's church, the speaker had emphasized the power and wisdom of older women. "Forget that hot flash talk. When that power surges through you, it's just time to impart some wisdom!" the woman with the short red afro had said. At the time, Jean had agreed. Now, as she placed her open hand in the middle of her husband's back and found it still fit perfectly in the space, she felt herself wanting to give him something more than wisdom.

A lot more.

Lord, help me.

Nigel recoiled at her touch, bringing a chill to her inner flame. "I apologize for Carmen sticking around this morning. And for what she said yesterday morning too. She overstepped," he said, the charcoal in his fingers sweeping out in arcs of mushroom and sage.

Jean sighed, taking in the sketch . . . and the artist. She shrugged out of her own jacket and grabbed a cranberry pencil out of the trays of art supplies that littered the table. She stood closer to Nigel, extending her hand to an empty space on his canvas. A silhouette much like her human model, with wide shoulders and nice-sized waist, emerged onto the page.

"Don't be sorry," she said. "I'm the one who should apologize for not introducing you to Chenille. I was startled to see you. Confused. So many feelings ran together . . ."

He nodded, leaning in to add a military cord to her design. "Too many feelings, probably. If I'd known I'd be working with you, I wouldn't have accepted the assignment."

Jean swallowed hard. What was he saying? That he hadn't wanted to see her again? Or did he think that was how she felt? To be honest, she had felt that way until lately. Now, this close to him, alone with him, her feelings were all confused. And though she didn't use the term anymore, *hot flash* would definitely describe what she was feeling.

40

Nigel looked into her eyes. "I never meant to hurt you again. I don't want to—"

Her lips swallowed his words. As their mouths met, the lost time melted between them. His mouth tasted of lemon and lettuce. She'd neglected lunch but hoped her last breath mint hadn't expired. His scent, a fruity variation on the same bay rum woodsy stuff he used to wear, made her pause. She opened her eyes to be sure he was really there, that she wasn't dreaming.

As if to reassure her, Nigel took her face in his hands, tracing the lines left by the years lost between them. He kissed the corners of her eyes, the furrow between her brows. The fire Jean had felt moments earlier easily returned as she twined her hands around her husband's neck before loosening his tie and top buttons. She raked her fingers through the tuft of hair she knew would be just inside his shirt . . .

He pulled away. "Let's not do something we both might regret. If you kiss me like that, touch me like that, I'll . . ."

She removed her hands from his shirt and dropped her arms at her sides. Too late Jean had attempted to surrender herself, to give her love to this man who had so long ago been her husband. Who was still her husband, wasn't he? Jean ignored her heart's question and tackled Nigel's comment instead. "If I kiss you like that, you'll what? Don't make me promises if you don't mean it." She covered her mouth then, realizing what she'd just said, what she'd just done.

So much for the quiet plan.

Nigel glared at her while buttoning his shirt, tying his tie. "I keep my promises, Jean. Out of anyone, you should know that."

His words hit her like a punch in the gut. Nigel had kept his promises. He'd come for her long after she'd left him behind. Her eyes traveled over the chairs until she found her own suit jacket, abandoned over one of the chairs at the conference table. She slipped into it quickly, buttoning herself in securely. The heat that came to her face this time wasn't hormones but humiliation. The shame and pain that had followed her for so many years nipped at her heels. He was right. She was the vow breaker, the one who ran away. She was the one who gave up.

Though a piece of paper still connected them, she and Nigel were long beyond repair. She could count her blessings for having seen him again, for knowing he was well and healthy. A little too healthy perhaps, she thought, refusing to take all of him in with her eyes again. Refusing to start thinking and acting like his wife. Instead, she needed to be his co-worker, no matter how painful the experience.

3

Carmen didn't show Thursday, but Jean stayed in her office until nine o'clock anyway, giving Nigel some time alone. In truth, she was just giving herself a break from being alone with him after the painful quiet that had been yesterday afternoon. They'd watched slides of the different NBA teams and taken notes without exchanging many words. At the end of the day, Nigel had made some vague reference to dinner, but she hadn't responded. She needed to get home and cancel some of the reservations for her granddaughter's birthday party. She'd lose quite a bit in deposits, but it was her own fault for planning it without being sure it was what Elena wanted. The girl had always commented on the quince parties of her other friends, so Jean had thought she wanted one too. Just like she'd misread her husband's feelings yesterday. She was batting zero at reading people lately.

This morning, instead of her usual apples and oatmeal, she'd scrambled herself an egg with some veggie links and whole grain toast. Today she wanted something a little more solid on her stomach before facing the day. Elena, who slept over most nights these days, had noted Jean's change in menu—and attitude.

"What's going on, *Abuela*? Something wrong?"

Jean had almost broken down then. How could she tell the girl in one breath that her grandfather had returned and explain in another that they'd probably be divorced soon and he'd be leaving town? Her own pain was one thing, but Elena had been through enough. "I'm fine," she told her granddaughter before leaving for work. Now, over an hour later, Jean knew it was a lie. She was not okay, nor would she be until that husband of hers was far, far away, preferably without that Carmen.

She checked the clock. 8:58. Time to face the music . . . and the man. She gathered her notes and swatches and headed down the hall. Nigel must have heard her heels in the hall, because the door opened just as she reached it. Jean entered slowly, surprised to find a coatrack on the wall and a vase of fresh flowers on the table.

Nigel shrugged. "I have no clue where it came from. It was all here this morning when I arrived."

"I think I have an idea where it might've come from," she said, eyeing a basket of snacks and fruit at the opposite end of the table. The Cheetos were noticeably missing from the assortment of chips. Definitely Chenille.

After a review of the team films from the day before, they watched films of menswear shows from past fashion weeks and noted details that appealed to both of them and would apply well to the line. The discussion left them standing close, a little too close. Nigel returned to his sketches from the previous day.

Jean swiveled her chair toward him, flipping through the notes she'd taken the past two days. Reebok wanted proto-

44

types by the New Year. With holiday production schedules, that'd be next to impossible unless things really started coming together. Today she'd have to worry less about her past with Nigel and more about her future in menswear. It was time to get down to business. "So we're focusing on the designs first? Is that it? Or are we going by NBA teams? I guess we could even focus on a player on each team like they do with the shoes." She stood and leaned around his shoulder to survey his drawing.

Nigel swallowed as if taking in the last of the closeness between them. "I'm just freehanding at this point. I have some ideas, but I really haven't chosen an approach." He pointed to the drawing Jean had added the day before. "Your sketch gave me an idea, though. The way you slanted the shoulders reminded me of David Robinson when he was with the Spurs. The Admiral, they called him. Let's look at a military feel for that team."

Jean paced away from him, keeping her eyes on the sketches they'd made. "That's a good thought. Let's expand on that. Maybe we should both work up an example for each team. We could start with the Spurs. You go with the military theme. I think I'm going to go preppy for them. Tim Duncan, maybe? Sort of a Kanye West meets *GQ*."

Color in hand again, Nigel drew as she spoke, making diamonds and stripes. "Yeah. I'm feeling that. An argyle and pinstripe sort of thing. Funky. That's good. Maybe we should just go with that. It doesn't really make sense to do two for each team even though we're not doing the whole league."

It made sense to Jean. She'd made a fool of herself yesterday inside of their first hour of total collaboration. She couldn't be sure what her upcoming "power surges" might give off if the two of them kept working so closely. Jean pulled up her glasses from the chain around her neck, reading through the project proposal again that she'd only skimmed earlier. "I think it's important that we give Reebok some options to pick from. Not put all our focus on one design. Time is a factor, of course. If we agree on something for a team and it works, one will be fine." She paused, forced herself to look into those beautiful eyes of his. "Things happen, you know? Let's just leave some room for different ideas. For starters, you stick with your military and I'll go preppy. I can go back to my office and—"

He shook his head. "No. That won't work." Nigel's tone echoed with finality as he ripped the page off the easel and tried to crease between the two sketches to rip them apart. There was no way to separate one image without tearing into the other. He laid it out on the table instead. "We need to stay in the same work space as much as possible. I don't want to have to search for you every time something comes to me. I mean, look at how easily this came together. We weren't even really trying. Think of what could happen when we really get going."

Jean didn't need to think. She knew. "All right. We'll try it." She sat down to the left of Nigel with a fresh piece of paper. While working, she mentally calculated how many teams they could possibly prototype. Thoughts of the grueling schedule pleased her. The work would leave less time for them to get sidetracked or for her to wonder when the divorce papers Carmen had mentioned might arrive at her door.

As Nigel rolled up his sleeves and moved closer to her to correct something on his design, Jean considered the salad she'd packed for lunch. She'd have to go for soup and a sandwich tomorrow. Her stomach was slowly turning into an incinerator. Nigel was right. The two of them had come together all too easily, all too naturally. That was what scared her most. Or at least she'd thought so, until her husband spoke again.

○

"So, how is Monica?" Nigel had meant to be more subtle, to take a few more days before discussing their daughter, but the words slipped from his mouth like warm butter. Underlying the words were other unspoken queries: "Did she miss me?" "Does she hate me?" "Does she know how much I love her?" He felt his teeth set on edge as the last question ripped through his mind. Not only did he still love his daughter, but he still loved his wife. He'd known it since that idiotic kiss when he arrived. Still, he couldn't let her destroy him again. God had brought him too far.

Jean pulled her scissors down a piece of electric blue rayon, shearing the material in two. If he hadn't been married to her, Nigel wouldn't have seen through her cutting and moving dance. The way she tapped her pen before answering and raked a hand through her hair told him she was as nervous as he. Perhaps more so if that was possible. "Monica is doing better. It's been a long road, not without its problems. After the baby—"

"And what a beautiful baby she was. Thank you for the picture. I still have it." He took Jean's free hand. She tried to pull her hand back to pick up a ruler, a pencil—anything, but Nigel kept his firm but gentle grip. Her hand trembled, then stilled as their fingers laced together.

"She is still beautiful, my Elena. So much like Monica was." Her voice cracked. "In every way. That girl both delights me and scares me to death. Sometimes I wish she was more like her brother."

It was Nigel's turn to pull away. "Her who?" He had a grandson too? It didn't seem possible.

47

Jean smudged her tears in the corner of her eyes. She paused, staring down at the black streaking her knuckle. Nigel heard her mutter something about switching to waterproof mascara.

She started across the room for the box of tissue. "Her brother. I guess you wouldn't have known about him. Anton is his name. He's nine. He lives with his father in Long Island now. I miss him."

He took a deep breath. "Wow. I've really missed out on a lot. I don't know where to start. I didn't expect the boy. I know this is hard for you, but I'd really like to see them. Monica too."

Jean mumbled something about it not being a good time. She dabbed at the corners of her eyes with the tissue, but black tears streamed down her face anyway. For some reason, that made Nigel smile. As he rounded the table to take her in his arms, he found himself laughing.

She didn't think it was funny. "What are you laughing about? It's a mess. All of it. I don't know how to do this. I can't do this."

Her defiance made Nigel laugh harder. Soon Jean let out a giggle too, shaking her head as they reached for each other in the same moment.

"I'm going to ruin your shirt," she whispered, trying to keep her makeup off his crisp cotton shirt.

"I know." Nigel pressed her face into his chest and stroked her hair. She had already ruined him. Didn't she know? He'd tried to accept the love of other women. Good women. Yet in his heart, he had always yearned for this woman, his peach. She was bruised in places and sometimes sour, the same as their marriage had been. Oh, but when things were sweet, like this . . .

His lips brushed the top of her head. "I was laughing because that mascara brings back so many memories. I never could get the stuff totally out of my shirts, but the making up was always worth buying another one."

Jean chuckled. She reached up and kissed his cheek. "Bring me the shirt tomorrow. I'll get it out. And I guess I'll have to get up with the times and buy some waterproof mascara. With you around, anyway." She took a step back from him. "As for the kids, you're just going to have to give me some time. We don't have visitation with Anton anyway—"

"What?" Nigel jammed his hands into his pockets. "No visitation? Why?"

"Monica has had her problems, okay? Just like all of us. She's in school now and seeing some guy. He seems really nice. Acts like he wants to marry her. Who knows?" Her eyes were dry this time.

Nigel wondered if he shouldn't ask her for a tissue of his own, just in case. How could things have gotten so mixed up? "She was a good girl, Peach. Hearing all this is killing me. This isn't how things were supposed to go." He shook his head. "I just want to see her, to tell her I'm sorry. To tell her that I never stopped loving her."

Jean pursed her lips. "I don't know if she's ready for that, Nigel. I don't know what she might say. It's been a long time . . ." She wanted to say something else, he could tell, but stopped herself.

His shoulders slumped. "Exactly. It's been too long. I don't think I'm asking too much. If she hates me, I can accept that. I just want to know her and my grandchildren. You got to decide before. It's my turn, don't you think?"

Jean reached for another tissue. She offered one to Nigel. He declined. She dabbed her remaining tears. "You're right. It is your turn. I just don't know how to give it to you."

Nigel's mind raced back to the design board; his hands

longed to sketch, to escape this moment. He held his head and his heart still, then dropped onto the conference room carpet. He extended a hand to Jean. "There's only one way we're going to get through this," he said.

Jean adjusted her skirt and joined her husband on the floor. She bowed her head and took his hand. When he squeezed her hand for her to begin, she found no words. Finally, he broke the silence, speaking to God as if she weren't there. As his sincere prayer washed over her, something inside her broke open like a seed unfolding in a dark field. In Jean's heart, two words echoed like a promise.

I WILL.

"So, how are things going?" Doug's voice sounded bright and cheery on the phone, but Nigel knew him well enough to hear something else too: worry and wonder. The guy wanted to know what was going on. And bad.

"Nothing new to report, really. We talked about the kids some today. Didn't go over so well. We prayed together—"

"You prayed together! That's great, man—yes, they did. In the conference room, I guess, Lil. I don't know—I'm really happy for you, man. Hang in there. I'm going to stop by as soon as we put this collection to bed."

Nigel looked at the door to see if Jean was coming. No one appeared and the hall sounded silent, so he risked a hearty laugh at his friend's response. "We weren't exactly praying for our marriage or anything, man. It was more like a let's-not-kill-each-other prayer, you know?"

Doug laughed right back. "Are you kidding? Those are

the best kind. Seriously, Nigel, you know as well as anyone that there is a connection when you pray with someone, especially your wife. Though I know it seems weird to think of it that way after so long, that's who she is to you. And all of us are praying that you two can somehow work things out."

Nigel sighed. "You told me yourself how she felt, okay? I'm just trying to get this work done without getting caught up in the rest of it. It's hard though. Very hard."

"It's supposed to be. Hey, do you still wear a size ten shoe?" Doug's voice blurred on the line as if he were running a marathon.

Oh boy. Shoes? What now? "I wear a ten and a half. Why?"

Lily's voice murmured in the background, but Doug emerged again. "No, this one. Here . . . Ten and a half. Perfect . . . Okay, well, I'm couriering over some sneakers and sweats for you. Raya's husband, Flex, will be there to pick you up after work. I wish I could make it, but my wife and my knees would make me pay for it tomorrow."

"Who? When? I have dinner plans tonight—"

"Cancel them. Flex'll take you out after. That guy eats like a newborn, round the clock, so I'm not worried about you going hungry."

Nigel didn't know whether to thank his friend or throttle him. He'd had friends here and there the past few years, but none who knew him as well or got on his nerves quite as much as Doug LaCroix. "Whatever, man. I need to go. Jean and I have a lot of work to do."

"And praying too. Don't forget the praying—"

"I'm hanging up now." And he did hang up, all the while wondering what he'd gotten himself into. He looked up just in time to find Jean coming through the door. Her face was full of questions.

51

Not up for playing games, he quickly answered them. "That was Doug. It seems that he's sending me over shoes and a sweat suit so I can go and play basketball with Flex. Raya's husband, he said? She seems like a trip. Whistles every time she sees me and asks if I've moved in with you yet."

Jean's eyes widened in horror.

Nigel laughed. "Hey, they're your friends. Don't look at me. Anyway, I can imagine that her husband will be just as interesting."

She agreed. "Flex is something else too. He's very competitive. Take it easy on him, okay?"

He took a step toward her. "Who? Old, defenseless me? I'm sure the young buck will beat me handily with little problem."

"Yeah, right. I know we're older, but your love of basketball will never change. You'll be playing at the old folks' home even if they have to strap your knees on." She hit his chest playfully, then drew back as if she realized how easily she'd touched him.

Nigel grabbed her elbow and drew her close. Seeing those little flares of hurt in her eyes every day hurt him too. His words, though, hurt worst. He wanted to take some of them back. "Before we get back to it, I wanted to apologize for that crack I made the other day about keeping my vows. I'm just as guilty as—"

She held a finger to his lips. "We're both guilty. Everyone is. That's what makes God so good. Now let's get to work. We don't want to keep Flex waiting."

4

Things fall apart. In prison, Nigel had read a novel by the same title, the story of a man whose life was turned upside down, whose human code had been bent. That man had been too strong to flex with the madness around him. Too straight to be broken. Nigel felt some of that rigidity coming to him now, infecting broken places that had never set properly, wounds left to mend in uncertainty.

Now, as he stepped out of the city snow and into Garments of Praise, there were not only the wounds but the questions. So many questions. Among them, what in the world was God up to? He searched the Scriptures daily for the answers. After basketball and a quick dinner, he'd attended midweek service at Chenille and Raya's casual but intense nondenominational congregation. The pastor had done time himself and had outreach ministries for veterans and their families, among many other programs targeted at every part of life. He'd been nervous at first, thinking that Jean might show up, but Flex said she went somewhere else and only showed up on Sundays here when she did come. The service and the quiet that followed had been healing. Until he arrived at work this morning, anyway. Then it all started again.

A hand hit Nigel across the back as he started down the hall. "Morning," the man said in a mock serious tone.

Recognizing the voice immediately, Nigel turned and smiled at Flex, who was known to show up around the firm at unexpected times. Nigel waved as he passed by, not wanting to get into some big restoration prayer session. When not on the road, Flex spent as much time with his wife and kids as possible. Though Nigel hadn't met Chenille's husband yet, both Doug and Flex seemed to be real family guys, something he once prided himself on too. All of that seemed far, far away as he wondered when he'd even talk to his daughter and granddaughter, let alone see them. If the prayer warriors around this place had anything to do with it, something was bound to happen. They let him know at every opportunity that they were "trying" to help all they could.

Nigel wondered whether he was "trying" too. He'd never tried on so many clothes to go to work in his life. He strained to remember what Jean had liked, always coming back to the clothes he pulled out first and putting them on. Much was the same, but much more was different. He couldn't come to her as anyone other than the man he was now, a man who until a few months ago would have identified himself as a street preacher, tailor, and urban missionary. He heard all the old identities whispering in his head: failure, ex-con, reject. Then, like now, the voice of God would come, even more still than the lies, saying, *You are mine*. He'd relax then, remembering God's grace, coming back to the beginning. Back to Jean.

Beautiful, stubborn Jean.

Seeing her every day was wonderful and torturous. Years

ago, he'd seen her sketches on napkins and cookbooks in their apartment. His work in the tailoring industry and her design jobs seemed worlds apart. Now, her insights often amazed him. She could revise an entire idea by changing one line or shade of color. Jean's knowledge of basketball surprised him too, especially since she'd often tired of his love for it while they were together. He knew from reading his granddaughter's online journal that Elena liked basketball, even played it, but he couldn't figure out if Jean had influenced the girl or if it was the other way around.

He prayed silently with each step, the way he and Jean often prayed now when tension drove them to their knees. The work that had come so effortlessly at first was a struggle now, especially the kisses of celebration or the laughter that impulsively became hugs. Even after so much time, the habits of marriage came back to them easily, both the affection and the lack of communication. He watched Elena's web space daily for some indication that Jean had said something about him, but the girl kept to her steady topics: boys, basketball, and beads. It seemed that she and her *abuela* made jewelry sometimes. He wondered how many of Jean's beautiful accessories had passed through Elena's hands. Did the girl even know her grandfather was here? He wondered what they'd told her about him. Even if they'd just given the facts, it wouldn't sound good. He wound down the hallway toward the conference room, convincing himself it didn't matter what the girl thought, and knowing it was a lie.

After taking a deep breath, he entered the conference room, unwinding his scarf onto the coatrack that had appeared yesterday. Remnants of the city's first snow still clung to his shoes despite his efforts to wipe them several times at the firm's front door. Though Jean usually spent the time before nine o'clock in her office, leaving him to work and pray alone, this morning she was waiting for him.

She wore camel-colored boots and a jersey coatdress in a shade somewhere between moss and pine. Orange and green beads hung from her waist, with a shorter strand of the same beads draping from her neck. Nigel wondered if Elena had helped her make them, but decided they'd probably come from some pricey boutique instead. She looked stunning as usual.

She greeted him with an unexpected and apologetic kiss on the cheek. "I know that you started on a Tuesday, and I don't know if anyone told you, but today we have a staff meeting. Anyway, you don't have to come. I just wanted you to know where I'll be this morning. You're welcome, of course, if—"

"I'll be there." He watched Jean shrug and steal a glance at him as she did each morning. She stopped at his feet and stared.

He laughed, inching his cowboy boots forward. "You like? I pulled out these jeans today and got this cowboy vibe. Doug lent me a tape of a Ralph Lauren fashion show for inspiration, and I've been trying rope stuff around the house ever since."

Jean scratched the side of her face and then pulled her nails through her hair. She shifted her weight onto one foot. "Very nice. You wear Lauren well. Those jeans are, well, a great fit." She'd moved on to her necklace now, fumbling with the beads. "The blazer too. The elbow patches are a great touch."

Nigel would have found Jean's fumbling amusing if it didn't hurt so much. There'd been so much to her that he hadn't seen when they were married. So much to him she hadn't known. She once bought him a Ralph Lauren suit, and he refused to try it on. What a fool he'd been. Did she remember those kinds of things the way he did? The little things? He hoped not. Dealing with today was enough to do them both in, without remembering the past. "Thanks. I liked the patches too. I know it must be weird to see me so interested in my own clothes when I wasn't before. It started out as an image thing for the customers, and then people started giving me things. I don't buy them all—"

"You don't have to explain." Jean brushed past him as if trying to escape a fire. She narrowly missed stepping on his foot. He let her pass, using all his resolve to keep from grabbing her by her waist and pulling her back to him. He gripped the table, knowing that if he got his hands on Jean, they wouldn't be making it to any meeting or even designing any clothes. He didn't know where something like that might leave them. Today, he didn't care.

God help me.

He followed Jean and leaned down toward her, sliding his face between her ear and shoulder. His hands circled her waist despite his best-laid plans. "Is there anything I should bring along, Peach?" he whispered, drinking in the fruity scent that clung to her skin. Mangoes, perhaps.

Jean went stiff at the sound of his old nickname for her, one he'd repeated on the first day when he'd planted his infamous kiss on her. His hands found his pockets easily as she jerked away and turned to face him.

Her look reminded Nigel that he'd crossed the same boundaries he'd put in place on that same day. Their forgetful embraces were one thing, but this was something else. "Your Bible might come in handy," she said before walking out the door and leaving him to consider her beauty and his own stupidity.

Nigel reached into the side pocket of his blazer and removed a pocket-sized Testament. He slipped it into the back pocket of his jeans. He hadn't been to a staff meeting where Bibles were required since conducting his own meetings back in LA. He grabbed a pen and a pad and stepped into the hall, finding himself thankful once again that Jean had found Garments of Praise, thankful that she now loved God, even if she could never again love him.

He shot off a quick prayer before jogging down the hall. Grateful for someone to follow, he fell in line behind Raya. "Hey. I guess I'm pretending to be one of the staff today. I'm going to follow along if you don't mind," he said, glad not to see that praying husband of hers anywhere around. It was no wonder he couldn't keep his hands off Jean, with most of the staff practically praying them back to the altar. Raya, however, hadn't brought up the subject too many times. She had her hands full chasing that cute little boy of hers.

Raya adjusted her sleeping toddler in the cloth slung around her shoulder and waist. "You're not pretending to be part of the staff, Nigel. You're one of us. And we're glad to have you. My husband says that if Jean wasn't married to you, he'd set you up with somebody around here. He really likes you."

Nigel laughed instead of cringing like he wanted to. He could only imagine what all of them said about him when he wasn't around, considering the things they said to his face. Aside from the reconciliation prayers and more prying than he thought was necessary, the men had been very accepting of him. He'd even had some fun with them on the basketball court. It seemed strange to have a growing group of friends again. He smiled at Raya. "I really like Flex too. Tell him I apologize for having to school him in ball the other night, me being an old man and all, but he brought it on himself."

She laughed, turning the corner as they headed toward Chenille's office. "I can believe that. He is so competitive. He and my oldest son turn a Monopoly game into an all-night real estate assault. Neither of them wants to lose."

Nobody wants to lose.

"I can't blame him there," Nigel said, pulling back the glass door so that Raya and the baby could get through. All the seats were filled, except for one—right next to Jean. She didn't look at him, but Chenille waved him over.

With all eyes on him, Nigel took his seat. As he did, the music started, playing one of his favorite hymns. The beautiful sounds coming from the CD player made him forget even Jean beside him. Twenty minutes and several songs later, Nigel's eyes were closed and his hands raised as a sweet silence washed over him. Over all of them.

"Lyle?" Chenille's voice cracked as she broke the silence.

Nigel opened his eyes to see a smiling man in a wheelchair join Chenille at the head of the table. Obviously, he was Chenille's husband, though all the employees greeted him with hand claps and whistles. His body looked weak, but his eyes . . . they were triumphant. Nigel leaned forward on his elbows to see this man better, to try to hear what his eyes were saying.

Welcome, the man's eyes seemed to say. *We've been waiting for you.*

"Honey, what are you doing here?" Chenille seemed both elated and alarmed, pulling Lyle's jacket around him, arranging the blanket covering his waist.

"He's come to get us in line!" a short, round man from production shouted through cupped hands.

Lyle laughed. "I don't have that much time, okay? I just came to say hello, both to my beautiful wife and to all of you." His eyes fixed on Nigel. "And especially you, Mr. Salvador. I've heard so much about you."

That's what worries me.

Nigel stood and rounded the table. He held out his hand. "Glad to meet you too."

The man smiled but didn't offer his hand. "I'd love to shake with you, but she's going to be furious with me as it is. My white count isn't the best, so I'm going to have to pass. I doubt that a handshake is going to make much of a difference in the long run, but you know the ladies . . ."

Swallowing hard, Nigel found something else to do with his hand and managed to nod his head as he moved back toward his seat. He hadn't meant to agree exactly, since he knew little about the ladies at all, but he didn't know what else to do. He sank down into his seat, ignoring some of the furrowed brows and dark glances. How was he to know not to try to shake hands? Lyle looked sick, but not that sick. What had he looked like before when his entire body matched the light in his eyes? Jean reached out and took Nigel's hand, leaving him plenty of other things to imagine.

The meeting marked the anniversary of the company's inception, and they celebrated with a slide show of all the children they had helped in some way. Nigel stifled a gasp as Flex's oldest son, whom he'd also schooled in basketball, flashed across the screen. A picture of Doug and Lily and three smiling Nigerian girls came next. Photos of Flex wearing their first designs in some sort of fashion show, followed by stills of Lily on that reality fashion design show she'd won, rounded out the slide show. A final picture, a snapshot of an unhappy-looking young woman in a wedding dress, came next. Nigel listened as Jean whispered an explanation in his ear.

"That's Megan. She ordered a million-dollar wedding dress from us a few years back, and she's still not married. We're supposed to finish her out in a few weeks. We didn't make the original price off the project, but it did really get us going. You'll know her when she comes around."

Nigel nodded. There were some people who didn't need introduction. You just knew who they were. He looked across the table again at Lyle, surprised to find the man looking directly at him. No one else seemed to notice, or perhaps they were used to it. Nigel normally would have felt uncomfortable, but Lyle had such a look of joy on his face that he didn't mind. He'd seen the same look on the faces of priests and homeless men, men whose homes were not of the world but of heaven.

Throughout the meeting, Nigel saw the men exchange knowing glances as their wives reported on the finances, production, and organization of the firm. Though he wasn't a financial wizard, what Nigel heard gave him some cause for concern. The numbers were good, but not great. The accounts receivable weren't being paid on time, while the bills seemed to be arriving like clockwork. He could see Lyle's jaw tighten during some of the departmental reports as well.

It was then that Nigel began to understand his new friend's intensive gaze. The firm needed help. His help. The ladies would never ask him for it, but a caring husband would. Nigel didn't know how far to go or even what he could really do, but he moved his head slightly to show Lyle that he understood. The other man smiled, then dropped back against his wheelchair and promptly fell asleep.

Chenille cut the meeting short at that moment as if a maestro had lowered his batons. "Let's leave it there, everyone. If there are any more comments, we can follow up by email."

After a soft prayer for healing and strength for the staff and their families, Jean started the chorus to "Amazing Grace." Nigel, who was halfway out of his seat, froze in midair, cherishing the sound he'd prayed for so many years to hear, the sound of his wife praising God.

He rose from his seat slowly, pausing to join the refrain.

Grace was amazing, indeed. From the time he'd woken up to see Jean's face in a Saigon army hospital, Nigel had vowed never to be without her, but God had kept the promise instead, staying by his wife's side. And now she knew it. That alone made everything else seem small, at least for a moment.

Though the burden of his broken family seemed more than Nigel could carry, he could see now why God had led him to stop looking for Jean, to release his own plans. But why would God bring him back to her after all this time? Pushing away the question, he could only rejoice as his wife's hand gripped his and the song ended. God's amazing grace had seen them this far. Surely he could get them through this assignment and whatever followed it as well.

5

It was an odd request. Jean's granddaughter, Elena, had sent a short email the day before asking to have lunch at Garments of Praise. Jean, who'd planned to talk with her granddaughter about Nigel at dinner the next night, wondered what had happened to make Elena request a "working lunch," as the young girl called them. She always protested when Jean wanted to stick around and eat in instead of going to a restaurant. Something was definitely up. Had the girl somehow gotten wind of her grandfather being in town? Or was it something more serious, something that Jean might not be ready to know? The handles of Jean's lunch bag cut into her fingers as she approached her office door, but she hardly noticed as the delicious smell of the special meal she'd ordered wafted around her.

Chenille rounded the corner and stood between Jean and the door, dusting her hands of Cheetos cheese. Normally, Chenille's hovering would have driven Jean crazy, but this time, she used it to her advantage. "So, how did she seem when she came in?"

"Great. Just the same. She asked about Lyle and offered some decorating advice for the foyer. 'That green is a little dark. Not quite popping. Maybe a little lime wash on the trim?' You know. Just like you, but with walls instead of clothes."

Jean shook her head. That was Elena for you. Not even Chenille could read that girl. "Well, thanks anyway."

Her boss shrugged. "No, thank you. And Elena too. I'm going online to find some paint colors. Lily and I were in sort of a dark period when we did those walls. I guess we can brighten things up a little."

"I know just what you mean," Jean said, pausing for a final prayer before entering her office. Her dark period had lasted over a decade and seemed to be revisiting her now along with a hormonal tidal wave. Humming a hymn she'd heard Nigel singing earlier in the day, Jean took a deep breath and reached for her doorknob, only to pull back.

Chenille was still standing there. "She's not pregnant, hon. Really. Go on in."

Was she that obvious? "Are you sure? I mean, I trust her. She really is a good girl. It's the boys I don't trust. Too many tattoos—"

The door swung open. Elena's head, full of black curls, poked out. "Grandma! Will you get in here already? Miss Chenille is right. I'm not pregnant. I just want to talk to you. Really."

Chenille let out a giggle and disappeared around the corner, leaving Jean with a mouthful of excuses. She pushed the food in front of her as a peace offering as she stepped inside.

Elena accepted the bag, opened it, and took a long whiff. After flashing a smile, she became serious again and offered her grandmother her own office chair. "I'm a little sad that you would even think I'm having sex, much less pregnant, *Abuela*. Despite this black fingernail polish, I really do listen to what you tell me. Mommy too. I'm not her, you know."

Or you. The thought went unsaid, but it passed between them nonetheless.

Was this a game of whack-the-grandma? Stinging comebacks were usually Jean's department. It was bad enough that Lily, Raya, and Chenille thought they had pulled one over on her lately. Now she had to deal with a smart-mouthed teenager too. And all she could do was laugh. "Okay, so I was wrong to think that, but you've got to admit, that nail polish is a little scary."

The girl laughed too, throwing up her hands as Jean sat down in her chair. "It's just polish. No big deal."

Jean pulled up the glasses hanging from a string of beads around her neck to take a closer look at her lunch guest. "I beg to differ. It's terrifying. And the lipstick too. When granddaughters paint themselves black and ask to have lunch in a place they usually don't like to have lunch, well . . . we grandmothers get a little uneasy." To put it mildly.

The girl reached out and took Jean's hand. "Remember what you tell me about Mom when I think she's starting to do something stupid? 'Just think the best,' you always say. Well, do the same for me, despite my cosmetics. I'm fine. Just think the best."

Jean pushed the bangs back from her granddaughter's face, remembering when she'd envied others' ability to keep that perspective. Though she and Elena didn't often discuss faith, her granddaughter's openness to change and her courage in dealing with her mother's less-than-stellar parenting always gave Jean courage.

"Yes, let's think the best. I'm sorry I let my fears take over and mess with my mind. I'm really glad you came today. I've just been a little preoccupied lately. Have you decided what you want for your birthday?" The ease of Jean's words surprised her.

Thoughts of her granddaughter's fifteenth birthday had been weighing on her mind for months as she planned a surprise celebration. A few nights ago, she'd intended to cancel some of the reservations for her granddaughter's quince, but the businesses were closed by the time she got home.

Elena had made it clear awhile ago that she didn't want one of those "lame traditional parties" that so many Puerto Rican and Dominican girls they knew celebrated. Jean was disappointed at first, then realized that she wanted the party as much for herself as for Elena. She wanted to somehow fix what she hadn't been able to give her own daughter. But as Elena so often reminded them all, she was not her mother or her grandmother either.

"About that," Elena said, pulling the cartons of organic vegetarian food out of the bag. "I know I said I didn't want one of those big parties, but I've changed my mind."

Almost in disbelief, Jean took a second before finding her voice. "Are you sure? I mean, it'll be a big thing. We'd have to invite a lot of people."

Elena nodded. "I know. Isn't it great? Do you mind praying over the food before we talk more? I always forget and interrupt you." Elena bowed her head.

Jean smiled. She'd had the same problem with her friends when she first started working here. Now, thanking God was part of her day, from the beginning to the middle and in between. Having Nigel around was turning her into a real prayer warrior, both for herself and for him. She blessed the food quickly, adding a short "Lord have mercy" at the end at the thought of trying to plan such a big party with so little time. And so close to Christmas too. But wasn't this her idea? She had been trying to talk Elena into it since she was twelve. Still, she liked to operate a certain way, with a certain amount of time.

Time. Jean seemed to have either too much of it, like the years she'd spent away from Nigel, or too little of it, like the time to plan this party.

Be ready in season and out of season.

"It may be a little hard to pull together since it's so late, but the party will be something to remember. Thank you for letting me do this for you. I love you, Elena." Jean leaned over and kissed the girl's blush-smeared cheek.

"There's just one catch though," Elena said, looking up from her salad plate. "I'd like for my grandfather to present me."

Jean let out a ragged breath. "Your who?"

Elena wiped her mouth. "Don't say it like that, *Abuela*. You sound like an owl. My grandfather. The Conquistador. He's been visiting my blog for a while now. It took me like forever to figure it out, but one time he slipped up and signed one of his comments 'Grandpa.' Must have been subconscious or something. Then Jay told me about him working here—"

"Raya's son, Jay? You two talk?" Jean pushed her plate away. Sure, Raya's son was about Elena's age, and they'd both hung around the firm some the past few years, but it never occurred to her that they were friends.

The girl laughed. "Yes, Grandma. Teenagers talk too. I knew something was up anyway. You've been eating eggs for breakfast. And you're wearing orange again. I'm glad of that. Those few months of black and white drove me nuts." She forked more spinach into her mouth, stabbing through her salad in a chase after a rolling cherry tomato.

Jean sat stunned. Kids. How could they act so innocent when in reality they were watching your every move and had spies everywhere taking notes for them. "I-I don't know what to say."

Elena pulled out her phone and flipped it open. A picture

appeared of Nigel wearing the winter white wool suit he'd come in wearing the week before. It was a one-in-a-million shot worthy of any men's magazine cover. She held it high, smiling in admiration. "I gotta give it to you, Grandma. He's hot, even by grandpa standards. That's kinda gross, I guess, but hey. I call 'em like I see 'em. Where is he, anyway? I have to get back to school in time for last period." She replaced her phone in her purse and stood, waving for Jean to follow.

"So you want him to come to the party?" she asked, standing now but not ready to leave her office.

Elena stopped at the door. "Stop stalling, will you? Of course I want him at the party. I want him in the party. Now come on. I'm like fourteen years behind on hugs, and time is short—"

Jean tucked the girl's arm under hers and pulled her out the door and down the hall. Anything to get that kid to be quiet. Goodness. She punched open the conference room door, half hoping that Nigel had taken lunch like a normal human being.

He had.

With Carmen.

In the room.

The shock on Nigel's face at the sight of Elena strangled Carmen's high-pitched laughter. He stood as if to salute her, then managed to find his voice. "Hello."

Carmen stood too. "He's still on lunch, Jean. Can you come back?"

Nigel started to speak, but Elena, who must have expected this from the way she smacked her lips together, beat him to it. "I guess I had to meet her sometime. Now's as good a time as any," she said before walking over to Nigel and throwing her arms around him. She planted a big kiss on his cheek before releasing him and extending a hand to Carmen.

"Hi, I'm Elena. His granddaughter. Nice to meet you."

Nigel was still holding Elena's other hand and staring at her in wonder. Jean lowered her head, knowing who was probably on his mind: his grandmother. From the few pictures that Jean had seen, Elena was the spitting image of her, only taller.

Elena kissed the top of her grandfather's hand and waved at his now quiet guest. "Well, gotta run. You all have fun making stuff. I'll be back soon." She pointed at Carmen. "We'll have to have you over for dinner . . . or something."

Jean closed her eyes. Where did this kid get this from? "Elena . . ."

She shot her grandmother a huge smile. "Don't worry. It'll be fine. Don't forget to tell him about the party. If he doesn't come, I don't either."

Carmen rolled her eyes as Elena disappeared out the door. "Party? He won't have time for that. When this project is finished—"

"Carmen?" Nigel's voice was steady. Calm. His eyes were fastened on Jean.

"What? I'm just saying—"

He turned to his guest. "Can you wait outside for a moment, please? Thanks. We'll talk about this later."

She shot Jean a sharp look and gathered her shawl from the chair. "Call me tonight. I have a plane to catch now. I just stopped through to say hello and to see how things were progressing with the divorce. Obviously, nothing's going to get done unless I do it myself." She kissed his cheek before hurrying out past both of them.

Nigel, who'd tensed when she kissed him, closed his eyes for a moment. Jean kept hers open, watching as her already flimsy marriage slipped away. She turned to go.

His fingers felt warm through her sweater as he took her

arm and held it, gently turning her back to him. "Thank you," he said quietly. "Thank you for bringing her to me. I know it wasn't easy."

Jean smiled and pulled open the door, forcing herself not to run down the hall. He had no idea how hard any of this was.

"Wow, Mom. You look great." Monica's surprise at the sight of Jean showed on her face. They talked regularly by phone but kept up mostly by email. Though Jean had lost a significant amount of weight in the past few years, it was the soft, shapely muscles, now where her rolls had been, that left people ogling. Monica kept staring as her mother came inside. "Seriously. Look at you. You're almost smaller than me now. I can't believe it. You used to look so . . ."

Jean laughed. "Old?"

Monica shrugged before taking a seat. "Not old, exactly. Just older. Not that there's anything wrong with old. Having you look like this is a little creepy. Like you might get a boyfriend or something. The thought of that sort of freaks me out."

Tell me about it.

Jean brushed past her daughter, taking in the disarray of the apartment. With Elena practically living at her place now, she knew that Monica was having a hard time, but she didn't know things were this bad. Monica's depression had set in after her second child and seemed to return more often than not. There were up times and down times, the ups usually associated with a man's arrival and the downs with his departure. The last guy, the one who proposed marriage, was nowhere to be seen, but that didn't necessarily mean anything either. Jean rolled up her sleeves and headed for the kitchen, glad she'd taken off early. If she went for it, she

70

could get through the kitchen and get home before Elena got home from basketball practice.

"Oh, come on. I can do that." Monica watched Jean push aside the dishes and turn on the faucet. "Look, what are you here for? I know you didn't come just to wash my dishes. Is it Elena? Is she in trouble? 'Cause I don't know if I can take it—"

Jean took her daughter's hand. "Elena is not in trouble. This is about something else." She paused as if to measure the contact between them. Was a hug required? No, washing the dishes would be better. She'd hug her on the way out. Bubbles filled the sink.

Monica sighed and started out of the room, coming back immediately with a cup and two plates and plunging them into the water. "I can do that, Mom. Really. And it's not what you think. It's just finals. I'm doing better. A lot better."

Jean stared at her daughter, assessing her splotchy skin and red eyes. She might have been doing better, but there was a lot more going on than finals. Still, she looked better than the last time they'd been face-to-face. Jean attacked the dishes, trying to think of where to start. Finally, she decided that only the beginning would do. "Your father is here."

Monica backed up against the refrigerator. "Here? Where? What are you talking about?"

Jean grabbed a saucer, setting into a baked-on bit of cheese with a vengeance. All her excuses seemed silly now. Why had she waited so long to let Monica know? What was she trying to hide?

"Mom? What are you saying?" Monica's eyes widened, showing red lines Jean had missed before. She was about to cry. Jean knew it only because she was about to cry too.

"He's here. In New York. I'm working with him at the firm. I didn't know if I should—"

"How long?" Monica's voice rose, as it had the last time they were together. Then, they'd argued over faith, over truth. Now, it seemed that Jean's lack of truth would be the source of tonight's conflict.

The right side of the sink filled with warm rinse water that Jean had forgotten in her haste. Though Monica was in her thirties now, the dynamics between them always came back to her fifteenth year. It was as if they were stuck there like a broken record. Tonight Jean didn't want to play this song. "A few days. It's complicated. I'm still processing it myself."

Monica sighed and slumped back against the refrigerator. "Processing it? Are you kidding me? Did you even give him my number or anything? Didn't he ask about me at all?"

Jean swallowed, disheartened by the speed in which the dishes were disappearing. She could always empty out the pots. Monica never did wash those right . . .

"Mom! Did he ask about me?" Monica took the rag from her mother's hands and released the sink stopper.

Jean watched the water flow out, wishing that she'd waited until later and brought Elena along. Maybe even Nigel himself. That's who Monica needed to be mad at, not Jean, who had given up everything to take care of her. "Yes, he did. Okay? He did. Now I'm going. I don't have to be yelled at. I'll give him your number, and you two can ride off into the moonlight happily ever after while I raise your kid."

Monica was crying hard now. Her shoulders jerked with the sobs. "Why do you have to do this, Mom? I know you loved him, but I loved him too. Why can't you ever let me have any of him? Of anything?"

Jean tightened the belt around her jacket, thinking of the prayer she'd shared with Elena at lunch today. That extra "have mercy" was for this. She should have added a couple more. Though she knew that praying aloud would start another fight, she risked taking Monica's hand and then her whole body, absorbing her tears and adding her own. The two of them never seemed to agree on anything but loving Nigel, the one thing they never discussed. Until now.

When Jean let go, Monica hung on. "You were praying, weren't you?"

Jean heaved a sigh. "Yes. I'm sorry."

"It's okay," Monica said, wiping away a tear. "It was kind of nice. I know I got all mad about that God stuff the last time we talked . . . and I'm sorry about that. This thing with Dad, though, you really caught me off guard. I mean, maybe there is a God after all. Not that I'm ready to, uh . . ."

"I know. And I'm not pushing you. Being able to pray for you is enough for now. And you're right about your father and about us. I guess I never really let you grow up. I never let you be a mother. In my head, you're still that fifteen-year-old—"

"Screwup." Monica finished the sentence with regret.

Jean pressed her lips together. "No. That's not it at all."

Monica smiled a little. "That's it exactly, Mom. It's okay. I've done my share of stuff to live up to it. I always hoped, though, that I'd get it together and Dad would come back somehow. That he'd find me."

What have I done? To all of us?

"Look, your father tried very hard to find you, to find us. I just didn't know what to do. When you got pregnant, I felt like I had to choose. I was just hanging on as it was, and there was only one of me. I should have asked for help. Even the way you feel about God now is my fault, I'm afraid. I went through some hard times while you were growing up, and sometimes I said things I should have kept to myself. Now I'm stuck with the consequences."

Or at least that's what she'd thought. Looking at Monica now, she realized that they'd all paid a price.

Monica's eyes lingered on Jean a few seconds more. "Come here again, Mom, and let me smell you again. With that short hair and those long legs, it's like you're someone else."

Jean chuckled as her daughter sniffed her wrists for Chanel No. 5, her signature scent. It was Monica's way of releasing her from the subject, of letting her off the hook the same way Jean had done with her so many times. Grace was even sweeter on the receiving end.

"You're still you, I guess," she said.

Leaning forward to kiss Monica's cheek, Jean laughed a little. "You're still you too." She pulled a piece of paper from her pocket. Nigel had scrawled his phone number and address on it a few hours earlier. Despite her attempts not to, Jean had already memorized the information. "Here. He's going to call you tonight."

Monica smoothed both hands against her dark hair, brushed flat against her scalp up into a ponytail of wayward curls. Elena often wore her hair in the same style. "Thanks for coming over, Mom. I know this hasn't been easy."

Jean blinked. "It hasn't. None of it has." She wiped her face and started toward the door, turning back when she remembered what else she'd come to tell her daughter. "One more thing. You know that fifteenth birthday party I wanted to give you? Well, Elena changed her mind about waiting until next year to do a sweet sixteen party. She wants a quince, the Latin way. To celebrate her becoming a woman."

"Becoming a woman," Monica repeated. Tears welled again in the younger woman's eyes, but she fought them back. "I hope it's a great party, then. It's quite obvious I missed mine. I'm still trying to become a woman."

"Monica."

Jean watched as her daughter shook her head and shoved books off the couch to find the TV remote. Their little moment was over, leaving Jean to sort out the truths her daughter had spoken. Though she knew better than to think that a birthday party could have made a difference in Monica's life, she did know now how much hinged on these years. Even if Elena didn't know what this really meant to all three of them, this time Jean would make it happen, even with almost no time to plan. She'd hoped that Monica might be excited and want to help too, but she realized now that it was too much to ask.

Sometimes people could give only the love they had, and sometimes it wasn't enough. If anyone should've known that, it was Jean.

6

"Let me guess, this is the Miami Heat collection, right?" Nigel's granddaughter surveyed his sketch with a critical eye.

He watched Elena just as warily, taking in her every move. How could a child over a generation removed from Nigel think so much like him? She was hilarious. And spunky just like Jean and Monica. "Yeah, those are my 'Flame On' sketches. What do you think? Too much?" He joined her at the easel where his burnt orange blazer and red pants were sketched on the page.

Elena gave a slight nod. "It's a good start. You're holding back though. Too conservative. This is Shaq we're talking about. Think big. Bold." Without another thought, she tugged the sketch off the easel and wadded it up in her hands. With perfect form, she shot the paper into a wastebasket several feet away.

Nigel froze. "I can't believe you just did that. Do you know how long that took me to do?" He shook his head and sighed. "You're just like your *abuela*, you know

76

that? Nervy. Here we just met, and already you're tossing my sketches and telling me how to do my work." He arrived at the trash in three strides and retrieved the paper. He held it for a moment and then dropped it back in, laughing to himself. The girl was right. This line really wasn't about mass appeal. NBA products had their own market, and each of them was looking to make a statement. Why not let them? Having Elena here was like having instant market feedback. Her friends would likely be the ones buying these suits. Or at least he hoped so.

He held up his hands. "I give. You got me. What would you suggest?"

With her grandmother's smile, Elena gave him an approving glance before settling down in one of the conference chairs. "First things first. About this whole we-just-met thing. We did not just meet. You've been coming to my blog for like, what, two years now? I mean, hello, you could have said something." She leaned over the table, searching through his set of art supplies. She settled on a ruby red, a canary yellow, and a bright, full orange. Fire.

Nigel took a deep breath. He'd known this question would come someday. "For one thing, I didn't want you to think I was some dirty old man and freak out. Even though I'm really your grandfather, I could have been some weirdo online. Also, I hadn't talked to your mother or your grandma, and I didn't want them to think I was trying to go to you instead of them." He watched as Elena approached the page. She stared at it for a few seconds before copying almost exactly his previous design, only with all three colors blending—orange, red, yellow. Then she added another ensemble of her own with the colors reversed.

"Wow," Nigel said, truly impressed. "I can feel the heat there. The color made all the difference. This really gives me something to work from. Thanks." He accepted the colors as his granddaughter passed them his way. After talking to his daughter for the first time, he'd had a hard time concentrating at work. He'd invited Monica to dinner at his place on Saturday, and she said she'd think about it. That had disappointed him, given how excited she'd sounded to hear his voice, but in a way, he could understand. Some things needed to be digested a little at a time.

He must have been staring off into space, because Elena waved her hand in front of his face. "*Abuelo*, are you sleeping? Wake up. I have to go. Before I do, though, I wanted to tell you to come by for dinner this Saturday night."

Nigel stared at the girl in disbelief. "I was just going to invite you. I invited your mom, but she said—"

"Forget that," Elena said, going to the trash for his old sketch and stuffing it into her backpack. "They'll never come to your place. You have to hit them on the home turf. In their comfort zone. We'll discuss the party plans too. *Abuela* had some great plans for my quince, but none of them will probably work now. So . . . I'll need some of your magic on picking tuxes and men's stuff. Got it?" She pulled out a card-stock invitation and placed it in his hand.

Family Fiesta, the heading read. Nigel couldn't do anything but smile. This kid was something. Really something. "I think I've got it. Anything else?"

She gave a nod toward the door. "Give Grandma a chance. She never stopped loving you. Ever. It was because of me that she left you. It's sort of messed up, I know, but she tried to do the right thing. She's been good to me, so try and be good to her. Okay?"

Nigel scratched at his forehead. "Um, okay."

She waved good-bye and checked her phone. "If you need me before the weekend, email me or hit me on the cell. After school hours, of course. Oh, and dress nice on Saturday. Wear the cowboy boots and those tight jeans. She's still talking about that. I'll text you the menu tomorrow."

"Huh? Wait—" Jean was talking about his pants? And who said they were tight? They weren't tight. And how could this girl talk so fast?

"Gotta go," she said, disappearing out the door. "Just remember. Be good to Grandma, even if she acts a little crazy now and then. And don't worry about Mom. She is crazy, but she knows it and she takes her medicine. She'll come around. TTFN!"

TTFN? Nigel pulled out a chair and dropped into it. He'd been so afraid that Elena would hate him or be ashamed of him. Instead, she was giving him work pointers and fashion advice. And what did she mean about Monica being crazy? Not that it mattered, whatever it was. In his mind, Monica was still that curly-haired princess he'd left behind, though he knew in his heart she'd long since grown up. He had mixed feelings about Elena's fiesta plans, but he couldn't argue with the girl's logic.

As for her advice about Jean, he didn't know what to think. Since waking up to his wife's brown eyes in an army hospital in Saigon, Nigel had vowed never to be without Jean. That vow had long been broken, and seeing her again, let alone thinking about being with her, was taking Nigel to his limits. Though God promised not to burden him with more than he could bear, the load of Nigel's broken family seemed heavier every day. Hadn't the Lord led him to stop looking for Jean, to release his own plans? Why, then, had he brought them back together now? Was it possible for them to find love after all this time? Or was this just another jagged stitch in the fabric of Nigel's faith? For some reason, his granddaughter seemed to think that love was still possible. He folded his elbows on the table.

With God, anything is possible.

Jean took one last breath before entering the conference room. She'd spent the past hour having lunch with Raya and Chenille, but as much as they'd talked about Nigel, she might as well have stayed in the conference room and eaten with him. Upon entering the room, she stared at the two plates of food and the lipstick on a plastic glass. Nigel sat with his head down on the table.

Probably praying for forgiveness. Hadn't that Carmen woman said she was going to be out of town? It was bad enough how she'd treated Elena earlier and he hadn't called her on it. Now he had her back in here again? Well, Jean was too old for playing games, but obviously Nigel wasn't. She had a mind to go back down the hall and tell her friends what their little angel man was up to, but it wasn't worth the effort or the time. They had work to do.

Nigel raised his head and offered a weak smile. "Hey. You're back."

She kept a blank expression. "Hey yourself." She walked over to the easel and surveyed the tricolor calamity on the page. The lines looked similar to Nigel's, but the technique was more crude. Had he let that woman work on their project too?

This is not about you.

It wasn't about her. It was work, or at least it was supposed to be. She'd made a mistake by thinking she could set aside her personal feelings and complete this project. If she wasn't careful, not only would the prototypes go undone, but Nigel and that silly twit of his would be needing medical attention.

The weapons of our warfare are not carnal.

Jean took a deep breath. So many of her life's battles were waged in her mind. What did it matter what Nigel did? Or who he was with? It was what God did that made the difference, and how Jean responded to it. "So what is this supposed to be?" She wanted to add that it looked like a clown suit, but she held her tongue.

"That was designed by our—" Nigel shook his head as he stopped short of an explanation. "It's nothing, okay. It's just some fooling around. Some brainstorming."

Jean tried to focus herself on the real question, how to do the best work. "I guess I do see some good in it. The Miami Heat, right?"

"Right," Nigel said. "I guess the fact that you know that immediately, says something."

She rounded the table to choose some colors of her own. "It says something, all right. I'm tacky and on fire." She turned back sharply at the sound of Nigel's laughter.

He met her around the table and closed his arms around her, chuckling against her ear. Jean tried to move him, to slip away, but despite all her workouts, he held her still. "That's funny. Really funny. I tell you, I am no match for the women in this family."

She stopped struggling and turned to face Nigel. "What family?"

His hands laced around her waist. "Our family. Elena drew that sketch a few minutes ago when she surprised me for lunch. I'd done another sketch, but she tossed it. Said I was holding back. Too conservative. I think she was right."

Elena? That was who Nigel had eaten lunch with? She held a hand to her chest, feeling one of those despised coughing fits coming on. Sure enough, it started, and the force of the coughs got her out of Nigel's grip easily.

He ran for water. "Here. Are you all right?"

She managed to nod her head up and down before downing the water in one gulp and finding her voice again. "Sorry.

81

That just happens sometimes. We had tomato soup at lunch. That always does it. A little reflux, I think." Immediately she regretted her words. She sounded like some complaining old lady at an old folks' home. She put the glass in Nigel's extended hand, giving him a sheepish look. "It's not that big of a deal. Don't worry, I won't start telling you about my arthritis or anything."

Nigel came to her again, this time placing his hand on her cheek. She closed her eyes as his fingers feathered against her skin. He kissed her forehead. "If you started on arthritis, I'd have plenty to say. I've got to put on extra cologne to cover up the smell of my menthol rub. I beat Flex in basketball, but then basketball beat me."

They both laughed.

Jean pulled away and took a seat. "Elena. I should have known. That girl turns up everywhere. I have to call the school all the time to make sure she's not in trouble, but somehow she ends up where she's supposed to be. It's amazing. You go ahead and work on that. I have some other things to catch up on. You can call me if you want my opinion."

Or if you don't.

Nigel crossed his arms. "Okay, but aren't you going to do your own design for this team as well? Having options and all that jazz, remember?" he asked, sounding a little defensive.

Jean ignored him, opening her portfolio to check her list for the *quinceañera* party for Elena. Though she hadn't received confirmations that her phone cancellations had been accepted, she had called everyone by phone when her granddaughter first decided against the party. Now all the places were unable to accommodate her on-again plans, and most of Elena's court had made plans to go out of town. That fact would probably make Elena happy since, despite having attended functions with the girls from the neighborhood most of her life, she didn't feel that any of them were her true friends. To hear Raya tell it at lunch today, Elena and Jay were very good friends now. Jean wondered exactly what that meant but made a note to talk to Elena about it later. "We can let your design fill in for this team if you want. Otherwise, I'll start my sketches as soon as you're done. Chenille has a few things she needs me to check on with one of our suppliers."

Nigel had started on a new sheet of paper, drawing flames, fireplaces. Everything but clothes. "Oh yeah. Flex told me about that. The fabric from Italy. I can check on that when I'm done here."

Jean felt as if her blood would boil. Weren't her co-workers and their families supposed to be her friends? Didn't they understand what she'd been through? Probably not, since, unlike Nigel who had no doubt spilled his guts to Flex, she didn't feel comfortable sharing every unpleasant aspect of her life. If Jean knew for sure what happened between them, she'd be glad to share. For now, though, she was still sorting through things herself. One thing she did have straight was her job position. She was consulting with Reebok, but she worked for Garments of Praise. Nigel did not. "That won't be necessary, Nigel. I wouldn't want to cut into Reebok's time. Let's just get down to business here, and I'll take care of company business."

Nigel put down his colors and took the seat beside her. He took Jean's hand and kissed the top of it. "So they didn't tell you, then?"

Her heart began to pound. Who was Nigel talking about, and what hadn't they told her? She thought back to lunch and that faraway look in Chenille's eye. What was she up to now? "No, nobody told me anything. What is there to tell?"

Her husband gave her another gorgeous smile. "There's not too much to tell, really. Just that Chenille has offered me a position here once my contract with Reebok is up. That's

83

all. I figured I'd better get a head start on learning some of my tasks—"

Jean didn't hear any more. She was on her feet, out the door, and down the hall. She knew what her friends were trying to do, but this time they'd gone too far. Way too far. She made it to Chenille's office in record time.

"Just who do you think you are?" Jean asked Chenille as she stormed into her office. She'd been so pressed to get in the office and say her piece that she hardly noticed Chenille's husband, Lyle, quietly resting in the corner.

Her boss held a finger to her lips, then stood. "I don't know what's going on, Jean, but I think you'd better lower your voice. As for who I think I am, the last time I checked, I was your boss. Now, would you like to go out and come in again?"

Jean lifted her glasses and stared at her friend. "Whoa. I guess I really don't know who you are. I don't know where all that fire came from, but I like it."

"Me too," Lyle said weakly from the sofa.

Immediately, Jean was sorry she'd wakened him. "I'm so sorry. I didn't mean to burst in like that."

Chenille handed Jean a stack of profit-and-loss forecasts for the upcoming spring line. "I'm glad you're here, frankly, even if I didn't care too much for your entrance. Look at this. If this is correct, this could be our bestselling line ever."

Jean glanced at the figures. "Wonderful."

Chenille pointed to the chair across from her desk, inviting Jean to sit. She sat down too. "Not wonderful. If orders come in like this predicts, we'll never be able to fill the orders. All of us are doing all we can on the design end, but we really need someone to oversee the production and keep things flowing. Lyle and I have prayed about it for the past few days, and we think Nigel might be the person for the job."

Jean leaned forward in her chair. "That's exactly why I came down here. You can't do that. He's got to leave once this project is over."

"Let me get this straight. You're okay with working with Mr. Salvador when it benefits you, but not when it benefits the company? At lunch today, you said there was nothing between you, so what's the problem?"

What's *your* problem, was the question that came to Jean's mind. This wasn't like Chenille at all. As if to confirm it, Lyle waved a hand from the corner, some sort of signal between them.

Still, Chenille didn't back down. "There's a lot going on, Jean. I know this is a sacrifice for you to work with him at all, but we're all making sacrifices, okay? People are depending on me for their livelihoods, and I want to continue to live up to the expectations and even surpass them. To do that, there may be some decisions made that make us all a little uncomfortable. What I need to know is, can you handle that?"

Jean stood and gave the only answer she could think of. "I honestly don't know."

7

"You've got to be kidding me," Jean said as she read the memo that had just been delivered to the conference room. It'd been three days since her run-in with Chenille about Nigel, and now Jean wasn't too keen on talking to either of them. Still, having a memo delivered by another employee instead of walking it down herself or calling for Jean to get it seemed a little cold. Reading it over, though, Jean could see why Chenille had stayed as far away as possible.

Please be advised that our former client Megan Ariatta has once again requested our services in the completion of her wedding gown project. The design and pattern phases were completed previously and a prototype created and accepted. The dress will now go to full production with only department heads completing the remaining tasks. Jean Guerra will complete the cutting of the pieces, and I, Chenille Rizzo, will put the piece together. Estimated production time is ninety days with the cutting completed by January 1. I apologize in advance for any inconvenience this may cause with deadlines already in place. Lily Chau will be back in the office one day a week starting next week to work on the marketing plans for the fall line. I'm currently working through production for the spring line. Please call me if you have any questions.

Jean wasn't sure what bothered her more, Chenille's professional tone or the fact that they were still working on a wedding dress three years later. Not only was the bride more than a little crazy, it was unlikely that she'd ever get married, let alone anytime soon. She was just insisting on completing the dress to torture them. Jean put the paper down on the desk and pinched her eyes shut.

Nigel reached down and took the paper. He scanned it quickly. "More work, huh?"

She lifted her head and looked into his eyes, something she'd avoided the last few days. "Yes, more work. That usually makes me happy, since the time passes faster, but there's just so much going on right now. I've had no luck finding another place for Elena's party. My apartment is too small—"

"No problem. The place they're renting for me is big enough. There's even some space next door they said I could use as a studio if I needed it. I can call today and see if it's okay to use it. I'm sure it's not a big deal." He touched her shoulders one at a time and began to knead them gently. She was too tired to try to rouse a complaint. He seemed encouraged by her silence. "Really. I'd love to do it."

Jean was too stunned by her husband's touch and his words to respond. Just as he reached a band of tightness around her neck, she pulled away. "We couldn't impose on you like that. There'll be kids everywhere. And the food. Without a caterer, I'll have to make everything myself. I couldn't cart all that stuff uptown. It'll never work."

Nigel's forehead creased, and redness that probably only

Jean would notice against his dark skin blushed the tops of his ears. "Never work? Of course it can work. The kids can have their run of the place. What do I care? I'll clean up everything. As for the food, you can cook at my place. Better yet, we can do the food together the week before. I don't know why they gave me such a big refrigerator. It's one of those stainless steel types."

Jean walked to one of the mannequins that now graced the conference table. She unbuttoned one of the jackets that had just come back from production. It was Nigel's military idea with double buttons down the front. She'd liked it on paper, but seeing it now, she knew it was probably the better idea of the two. And now she'd be willing to admit it if he'd stop all this talk of them cooking and having the party at his place. She'd given a lot of energy to not thinking about Nigel's place, despite having his address burned into her memory from the info she'd given to Monica. Now she could see the big stainless refrigerator he described, a comfortable couch with one of his shirts draped over the arm, and somewhere in the place . . . his bedroom. "I'll keep trying to find a place, but thanks for offering. I keep coming back to this jacket. It's amazing, really. Maybe we should go with your pick for the Spurs."

He slipped a finger into his cocoa-colored turtleneck and tugged, as if to give himself some room to breathe. "I like the coat too, but I'm not going to let you push me away so easily. It's my turn, remember? I want to help, and from what I gather, Elena wants me to be a part of the celebration too. I've wanted so long to have something to give to you, to all of you. Please don't turn me down so easily. Really think about it. We used to make a good team for holiday cooking, as I recall."

His words brought memories of melted chocolate and a

whirlwind of spices: cardamom, cumin, red pepper. Born to a Mexican father and an African-American mother, Nigel brought high notes and sweet spiciness to Jean's Dominican fare. When they'd first married, Nigel had spent the days leading up to the advent making a Tree of Jesse in their living room. Each day, he made an ornament and one of Jean's favorite dishes. Jean had caught on after the first year and joined in too, sharing the Christmas season with her husband even though she hadn't shared his faith. What could things be like now with them both celebrating Christ's birth? Jean wasn't sure she wanted to find out.

"Okay. I guess we can do it at your place if you really think it's okay. Today was about the last day to send invitations if we want anyone to show up, so I guess it's best to go ahead and accept your offer. As for the cooking, I don't know if you've still got it. I might have to sample something just to be sure." When Nigel started choking on his coffee, Jean realized what she'd just said and how it must have sounded. She slapped him on the back.

"Are you okay? I didn't mean it like that. I was talking about food."

Nigel took another swig of coffee, unable to hide the mischievous grin curving his lips. "Sure. I got that. And I suppose that a sampling is only fair after all this time. However, I warn you that if your food is better than mine, I will be forced to take it home for leftovers."

Jean couldn't help but smile at that. She inspected another mannequin next, the one with her preppy/funky look. The pink sweater and slate gray tie went well with the jacket, also gray, with a recessed argyle pattern on both front panels. It didn't have the immediate eye appeal that Nigel's design did, but there was something alluring about it. With each second she looked at it, it was growing on her.

"My thoughts exactly," Nigel said, rubbing a hand down one of the lapels. "I'm not sure if the pants work with it, but I'm very pleased with your jacket. It's a conversation piece and it's comfortable."

She took her hand away from the mannequin. "Comfortable? Don't tell me you tried them on."

He unbuttoned the suit jacket from the display and slipped it onto his shoulders. "Of course. I had them all cut 40 regular so I could try them on. Mannequins just don't do menswear justice in my opinion."

Looking at the way the fabric eased along Nigel's trim frame, Jean had to agree. The human model brought out something in the piece that she could never have conceived.

Power.

Though the jacket had young and fun accents, on Nigel's body it became strong and subdued. It didn't bunch eagerly around his body or hang slack. The jacket closed in the right places and curved away in others. Relaxed but controlled. Jean wondered how long her mouth had been hanging open. "It looks amazing on you. If it feels comfortable too, it's a winner."

He took it off quickly and replaced it on the table display. "It's definitely comfortable. The buttons work easily and the sleeve is cut just right. I can keep an eye on my watch without looking like it. Little things like that."

Jean turned away from him to grab her notes and the original proposal. She tapped her pen against the page. "What if we're going about this all wrong?" she asked, looking over their prior meetings.

Nigel ran a hand across his belt, no doubt thinking of how it would impact something in one of the designs. "Going about what wrong? I don't know what you mean—" He stopped for a second, then looked at her. "You mean the market, don't you? Your jacket was meant for a young person but turned out perfect for me because of its simplicity. My jacket looks great with all those buttons and bling, but it's really not something that I'd personally wear. One of Elena's friends might love it though."

Jean walked back to the easel and turned back the pages, surveying their sketches. "Exactly. We were both shooting for the same market, but it seems that we've ended up with products for two different markets. How can we help them get these pieces?"

Nigel snapped his fingers. "I have an idea that I think will work, but it's going to be more work instead of less. With that wedding dress, the party, and your other work, I don't know . . ."

She was still flipping sketches. "Just tell me what's on your mind. I'll worry about the work later," she said, pausing at Elena's tricolor suit sketch. It'd seemed clownish before, but now Jean could see the possibilities.

Waving his arms, Nigel paced the front of the room. "Okay, what about a fashion show for our presentation to Reebok? Nothing big, just two models, say me and, uh, Flex, if he can do it. I show the timeless simplicity of one style, and Flex shows the trendy flair of another piece. What do you think?"

Jean collapsed into the closest chair as she let out a scream. "Ahh! Yes! That's it. I just don't know how we can do it. Everything seems so . . . impossible."

Nigel stuffed his hands into the pockets of his tan cashmere pants, then pulled them out again. "Nothing is impossible with God, Peach. Nothing." He pushed the chair beside her out of the way and knelt down near her chair.

"But—"

He shook his head and rested back on his heels before

motioning for her to join him. Though he wasn't sure that his marriage could be saved, Nigel was certain that he and Jean made a great team and they could make this project work. There was a lot to be done, but perhaps, if they could stick together awhile longer, some great things could happen. As his wife slipped to her knees beside him, Nigel bowed his head, taking her hand in his. As he did, he thought of Doug and his excitement upon hearing about the first time they'd prayed together. As Jean's voice began to address God, he had to agree with his old friend. Prayer was a powerful thing.

Saturday came with a light dusting of snow, scattered like powdered sugar on the streets below Nigel's window. With so much going on at Garments of Praise, he'd forgotten to ask Jean what he should bring to Elena's little fiesta. He'd cleaned his place several times in case the girls wanted to come back with him on the train and check out the kitchen.

Until a knock sounded at the door, he'd forgotten that he offered to host Saturday morning prayer time for his new friends: Flex, Doug, and Lyle. Thank God he went shopping last night.

"Hey. Come on in," he said, opening the door for Flex and Doug. "To be honest, I forgot about today, but I can throw together some omelets while you guys are getting settled."

"You'd better think that one through, partner," Doug said with a wry smile. "We brought the little one along. You might not have enough eggs."

Just then, the door cracked again and Flex's older son, Jay, came in with a scarf wrapped around his face. As when he'd first met him, Nigel marveled at the boy's height, six feet at least. According to Flex, the kid had grown five inches over the summer and stunned them all. And now, he was eating them out of house and home. That said, Nigel had to give the boy some points for style at such a young age. He wore a burgundy cable-knit sweater, a coordinating pair of corduroys, and a tweed jacket woven with gold, burgundy, and green. Bone-colored suede boots topped off the ensemble.

Jay wiped his feet at the door and shook out of his jacket before making a beeline for Nigel. "Good morning, sir," he said, extending a hand with long, graceful fingers. A basketball hand. "Thanks for having us this morning . . . and whatever these two gentlemen said about me before I came is totally untrue."

Surprised again by the boy's open, polite manner and ease with adults, Nigel took Jay's hand and shook it. Flex made a sound of mock disgust at the table behind them.

Doug, who'd started hanging up coats, shouted down the hall. "We told him he probably didn't have enough eggs when he offered to make breakfast, Jay. Was that a lie?"

The boy gave a knowing nod, reverting to a more normal tone than his original salutation. "Naw, Mr. Doug. You ain't lie to him there." He rubbed his stomach. "I can eat some eggs now. For real. You too, right, Dad?" He punched Flex on the shoulder.

Jay's father pointed to a chair at the kitchen table. "Sit down, boy. And hush." He turned to Nigel. "Don't let his smooth talking fool you. We just rolled that boy out of bed a few minutes ago. I don't know if he brought his Bible along or his game controller. He barely made it up the stairs. As for breakfast, point me to the blender. I just happened to bring some protein shake mix—"

"No!" Both Jay and Doug, who had just reentered the room, seemed none too keen on the idea of one of Flex's shakes. Their voices clanged together like two iron pots.

Nigel went to his oversized refrigerator and brought out one of the egg cartons he'd purchased from the market the night before. He'd considered making a cake for Elena's dinner tonight and had stocked up on eggs, butter, and milk just in case. He gathered a wheel of cheese also and a few fresh peppers and an onion before turning back to his guests. "I've got the breakfast. You guys just get comfortable. Is Lyle coming?"

The jovial mood in the room was cut short at the mention of Lyle. Even Jay stared at the floor. Flex, however, mustered a broad smile. "We're going to put a call in to Lyle to get his requests. You've got a speakerphone, right?"

Nigel nodded yes.

"Right. Well, Lyle's in the hospital overnight for some tests, but he specifically asked us to call him. He hates that he had to miss it. We usually meet at his place. Last week, he must have known he wasn't feeling well, because he told us to ask you if we could come over here. It didn't occur to me at the time that he was trying to look out for us, knowing that he'd probably be at the hospital, but that's just how he is."

Jay disappeared into the bathroom down the hall. Nigel rinsed his hands and gathered his utensils. "This'll only take a few minutes."

Doug joined him at the sink, rinsing his hands and grabbing a paring knife. "Many hands make light work. I call veggies."

"But—" Nigel stared in wonder as Flex took the cheese and Jay, who'd reappeared, reached over him for a bowl and began cracking eggs. He stepped back from them, watching as they worked, each passing his ingredients to the next. By the time he put the pan on the gas and the butter started to melt, they were handing him a bowl. "You guys are pretty good."

Jay shrugged. "Mr. Doug taught us. Dad is pretty much a protein bar and chicken breast sort of guy, so I'm glad I can do a little something on my own now."

Flex grabbed a bag of oranges from the refrigerator and began squeezing them into a glass pitcher sitting on the counter. "A little something? Boy, from the look of my grocery bills, Doug may have ruined us all, teaching your behind how to cook. I can't lie though. The boy can make a mean cake. Make you want to bite your fingers off."

Nigel watched the edges of the egg mixture for signs that it was ready to fold over. Flex had grated some extra cheese for the middle and top of the omelet, and Nigel planned to use it. Seeing that breakfast still had a way to go, he turned to Jay for a moment. "Cake, huh? That's pretty cool. I'm considering making one myself today. It's a little complicated though, so I'm not sure if I want to go with something simpler. You know. Play it safe."

Doug pointed to the pan. The eggs were ready to move. As Nigel finished them up and garnished them with the extra cheese, he noticed that Jay had found some bread and made toast as well. "Glad to see that y'all are making yourselves at home," he said, walking over to the counter where Doug had four plates waiting.

Flex stopped pouring juice into the glasses he'd gathered to laugh at Nigel's comment. "We just came right in and housed your junk, right? We're just slicing and dicing and going on. Hey, sorry, man, but we're married and we have kids. We only get to hang out so often, and this prayer thing is a gem. We can't mess it up now."

Carrying two of the plates to the table while Nigel carried the other two, Doug joined in on the laughter. "Preach, preacher! 'Cause you know you're telling the truth. Those women of ours run a tight ship. You should know that better than anyone."

That was definitely true. In the two weeks he'd worked with Jean, Nigel had gotten more work done than when he ran his own shop. Many of the things he did Jean never knew about, but when he saw a lightbulb that needed changing or something out of order, he dealt with it, just as he had at his own place. Though he didn't officially work for Chenille yet and wasn't sure if he wanted to work there permanently, the place felt like home to him.

As they sat down to eat, it was Jay who almost made Nigel drop his steaming hot plate onto the table. The boy, who'd been silent since Nigel's cake comments, now came to life as if he'd been plugged back in. "I say go for it, man. With the cake, I mean. I could even help you out if you want. My grandmother gave me the recipe for this great Dominican cake, and I know Elena would love it. You were taking it to Elena's fiesta tonight, right? If my dad doesn't mind, we can even go together."

Nigel rubbed his chin, once more astonished at just how little he knew about his own family. Flex looked ready to scold his son, but Nigel shook his head. He had a feeling this was a boy he should get to know better.

A lot better.

8

They'd passed most of the train ride to East Harlem in silence, but both Jay and Nigel perked up as they exited the "6" train and entered the world of street vendors, Spanish markets, and people of every shade of brown. Jay responded easily in Spanish to the cryptic greetings of the other guys his age. Nigel watched as the boy's height slouched with every step they took.

Jay spoke first. "I think the cake came out good. That pineapple jam stuff was kind of hard to spread, but it's going to be tight, like the best ever. I can tell by the way it rose up out of the pan. That meringue stuff you made for the top had me scared at first, but that's looking really nice."

Nigel had to agree. They'd rigged the cake up with toothpicks and Saran Wrap. That was when they'd still been talking, of course. Laughing even. That was before Jay answered the ill-fated question that Nigel had promised himself he wouldn't ask—"So, does Elena have a boyfriend?"

Jay's answer? "Of course she has a boyfriend, Mr. Nigel. Me. Duh . . . How do you think she found out about you, anyway? If it was up to Miss Jean, you'd still be a secret." With that, the kid had commenced slicing the cake perfectly in half and filling it with pineapple jam while Nigel stood shocked and silent.

Now, though, with the cold gusting around them and the adrenaline pumping in his veins, Nigel felt brave. Until they came to a liquor store. Thoughts of how much of his life he'd missed while in prison flickered through Nigel's mind as he stared at the neon sign of bottles flashing on the store window. Inside, he saw a vet he'd known on the street. The sight both repelled Nigel and drew him in. Was he really worthy of a family? Was anyone? Nigel's feet paused despite his mental demands for them to keep moving. Jay, who'd walked on ahead, came back and stood behind him.

Lord, I don't know if I can really do this.

Jay tugged at Nigel the best he could while still keeping hold of the dish of corn pudding under his arm. "Come on, Mr. Nigel. Forget about that old stuff. If I'd been thinking, we would have gone another way."

Nigel felt himself moving, probably more out of shock than anything. He would have taken him another way? Just how much did this kid know? Worse yet, how much did Elena know?

That Internet. It's going to ruin us all.

When they were almost at the address on Nigel's invitation, it occurred to him that Elena had used a Mexican word to describe their dinner. *Fiesta.* Maybe she'd only meant party, but if not, he'd be making a fool of himself again with all this Dominican food. He let his breath fog out of his mouth as they walked up to the door. He could just take away all the tension and ask Jay what the dinner menu was. The kid seemed to know everything else.

Inside, colored lights showed through the curtains. Not

Christmas lights though. More like some kind of lantern. There was music playing, the happy kind that made Jean dance, with a grinding beat and a lot of words Nigel never quite understood except that it was usually something about love. He felt warm just listening to it, despite the cold evening. With a nod from Jay, he reached out and knocked on the door.

No response.

Jay smiled. "You being too polite, man. When you come over here, you really have to bang—"

"I don't like the sound of that word, young man." Nigel knew that he sounded old, but he was just being honest. He didn't have much right to be a worried grandfather, and if Elena was dating, Jay was about the best kid he'd ever met and definitely the one he'd choose. Still . . . he was fifteen. Nigel remembered when he was that age, and just the flashes of it made him shudder.

"Okay, knock then, Mr. Nigel. You have to knock really hard. Only Elena is listening for the door, and she gets distracted." He unzipped the large coat he'd worn over his jacket, borrowed from Nigel's closet when the weather took a turn for the worse.

Nigel reached out and rapped on the door hard and fast with his knuckles, military style. Immediately, the music stopped.

"See?" Jay said, balancing his dish in front of him. "Now smile, no matter what Miss Jean says."

The cake almost slid out of Nigel's hands. "What do you mean? What's she gonna say?"

Jay shrugged. "Well, there's no telling with her. You see, she doesn't know that either of us is coming."

Before Nigel could process the boy's words, Jean opened the door. She had an orange flower in her hair, some kind of rose Nigel had never seen. She must have been dancing before they'd arrived because there was a light sheen of sweat across the bridge of her nose and her lipstick was half gone. She looked beautiful.

Evidently Nigel did not. At the sight of him, Jean grabbed at her throat first and then at her skirt, as though a family of mice was standing on her porch instead of her husband and her granddaughter's boyfriend. Or was she clueless about that too?

Before she could start asking questions or Nigel could explain, Elena went under her grandmother's arm and welcomed them inside. She wore a similar outfit and a pink flower tucked into her curly ponytail. She took Jay by the hand and led him to the kitchen, but neither Nigel nor Jean said a word. They were both focused on the other woman in the room.

Their daughter, Monica.

Without thinking, Nigel passed the cake to Jean and started toward his daughter with his arms open wide. Some hard years had put weight on his angel and given her a scowling, suspicious look, but with every step he took toward her, Monica softened, straightened into the girl he'd left behind. They came together with a thud, her head against his chest, his arms tight around her body.

As his eyes filled with tears, Nigel tried to think of something to say, anything. Only one thing came to mind, the same thing as always. "I am so sorry, baby girl. So, so sorry."

She looked up at him with a weary smile. "It's okay, Papi. I'm sorry too."

They stood there for a long time like that, his forehead to hers, his hands in her hair. She was a woman now. A mother. "That's a beautiful girl you gave us in there," he said softly.

"*Sí*," she said in a trembling voice, speaking Spanish to

him. As a child, she'd been determined to teach him more of the language. They laughed softly together, and another set of arms surrounded them along with soft skin smelling of mangoes. Jean. She kissed them both on the cheek, father and daughter, before straightening and spinning on her heels.

Nigel and Monica watched as she strode toward the kitchen with purpose.

"So this is your little boyfriend, huh?" Jean wagged a finger at Elena and Jay, her other hand on her hip. "And all this time, I've been stupid enough to feed this child. Well, I guess you could do a whole lot worse. Get away from him, though. You're still fourteen. Don't look at me like that, Jay. I'll call your mother."

Monica shrugged. "I don't know how I got pregnant with her on the job, but poor Elena has her work cut out for her if she thinks this boyfriend thing is going to work out."

Nigel kissed his daughter's hair before letting her go. Just as quickly, he took her hand, unwilling to be anything but close to her after waiting all this time. "We've all got our work cut out for us, I'm afraid."

"So how'd she get you here?" Jean asked as they walked toward the kitchen together in search of a cool drink after a hot, close dance.

It took Nigel a second to realize that she was asking how their granddaughter had invited him. *You*, Nigel wanted to whisper in her ear. *She told me that you'd be here*. Instead, he dug into his pocket for his fiesta invitation.

Jean took it, read it, and laughed so hard that Nigel laughed too. She held the paper high and shook it in the air. "She should be arrested, this girl, or hired by somebody. Which I don't know. Come on." She took Nigel's hand and dragged him into the kitchen. He let her pull him, glad to be along for the ride. A few neighbors had been drawn in by the music, and the living room was now filling with people. Nigel wondered for a moment if they all would stay and if there'd be enough food. And then he remembered whose house he was in and who he was married to. Wherever Jean lived, there was always enough food, no matter how many unexpected guests showed up. And wasn't he one of the party crashers too? She definitely hadn't known Nigel was coming, but she hadn't asked him to leave either. Quite the opposite, in fact.

Nigel smiled to himself as Jean pulled out a vellum invitation inviting her to a practice *quinceañera* party at her own house. "Can you believe the nerve of that kid? And it came to my mailbox, no less. Living right here in the house with me and I get home last night and find this among my mail. She says she's not really inviting anybody and that we'll just see how the food might go and that Monica and I can dress up and pretend to be her court. When I got up this morning, the girl was already cooking and Monica was here cleaning. I couldn't believe it."

He stared into her happy face, listening as Jean's speech blurred past him. Something about the night was so healing, so wonderful that he felt he'd waited all this time just for this. This wasn't their apartment exactly, the one where they'd lived together, but the neighborhood was close by and some of the people were the same. When they saw him there, with Jean, they'd cried out with joy, some of them. Others had run outside to tell someone to go get a friend and come and see "Jean's *mestizo*," as some had called him. Elena beamed proudly as friends commented on how good her abuelos looked together.

Noting that the place was filling up, Jean started to look at the food. "I guess we should go ahead and get the tables going. Looks like this one will go late."

He could only hope so. Nigel didn't want to leave here for anything. Not tonight. Probably not ever. But ever was too long to think about. Tonight was all he wanted to take in.

"I can help you with that. Let me get Jay, and we'll take some tables out there. Just don't drop our cake. He and I almost came to blows over that thing."

Jean covered her mouth. "You made it? That big cake like that? You and that boy in there? It looks like a real Bizcocha Criolla. A real vanilla cake like from home. With the pine-apple and everything."

Nigel caught Jay's attention and waved the boy toward the kitchen. "It is."

She gasped, peeling back the plastic to survey it up close. "And this? Is it your meringue?"

He looked at her smile and felt full before taking even one bite of the food. "It is. The same meringue I put on our wedding cake. Jay's grandmother sent over the jam filling, and she mentioned that sometimes people put meringue on it. Jay thought I would ruin it, but I convinced him somehow." Nigel paused to nod at Jay as he approached.

"You get that end, son," he said, as Jean quickly cleared the food off the table.

They carried the table into the other room easily, with Jean following behind with both arms full of food. Chicken and rice seemed to be the main entrée from what Nigel could see and smell now. One of his favorites. If Elena had really cooked it all like Jean said, the girl was bound to be a great cook.

Not having to be told twice, the crowd swarmed around the table. Several women complimented the corn pudding he and Jay had made, and Nigel could see the boy towering over them, sharing Nigel's secret of cooking it with a vanilla bean. Nigel shook his head. That boy couldn't hold anything in, despite cool-guy façade.

Maybe I should be more like him.

Jean fluttered between the guests like a butterfly, but Elena followed close behind, reminding her grandparents, mother, and boyfriend-in-training to fill their plates and meet her in the kitchen. Knowing better than to keep that little lady waiting, Nigel made a quick plate of chicken and rice and a few tamales someone had brought and headed for the kitchen. Inside, everyone was already sitting at the table. The vanilla cake he'd brought sat in the middle of the table.

He waved one hand in protest. "Hey, why'd you leave our cake in here? We worked really hard on that thing, didn't we, Jay?"

The boy nodded but didn't look up. He'd started eating and, from the looks of things, had no plans of stopping anytime soon.

Elena waved her grandfather to the chair beside her. "They're going to get some of this cake, but only after we all have some. This is a big day for me, a practice for my birthday and a time for all the people whom I love to be together." She paused and smiled at Jay. "Except you, of course. I like you though. Very much."

Jay rolled his eyes and kept eating, giving Elena a "whatever" sort of look.

Nigel wasn't fooled. His granddaughter had meant what she said the first time. He looked across the table at Jean, who was also surveying the two teens. She was definitely on to them too.

Elena pulled out a stack of papers as everyone but Jean and Nigel plowed into their food. As though he'd caught himself, Jay lowered his fork. "Hey, did anybody say the blessing?"

Jean shook her head. "We know you didn't. You were too busy eating. Would you like to say it now?"

The boy wiped his mouth and extended his hands in both

104

directions. "Sure. I can do that." He bowed his head. "Dear Lord, thank you for this time with Elena and her family. Please bless everyone here with peace, joy, and love. Help us to serve you better, and let Mr. Nigel and Miss Jean get back together so that my parents can stop making me pray for them every night. In Jesus' name, amen."

Nigel felt a kick under the table. "If you were shooting for him, honey, you got me," he said to Elena.

She looked doubly embarrassed. "Sorry. I can't believe he said that."

Already attending to his plate, Jay gave her a funny look. "Yes, you can believe it. At least I didn't say anything about what you—"

Another movement swiped Nigel's foot under the table, this time making contact with the desired target.

"Ow! Cut it out, okay? I'm trying to eat." Jay tried to tuck his long legs to the side of his chair so that Elena couldn't reach him. He held his plate on his lap like a mother protecting a child.

That made them all laugh, even Jean, who'd looked horrified after Jay's prayer. Things unwound after that as Elena compared party plans with Jean. The biggest fight of the evening proved to be the quince dress itself. Jean insisted on the traditional white wedding gown with the court of young ladies, or *damas*, wearing dark evening gowns and the young men, or *chambelanes*, wearing dark suits or tuxedos. While Elena appreciated her grandmother's sentiment, she insisted that she'd rather save choosing a wedding dress until she actually got married. "I'm just turning fifteen, Grandma," she said with a smile. "I'm becoming a woman, not a bride. I want to wear something bright. Vivid. Let the court wear white. Right, Grandpa?"

From the look on Jean's face, Nigel knew better than to

weigh in too much on the dress question. Still, it felt nice to be included even if Elena was just trying to get someone on her side. "I see both your points, but I'll defer to your grandmother's wisdom here. Perhaps you should too. You'll be beautiful no matter what you wear."

Jay, stuffed with food and silently reclining in his chair, gave a nod of agreement. "That's for sure. She looks good in anything." He swung his legs around in case Elena tried to get him under the table again.

Jean reached over and pinched him instead. On the way home, Nigel decided, he'd have to give that boy some training on what to say in front of women. He'd definitely been hanging out with the fellas too long.

By the time they settled the dress question with Jean reluctantly caving in, Jay was half asleep and Nigel was watching the guests dance in the living room. When he turned again, Elena had placed a chunk of cake on a plate in front of him, along with a glass of milk. "This is girl talk, *Abuelo*. I see that now. Eat your cake and go and dance. We will finish the rest."

Too relieved to protest, Nigel elbowed Jay awake and took a bite of the cake. The rich, subtle flavors of vanilla mixed with the tart, sweet pineapple took his breath away. Jay wasn't much on talking to the ladies, but the boy sure knew how to make a cake. "Wake up and eat some of this thing, man. It's amazing. You outdid yourself."

The boy revived long enough to take a few bites, followed by a swallow of milk. "Not bad at all," he said before nodding off again.

All of them looked at him dumbfounded. Elena, who was licking her fingers after every bite, couldn't seem to believe that Jay had made it at all. "Grandpa, are you sure he made this? I mean did you see him mix it up? I mean it's just so, so good."

Through with his dessert, Nigel assured his granddaughter that Jay had indeed mixed up the batter and provided the recipe as well. Monica suggested that this be the cake for the party, but Jean wasn't sure. How could someone so young make enough cake for over a hundred people? It wouldn't work.

Nigel disagreed, offering to help Jay with the cakes. "Now you'll just have to wait until he wakes up and ask him if he's willing to do it. Jean, the offer to use my place and my kitchen still stands. You all tell me what you want to do." With that, he'd joined the guests in the living room, dancing the evening away with old friends and new. It'd been a long time since he'd had something besides work to celebrate, something besides clothes to be proud of.

I'm proud of you, came a whisper as gentle as a breeze.

Nigel walked to the window and looked outside, staring up into the night sky. How he'd longed to see that sky those years he was locked away. How he'd longed to be here celebrating birthdays with his wife and child. How he wanted to be part of a community again, a church, friends, family . . .

"What are you looking at?" Jean's body pressed against his back. Her hands laced across his chest.

He held those hands, kissed them, not wanting the moment or the night to end. But it would. And soon. "I'm just looking at the sky. Looking at God. Thanking him for tonight. It means a lot to me to be here."

Even though Jean probably wouldn't have ever invited him on her own, Nigel no longer cared about the circumstances. If it took Elena's plots and plans to make tonight happen, so be it. At this point, he'd take this kind of happiness any way he could get it. It was never enough in the long run, these kinds of things, but for tonight it was more than enough. Tonight it meant everything.

Jean leaned forward on her tiptoes and kissed the back of

107

his ear. "Thank you for coming. Really. Elena drives me crazy sometimes, but this time I'm glad she is who she is. I was too afraid to do this, to have you here. I should have been the one to invite you, from the minute you arrived. I'm sorry." Her hands left his chest and went to his back, moving upward in small circles. Upon reaching his shoulders, she began to massage them, draining away the remainders of the fear and anxiety Nigel had brought along with him for the night.

Nigel felt himself melting in her hands despite his best efforts to focus on his family as a whole this evening instead of focusing on Jean. How could he not focus on her? She was beautiful, smart, funny . . . He turned to face her. She was his wife.

"I'd better be going," he said. "I need to get Jay home, not to mention myself." It would be a long, cold night with little sleep, but he had to face it just the same. The memories they'd made tonight would hold him. He'd learned in prison how to survive on a memory. Tonight he'd have to do it again.

Jean ran a hand through his hair and tugged at his neck, lowering his face to hers. She kissed him gently on the mouth as some of the partygoers started to leave. "Flex just came for Jay, and Elena is going home with Monica. So you don't have to rush home."

Still reeling from the kiss, Nigel knew he had to leave now or he'd do or say something that he might regret later. "It's late and cold out there. No sense prolonging the inevitable. I'm already too comfortable as it is. If I stay any longer, you won't be able to get rid of me."

"Good," she said, giving him a look that he still understood even after so many years apart. "Stay with me, then."

Heart racing, he leaned forward and kissed her neck. "I thought you'd never ask."

9

Like wine, love got better with age. Someone had told Nigel that once, but he hadn't believed it. When he and Jean were married, they'd spent most of their time working, parenting, and fighting Nigel's chasing after the God of his future and the pain of his past. Their intimate times together had been cinched from tight schedules and quick-stitched moments of passion, often to make up after a bad fight.

Last night was different. This love, so many years later, was something new, something wise and patient, something both kind and passionate. Though morning streamed through the upstairs windows of Jean's bedroom and the scent of sweet coffee beckoned to Nigel from the kitchen, he stayed still, trying to pray. Trying to think. Neither came easily. His only thought was to pull the blankets up around him and stay put a little longer. He couldn't leave that bed until he said what he had to say, something Jean probably didn't want to hear, from the look of both fear and wonder in her eyes before she'd gone downstairs.

She knew too that something extraordinary had happened between them and that no middle ground existed any longer. It couldn't. For the first time in a long time, maybe ever, they knew each other. Nigel chuckled, thinking that he finally understood the passage in Genesis where Adam "knew" his wife. God had packed nuggets of truth into those verses, truth that both he and his wife now had to face.

"Aren't you going to get up?" Jean came back into the room wearing a black robe with pastel florals and Asian accents. It looked lovely, but Nigel wanted to pull it off her shoulders and drag her back to bed so he could hold her a little longer. To look at her . . . to make her listen to what he had to say. As if she sensed his plan, Jean took a seat on the edge of the bed after setting a cup of coffee on the nightstand next to Nigel.

"I'm afraid to get up," he said matter-of-factly, wondering if Jay's dangerous honesty hadn't rubbed off on him after all. Those words were the last thing he'd wanted to say to Jean, though they were totally true.

From her stony expression, Nigel knew a scathing comeback was on the way, so he braced himself as he scanned the room for his clothes. He found them easily, folded neatly on a chair at the foot of the bed. He'd forgotten that about Jean too, her way of making even small things seem special. Nigel motioned for her to hand him his clothes.

"I'm afraid too," Jean said softly. "I don't know what to do now. We can't be just friends anymore." She passed Nigel his shirt.

"Definitely not," he said, nodding in agreement. "I think I knew that going in. Or at least I should have. Still, I'm not sorry I stayed."

Jean raised an eyebrow like he'd seen Raya do around the office many times. "You'd better not be sorry you stayed. I'd hate to think I had all that fun by myself."

Nigel stopped buttoning his shirt and leaned toward her for a kiss. "No, you did not enjoy yourself alone, but I think you know that."

Jean bit her lip. "Papi, I think the neighbors know it. I'm going to have to move after this."

Papi.

It had made his heart flip to hear Monica call him that, but to hear Jean say it again . . . He pulled the sheet over his head for a moment and then pulled it away. "Enough of that. You're just trying to distract me. What I want to know is how you want to do this. Do you want to move in with me uptown until I get my own place? Or do you want me to stay here? And our vows. Do you want to renew them—?"

Jean pressed a finger to his lips. "I was afraid of this. You're moving too fast. Taking things too seriously. You act as though you stole my virtue. We're already married, you know."

Anger welled up inside of Nigel, but he took a moment before he spoke. He took Jean's hand, now on his cheek, and placed it in his own. "I do know that we are married, Peach. More so now than ever. This is serious. We can't just enjoy the benefits of marriage when it suits us and not be together. It isn't right."

"Maybe not, but I don't see how it's wrong either." She pulled his hand to her lips and kissed it. "I failed as your wife when we lived together, but this I can give you. I know Carmen is younger than I am—"

"Don't." He swung his legs to the side of the bed and tugged on his pants. "Don't bring Carmen into this. It's about us. You are my wife. I want to be your husband. I want us to stand up before God and man and declare that we are together."

111

She stood. "Aren't we together now? Weren't we together last night? This is what I can give you right now. Just stay here on the weekends. Work is work. When the project is over, you can do what you need to do concerning our marriage. After all we've been through, isn't it enough just to be together?" She put her coffee on the table next to his and walked over to him, pulling his face to hers.

He held her hand still before pulling away. "Last night, the same people who told me you were better off without me when I came to find you came out to see me. I didn't know how to fight for you then. I believed what they said, that I'd messed your life up enough. I just figured that one day I'd get served with divorce papers because you'd found somebody who could make you happy. Well, those papers never came and now I'm here. I want to make you happy."

Her kiss brushed his ear. "So make me happy."

The air in the room even seemed to still as disappointment chilled Nigel to his bones. She didn't get it. He'd thought that with God, with time, with love, everything would be clear. Easy. Instead, it was all confused. His body wanted more than anything to stay, but his heart knew that it would take more than any love they might share in that bedroom to make things right between them. He still wanted to believe that what happened last night had been the start of something. His only regret was that he hadn't found Jean ten years earlier and that the last woman he'd been with hadn't been his wife instead of Carmen, who also managed to confuse his feelings, despite his best efforts to be clear with her as well.

"As much as I'd love to stay again, you know I can't. It wouldn't be enough now, just being here with you. I need to know how you feel about me, about our marriage. I need to know that you want to be my wife again." He tucked in

112

his shirt and slipped his belt through the loops. Where was his jacket? Probably downstairs.

Jean got up too, turning her back to Nigel. "I love you, that's all I can say. I guess I am your wife, even though I didn't do a good job at it. I don't know how to make that right for you. Or for me."

"That's God's job, babe. We can't make it right. Any of it. It just is what it is." Nigel tugged on his socks before taking some of the coffee Jean had brought up for him. He looked into her eyes, hoping she could see deep into his eyes too. Into his heart. "Look, I failed as a husband too. Before and after I got out of prison. I've lain here all morning wishing that I'd searched harder for you, that I'd waited for you, held out. Instead, I gave in to something, someone, that I shouldn't have."

"But you didn't know where I was. I'm the one who put you in that situation." They were both crying now.

He wiped her tears instead of his own. "That's no excuse. You were still my wife. I should have waited for you."

She pulled away and walked over to the window. "I did wait for you, only not in the ways that mattered." After a long sniff, she became silent. "This person you were with, that you gave in to, was it Carmen?"

Nigel stopped, shoes in hand. Carmen again? Where had that come from? "Does it matter? Carmen helped me get on my feet when I got to LA, and she still has a thing for me, but she knows how I feel about you. She knows that you are my wife." Even as he spoke the words, Nigel wondered to himself about the truth of them. Carmen was still out of town working on other projects, but she emailed and called him incessantly despite his telling her that nothing else was going to happen between them. He'd always used not knowing where Jean was as the excuse to keep them apart, so she

113

probably thought he only wanted to find Jean to divorce her. There'd been times, years, when he'd thought that too. But not now. Probably not ever again.

"Just tell me. Was it her? I know you have a weakness for hips, after all." Jean's voice rose this time. The steely edge that was often in her voice at work came out again now, cutting Nigel to the heart.

Angry that she'd fixated on Carmen when it was the two of them that they needed to be thinking about, Nigel blurted out his answer. "Yes, okay! It was Carmen. And if you must know, I got my hip-thing from being with you. In fact, it's probably what attracted me to her in the first place. She reminded me of you. Are you happy now? It was Carmen. Not that it makes any difference."

Jean turned slowly to face him. "The difference is that Carmen is downstairs getting out of a cab. And I doubt she's here to see me."

A few weeks ago, Nigel had reminded himself that things fall apart. Now he wondered if sometimes they didn't explode too. With his feet half in his shoes and his mind at half-mast, he downed the stairs two at a time, grabbing his coat from the couch where someone had placed it.

"I'm sorry, Jean. Really. I never even told her where you lived. I didn't know myself until Elena gave me that invitation. You have to know that I would never do anything like this."

It sounded silly, even to him, so he stopped himself from talking and focused on getting to that door and outside before Carmen tried to come in. Jean was ahead of him now, moving toward the door with purpose. More than anything, the feeling was impressed upon his mind that Carmen should not come into the house—

But as was Carmen's fashion, come inside she did. Wearing a white mink coat and red suede pants and matching boots. Her eyes seemed swollen, as though she'd been crying.

Jean closed the door and greeted Carmen stiffly before tightening her robe and starting for the stairs. "Lock up on your way out, Nigel," she said, her voice ringing with finality.

He ignored the comment, turning to Carmen instead. "What are you doing here? Have you lost your mind?"

"No," she said, aligning the zipper on his coat and yanking it upward. "My mind is fully intact. My heart, however, is a different matter. All these years, I thought this woman was your wife in name only. Now I see that it's more than that. It complicates things, but I'm not throwing in the towel yet. What I need to know from you is what you want."

He sighed. What Nigel wanted was what, according to Jean, he couldn't have. Though he and Carmen had been friends through lots of ups and downs, he didn't want to go through this with her. Not in Jean's living room. "Let me walk you to your cab, okay? This is my wife's home. I don't want to disrespect her any further."

The stairs creaked above them. He knew without looking that Jean had paused to listen. All the more reason for him to get this woman outside. Right now. He grabbed at a pile of fur where Carmen's elbow should have been, but she seemed to melt through his grasp.

Carmen's shrill laughter echoed through the room as she pulled away from him. She staggered toward the door, her finger pointed in the air, circling twice before turning to face him. "You're worried about disrespecting her? Oh, that's funny, see. Real, real funny. What about how she's disrespected you? She played you again, don't you see that? You'll never be good enough for her. You're no better off than me. Good enough for a booty call and nothing more. For all that

God stuff you talk, it's all the same. We're both in love with the wrong people." She lifted her chin toward the staircase, which had been silent since Jean's creaky pause. "Isn't that right, *mujer*? Never the right time."

Nigel stiffened at the sound of Jean's footsteps, this time coming down instead of up. The steps were slow, measured. Though she'd become a Christian now, Nigel still knew personally how rough Jean's fury could be. And then Carmen had to go and pull the Spanish card, at that?

"Girl, come on," he said, attacking the ball of fur again. This time he got her, but Carmen put every bit of her weight into resisting him. By the time he coaxed her to the door, he could sense Jean right behind them. Already he could imagine the face of a nosy neighbor between the curtain slits.

I'm way too old for this.

"Are you talking to me?" Jean asked calmly. Too calmly.

Carmen laughed again. "You could say that, I suppose. I'm talking to all of us here, but yeah, I'm talking to you. I don't get you. You left him in jail, then paid a PI to find him and never looked him up. Now he's here and you're playing head games?"

"What? You had somebody look me up? When? . . . Jean?"

She shook her head, refusing to answer.

Nigel felt behind him for the wall. He needed to get outside. Now.

"Nigel! Wait. Just wait. It's not that simple. There were things . . ." Jean batted the ends of her robe belt against each other like drumsticks.

Carmen took a step back and took Nigel's hand. "Things, huh? It's always something with you. Both of you." Carmen's icy stare rested on Jean. "But you're not my problem. He is."

Nigel jerked his hand free and stared at both of them in

116

disbelief. Jean said she loved him, but she didn't want to be with him. Carmen said she loved him, but she wouldn't let him go. Jesus and only Jesus had given him the kind of love he needed. Maybe that's what he'd been sent to New York to learn. If so, it'd been a painful lesson.

He opened the door and trudged outside, waving off the cab driver's invitation. He didn't want to go anywhere with Carmen right now or anytime soon. She'd gone too far. And Jean? She hadn't gone far enough. Nigel had wakened that morning prepared to be Jean's husband in every way. Now he realized that, from the time she'd stopped taking his calls from upstate, Jean had never planned to be his wife ever again.

He could hear Carmen behind him on the sidewalk, calling his name. He turned up his collar instead and disappeared onto a side street, steeling himself against a rusty fire escape ladder. Like his own relationships, the apparatus remained, giving the illusion of safety, but if fire ever came to the building, it would be useless. He fell to his knees in the snow, praying for help in his own fire, hoping that instead of burning him up, this pain that he felt would burn off the sludge that choked the truth from his life so many times. He still wasn't sure why he'd come back to New York, but he was now certain of one thing—God himself had led him to this wilderness, and God himself would bring him out.

10

It was Monday, staff meeting day. Still weary from the weekend, Nigel hadn't remembered. From the surprise on Jean's face after the announcement that the meeting would be in Chenille's office instead of the conference room, Jean had forgotten too.

Without any more talking from anyone, the room filled, leaving only two chairs next to each other for Jean and Nigel to sit in. He considered just leaving. After all, he wasn't really one of their staff, and he knew now that he could never be. Jean had built her own world with her own rules, her own friends, her own relationship with God. He was having enough trouble trying to accept that, and now more confusion assaulted him: Why was Doug's wife back at Garments of Praise? And why was everyone staring at him? What had Jean told them? He lowered his head. It didn't matter. It was a jumbled mess. The man always sounded like the bad guy. He couldn't win, not with these people. This was Jean's crowd.

Before the meeting began, Raya tapped

Nigel's shoulder. She pushed a note in front of him and pointed to Chenille. Besides that, she gave no other greeting, and her face had none of its usual expression. Nigel wasn't sure if that had something to do with Jay or Jean. Probably both. He unfolded the note.

Go into my office, please, and call my husband at this number. He's waiting to hear from you.

Glad to get away from the sea of eyes that seemed to be floating toward him, Nigel left the room with only a nod to Chenille. He made it to Chenille's corner office quickly, but paused at the door. Why was Lyle waiting to hear from him? Was everyone in on some kind of gang up on Nigel after what had happened over the weekend? Knowing that Chenille, Raya, and Lily probably knew the details was torture enough. Still, he went into the office and picked up the phone. He didn't know Lyle well, but something about the man was both encouraging and comforting. He had the look of a warrior but the voice of a sage. And Nigel could definitely use some wisdom right about now.

He sat on the edge of Chenille's chair, staring at her cheese puff stash for a moment before actually dialing.

Lyle picked up on the first ring. "Hello? Nigel?"

Nigel rested back farther into the chair, despite the faint smell of Chenille's perfume. "It's me."

"Great. Hit video if you want to see my pale mug. Second button from the bottom. Chenille uses it to watch me take my meds sometimes. I say she just wants to see if I'm still alive."

The leather burped as Nigel shifted in his seat. There it was again, that I'm-gonna-die-any-minute humor that Lyle seemed to inject into every conversation. He clicked the button for video and smiled as his new friend came into view. "Can you see me?"

119

Lyle nodded. "Sure can, dude. You're looking real suave today. As usual."

Nigel shrugged. "I'm not feeling suave. Far from it. I feel like an idiot."

"Ah. The weekend fling didn't turn out the way you thought it would? Bummer." The screen blurred for a moment as Lyle straightened himself up in the bed.

Nigel slouched down in the chair, eyes closed. "So you know about that? Me staying over at Jean's, I mean?"

Laughter interrupted by coughing came across the line. "Know about it? You don't know our wives very well yet, do you? Not to mention the fellas. Things were real good for all of us until Sunday."

Tell me about it.

"But later for that. We can pray on that if you want once we're done. What I want to know is if you're the man."

Nigel looked around the room. The man? "What man? I was declared innocent. I haven't done anything."

Lyle attempted to laugh again. "Cut it out, man. You're killing me. Literally. The next thing I know, you'll be over there with your hands up. That's not what I meant at all. I mean, are you the man that God sent here?"

The room felt warm all of a sudden. The image of Lyle across the room giving him that questioning look at the first staff meeting flashed back to Nigel's mind. That day, he'd been asking Nigel the same question he was asking now. And like then, he didn't have an answer. He wasn't even sure he understood the concept, though something within him agreed with the question. "I don't know what you want from me, Lyle, but I think I should tell you that I'm contacting Reebok today about being released from the contract. I really like all of you, but things just aren't working out. Jean is more than capable of finishing off the project herself."

"If she could finish the project by herself, you wouldn't be here. I know that seems obvious, but think on it awhile. Pray on it. On the other hand, that still may bode well for me and for what I need." Lyle's face came closer to the screen. "You see, I'm dying. I know that my jokes about it make you and other people uncomfortable, but it's a fact, so I try and get some fun out of it. It's a miracle that I've lived this long, and I know Chenille's love has a lot to do with that miracle. But this time, things are getting bad, and the Lord showed me that he is going to release me. He also showed me that he was going to bring a man to help carry the company, to be friends to my friends. I believe that man is you."

Nigel turned away from the small camera in the phone. He didn't know what to say. Sure he'd spent sleepless nights thinking up hundreds of ideas for Garments of Praise. Sure the people who worked there and their families had worked their way into his heart. But to stay would mean being around Jean every day, and after this weekend, he didn't see how that was possible.

With God, all things are possible.

It was one of his favorite Scriptures, that one, but it sounded so much better when he was saying it to someone else. Yesterday he'd stayed on his knees in the cold, wet snow trying to hear God, trying to enter his presence. The time had ended with Nigel surrendering to whatever God wanted for him, to whatever purpose he'd been brought to New York for. Had he been selfish to assume that it was all about him? About Jean? Could it be that him being at Garments of Praise had less to do with his marriage and more to do with a dying man's desire to make sure things were in order so that his wife and her friends could continue to do the thing that brought them joy?

He turned back to the camera. "This is crazy, you know?

When I saw Jean that first day, I was so sure why God had brought me here. I didn't know how it was going to play out, but I just knew that this was some kind of closure for me. Some kind of restoration. And now, listening to you, I'm wondering if it wasn't that at all. I mean, what if I'm just meant to be the answer to your prayers?"

Lyle didn't laugh this time. "The question is, will you be the answer to my prayers? Are you willing?"

Nigel bowed his head for a quick prayer, but this time it wasn't for direction or confirmation. This time God's leading seemed clear: a brother in the Lord needed something he could give. "I don't know if I can stay forever, but I'll give it five years."

A bit of color came to Lyle's cheeks and went away as fast as it had come. He disappeared from the camera, probably back on the bed. His voice, however, rang clear. "Thanks, man. Five years is enough. I'm going to have to go now and rest, but I want you to know that you didn't come here just for me. You came here for her, for you, for Elena, and Monica, for Jay, for Raya and Flex, for Doug and Lily, for Chenille, for me. God wants to do something big. Something crazy. And I'll be watching for it, whether it's from this bed or from heaven."

"Don't talk that way." Nigel knew he'd found someone different, someone genuine in Lyle. He wasn't ready to lose him yet.

"Okay, I'll go easy on you, but remember, you can't win God's battles with your hands. Stay on your knees, no matter what you see."

"Yeah," Nigel said as the line went dead. He used to know that, how to see God instead of circumstances. Since coming here, though, he hadn't seen past his own nose, his own fingertips. He hadn't seen past Jean's beautiful face. Now, he thought back over Jean's words. What had she said again and again? Failure. She hadn't been a good wife. She didn't think she could be one now.

He started down the hall, back to the meeting, sad that he could still hear voices behind the door. He'd hoped to melt into a rush of people heading back to their departments. Near the door, he took a deep breath, taking in what he'd just agreed to and what that would mean for his life. No more uptown apartment. No travel. He'd have to stay put, dig in his heels, and learn how to be friends again, how to be neighbors. It occurred to him then that he and Jean had never learned how to be married. They hadn't had loving relationships modeled for them or an understanding of what a godly marriage was supposed to be. Regardless of what happened to the two of them, these were things he wanted Elena to learn.

Instead of the silence he'd encountered when leaving the meeting, Nigel's arrival brought waves of applause. He looked confused, turning to Jean for a clue, but she wouldn't meet his eyes.

Chenille cleared up the mystery. "And here he is, ladies and gentlemen, Nigel Salvador, the new general manager of Garments of Praise. He'll be effective after the New Year, when I'll be taking an indefinite leave of absence to be with my husband. I'll still be chief executive officer, and I hope to have some of my original design team step up into leadership as well."

Nigel slid into his seat. Chenille's eyes rested on Jean and then panned the room.

"Until then, our own Lily Chau of Worlds Apart Fashions will be moonlighting with us one day a week."

The applause was deafening, but it couldn't drown out the low, deep hiss of Jean's words as she turned to face him.

"If you did this to hurt me, be proud. You outdid yourself

this time," she said, her words trembling with her pending tears.

With that, Jean stood and ran from the room.

Nigel did not follow.

They got a lot of work done. With the laughter and flirting gone and only the work left, Nigel and Jean's days became much more productive. Though Nigel had advised against it in the beginning, Jean spent more time working in her office, emailing and faxing Nigel down the hall with sketches and ideas. On the weekends, Nigel went over Chenille's plans for the spring and summer lines and reviewed the marketing campaigns and fashion shows from previous years.

November wound down like a worn clock, and the holidays pulled tighter and closer, daring to spring at any moment. Elena, Monica, and even Jay emailed and texted Nigel daily with inquiries about Thanksgiving dinner. To make things simple for Jean, he'd decided to have a dinner at his house on the Saturday after Thanksgiving and skip the dinner at her house. Despite assurances by his daughter and granddaughter that he was welcome, the icy quiet between him and Jean was enough to deal with at work. He'd spend Thanksgiving as he usually did, at a mission somewhere feeding vets or homeless people. There was always plenty of work to do and enough food to keep him for a week.

It was Wednesday, and the break from work looked stressful enough without Carmen's unexpected arrival. Nigel's only consolation was that Jean had been in her office most of the day working on the infamous "Megan dress" and was likely to stay there. He hadn't seen or heard from Carmen since that day at Jean's, and he wasn't any happier to see her now.

"I just came to apologize," she said, staying at the door

instead of gushing her usual affectionate greeting. "I'll be out of the country for a while and don't know when I'll return, but I needed to come and say good-bye and I'm sorry. I had no right . . ."

His jaw tensed as he tried to be polite, despite his desire to raise his voice. "Good-bye, Carmen. I pray the best for you. And no, you didn't have a right. I don't know how you found out what you did, but it wasn't your business. Anyway, I'm sorry too. I didn't mean to string you along, but I did."

For once, Carmen stayed quiet. "You didn't know?"

Nigel blew out a breath and picked up a stack of sketches. He'd sent several preliminary ideas to Reebok, and they'd sent back revisions on some but seemed pleased with the work so far. He was ready to wrap up this conversation.

"I didn't know what? About the private investigator? No. How would I have known? I'm not like you, checking up on everybody in my life. When I was at a point to hire somebody like that, I didn't have the money. When I got the money, I was too scared of what I might find."

Carmen walked into the room and took a seat in the first chair she came to. "I didn't investigate you, okay? True enough, I thought about it, but like you, I wasn't sure what I'd find. A year ago, a guy came up and hit on me in a bar. He knew that I'd lived in LA. Said he used to be a private investigator and that he'd helped a wife find her husband. He'd found the guy, all right, he said. In my bed. When he described the man, I knew it was you and thought it was time now for me to look for your wife. I figured if she never came for you after seeing the pictures the man said he took, then she was done with the whole thing and you two could get divorced and we could finally be together."

Nigel froze, watching as the sketches slipped from his hand and drifted across the table. Pictures? No wonder Jean had been so fixated on Carmen. She'd come for him after all and found him in someone else's arms.

Lord . . .

He didn't even know what to pray. What to say, either. He did know that Carmen had to exit the building and never, ever come back. "If you've ever cared about me, please go. I thank you for everything you ever did, including bringing me here, which I see now you must have had a part in."

She nodded yes. "I'm going. All that I ask is that you fight for her the way I fought for you. There's definitely something strong between you. Pray for me, will you?"

Nigel's eyes narrowed in surprise. "That I can do."

With that, she was gone, but not before Jean emerged in the doorway. She'd opened her mouth to say something, but at the sight of Carmen, she pivoted on her heel and turned away. Nigel checked the battery level on his laptop and phone, knowing that the rest of the day with Jean would likely be spent in electronic communications. Suddenly, that didn't bother him. He reached into his pocket for the intercessory prayer verses that Flex had passed out at their prayer meeting at Lyle's the weekend before. His finger traced the last words on the page.

. . . having done all, to stand. Stand therefore . . .

And as they did in prayer meeting after reciting those words, Nigel sank to his knees, knowing now more than ever that the best way for him to stand strong for his family, for his faith, for his marriage, was to kneel.

Nothing could have surprised him more than when he felt a hand grasp his and join in as he recited the Lord's Prayer and the Twenty-third Psalm. As Jean's new fruity scent drew him in, another prayer, silent and singular, echoed in Nigel's heart.

Thank you.

126

11

He'd been right about one thing. There was a lot to do. He'd chosen the Bowery Mission to help out at for Thanksgiving, and some of the people who'd come through the line had tugged Nigel's heart in every direction. What he enjoyed most about the day, though, were the smiles. Despite the situations that many of the people were obviously dealing with, he sensed inside many of them a deep abiding joy, the same infectious joy that Lyle had in the face of death and pain. Though he and Jean hadn't talked over their break from work, some of the ice had melted between them after their prayer yesterday. When he went to her office for a mock-up sheet that he was missing, Nigel noticed a Bible, pad, and pen on Jean's desk. He'd turned away, committed to praying for her more and focusing on himself less. More than anything now, he wanted God's best. He wanted peace.

Looking into the faces of these people who were so thankful for a simple meal, he remembered how thankful he had been to stand outside with the wind on his face, to finally be able to go where he wanted when he wanted to go there. Simple things that many people took for granted. Nigel never did. He still kept in touch with some of the inmates and ex-cons. Someday maybe he could go back to Eastern Correctional and share what God had done in his life, but right now the "doing" was still in full swing.

A kind-faced older woman who'd known all the dinner guests by name shooed Nigel off the food line. "You can go now, you know. Go on home and eat with your family. You did a great job today. We appreciate it. Everyone did."

He slipped on his coat and waved to everyone on his way through the dining hall. He left only because he wanted to get home and rest before rising early tomorrow to start on his own dinner. He could only hope that the girls wouldn't have eaten so much at Jean's that they wouldn't want his food. He'd invited Jay and his family also, so at least he knew that someone would be eating.

As he ventured out into the cold, his thoughts drifted to Elena's *quinceañera* party. He'd asked her a few times if there was anything he could do, but she assured him that things were under control. Although he hadn't known his grand-daughter long, he'd talked to her enough on the phone to know that she was being more hopeful than truthful. A few days later, though, his bright, beautiful invitation had arrived. There would be a service at Jean's church and a reception to follow in the basement. He was relieved that they'd found a place, but sorry that he wasn't more a part of it. Instead of worrying about it, he committed it to prayer.

When he got home, the phone was ringing, but he didn't make it in time to answer. On his machine, the light was blinking wildly, and it looked like he had six or seven messages. Knowing something was up, he pushed PLAY. Hard.

"Um, Mr. Nigel? This is Jay. I'm just trying to see if you've talked to Elena or anything. We sort of had a little falling-out because I told her that maybe we should wait until next year to actually date, and she's been acting kind of weird. Hanging out with some guy I used to know from before. He's bad news. She hasn't called me since last night, and she didn't go to Thanksgiving at Miss Jean's. Her mom doesn't know where she is. Just thought maybe she was with you. Anyway, Happy Thanksgiving."

Nigel played the message again before going on to the next one. Jean had told him a little bit of Jay's background the night he had stayed over, how both his parents had died from AIDS and he'd fallen in with a bad crowd. He'd been staying with a distant elderly relative when Chenille showcased him in one of their staff meetings, and the firm vowed to help by designing the uniforms for his church basketball team. Raya was the designer and Flex the coach. By the end of the season, they ended up engaged, and adopted Jay not long after. Nigel had been surprised at first, since he'd thought that Flex and Jay resembled each other. The more he was around them, he saw that they acted alike more than looked alike. The kid was growing on him every week. This message, though, made Nigel nervous. Where was Elena? It was a holiday. This didn't seem like her.

Before calling Jean, he played the other messages, most of them also from Jay, checking in a few more times and saying that he was going out to look around and would call Nigel back. One from Doug, inviting him over for dinner if he wasn't already stuffed. Normally, Nigel would have stopped to call Doug back, but his mind was in knots about Elena. Had she hooked up with some girlfriends and forgotten to call? He hadn't heard much from her about girls except to voice her disapproval of most of them at her school. To hear her tell it, they wore high heels every day and tried to act dumber than they were so people would like them more.

Some of the "dunces," as she called them, would be part of the court at her party, which was why she wanted it to be different. Ever the teacher, Nigel had commented then, but he wondered now if the teacher hadn't failed one of life's primary lessons—don't talk to strangers.

As he picked up his keys from where he'd laid them and checked for his phone, Nigel pressed the button to hear the last message. It stole his breath.

"I, um, can't get Grandma. I guess maybe she's out looking for me." Elena's voice choked up. "I'm in Central Park, Grandpa. A boy, he tried to hurt me. I'm by the sign. Come and get—"

Nigel didn't hear the rest of the message. He only heard the door slam behind him and the click of his heels against the cement. As he ran, only one thing came to his mind, to his mouth.

"Lord Jesus, please. Let her be all right."

"Where is he?" It was the only question Nigel could think of as he held his granddaughter's head against his chest. The other questions . . . well, they'd only upset him more.

Elena's shoulders shook against him. "I-I don't know. He had me down and he was reaching for something, but I bit his hand and kicked him as hard as I could. I ran here, to the front of the park where there was a lot of people."

Nigel's breathing slowed. She'd bit him and kicked him. Sounded a lot like what he wanted to do to the kid too. "Did you tell the police? I know there have to be plenty of cops on this beat. Come on, let's go find one."

His granddaughter pulled away. "Can't we just go home? Back to Abuela's? I saw the police, but I called you instead. I'm okay."

She might have been okay, but Nigel wasn't. He led Elena over to a bench, keeping a sharp eye out for any signs of trouble. "Look, sweetheart. You're not okay. Having someone try to hurt you in any way is not okay. I really would like for us to talk to the police." He spoke softly, smoothing the leaves and twigs out of her hair. She was shaken, he knew, but refused to show it. Or was that just what he wanted to believe? Had something like this happened to her before?

Elena slouched forward, the puffy sleeves of her nylon jacket sliding down her thighs as she hid her face in her hands. A moment later, she sat up and slipped off her hair scrunchie before arranging her curly tresses into a tight bun. "Thanks for coming for me, Grandpa. Seriously. But I can take it from here. No police. The guy, he's in a gang. I don't want any trouble."

Nigel swallowed hard. A gang. How could he have been so stupid. Here he'd been worried about Jay, and now some gangbanger was on the scene. He knew enough about gangs and the fear they held over people to know that he wouldn't be able to convince Elena to talk to the police. If he was honest with himself, maybe he didn't want her to now either. There were things that worked outside the law, things that he didn't want his family to be a part of. He pulled his scarf from around his neck and looped it around Elena's. It was only when he leaned in to tighten it that he saw the red ring around her throat. She had definitely defended herself, but she'd left out some of the story. Looking left to right, he took her hand. "Come on."

They moved quickly through the Thanksgiving crowd of people strolling through the park. Neither of them feigned a holiday face but moved purposely to the nearest subway stop. Once on the train, Nigel kept hold of her hand, walking until they came to an empty car.

131

It was then that Elena broke down. The remainder of her dark lipstick smudged against the back of her hand as she wiped her mouth with her fist. Her lips pouted upward as the tears rained down her face. "I can't believe I was so stupid. Jay tried to tell me about LJ, but I didn't want to hear him, you know? LJ told me he didn't roll with any gang, and I believed him. I should have known that something was up when he called on Thanksgiving asking me to meet him."

Nigel had questions, but he decided they were best left for later. He, not the police, was the one hearing her testimony, and he wanted to get as much of it as she was willing to give without shutting her down. He fumbled in his pocket for his phone, knowing there was one question he had to ask before they talked to Jean, much less saw her. "I hate to ask this, sweetheart, but do you think you need to go to the hospital? There could be injuries that you don't feel right now because your adrenaline is pumping and everything."

His own adrenaline surged as he waited for her answer, knowing that if it was a yes, he'd have to call the police, gang or no gang. Helplessness settled over him as she paused before answering.

Elena pressed the scarf against her throat. "No, I don't think so. He choked me after I bit him and tripped me as I ran away, but nothing . . . nothing inside me is hurt."

He pulled the girl to him and covered her head with his. He was rocking his head back and forth with hers, saying, "Okay . . . okay . . ."

Finally, he released her, but she held on, burying her face in his side. "I'm not hurt there on the inside, but it was close." She pulled up her baggy jacket and showed him her jeans. The buttons were gone and the zipper was broken. "He almost . . ." Sobs overtook her before she could finish.

Nigel pulled down her jacket and pulled her into his side.

132

He let his head fall back but stopped himself from screaming the way he wanted to. Why hadn't he just come to dinner today like she'd asked him? Why hadn't he tried harder to find them in the beginning? Why hadn't he been able to keep this from happening? "I am so, so sorry, little one."

They sat quietly for what seemed like forever before Elena sat back in the plastic subway seat and wiped her mascara-stained eyes. "Call them. All of them. I know they're worried. Tell them that we're coming and I'm okay."

Nigel nodded. He'd called Jean several times on the way to the park and left messages about where Elena was and that he was going to get her and bring her back to the house. Jean had probably been out searching too, but hopefully she'd gotten the messages and returned home.

He would find out now. He pressed "1" on speed dial and waited for an answer.

Elena smiled. "Speed dial, huh? I hope I'm on there."

Nigel held up two fingers. "Yeah. It's me. I've got her—please, don't cry . . . I know. Who is that? Jay? . . . I thought so. We're almost there. We'll probably get off at the next stop and get the bus . . . No? . . . Okay. We'll stay on here and meet you at the station. You want to talk to her?"

Elena shook her head and pulled a finger across her throat. "No. She's going to kill me as it is."

"Well, um, she's sort of still in shock, but she's fine." He paused and nodded before answering in a quieter voice. "Yes, I asked about that . . . No. He tried, but no. She got away." He paused to look at Elena, trying not to imagine what could have happened. What almost had happened. The voice on the phone pulled Nigel from his thoughts. "No, we did not file a report—talk to Jay. We'll see you soon."

At the next stop, other passengers filled the car. Nigel and Elena rode on in silence, both of them occupied by their thoughts. Nigel was thinking of his own adolescence as a young black boy with a Latino name. Rejected by his mother's family because of their dislike of his father, Nigel was ignored by the Mexicans he knew as well. He spoke no Spanish and knew nothing of his father other than the worn picture his mother kept of a smiling man with a thick mustache and glossy black hair. His mother had worked two jobs to try to get them out of the projects before he hit puberty, but she hadn't made it in time. At thirteen, he'd fallen in with the wrong people in the neighborhood, trying to find an identity that fit, a place to belong. His mother had moved him out of the projects, but he continued to hang out with people who stayed in trouble, often bringing trouble to him. On the day he graduated from high school, his mother had dragged him to the army recruiter, hopeful to save her son from prison life. Little did she know then that she'd actually sent him to war.

Still, the army had given Nigel somewhere to belong, something to believe in. The black guys named him "Conquistador" and called on Nigel to sing their favorite songs from home when they got homesick. Hispanic guys who might have ignored him back in Detroit now cared for him like family, nodding in pride at the worn picture of his father. "You should go there sometime, to Mexico," one of them had said. "When all of this is over. You should find him. He'd be glad to see you. They all would." That thought seeded deep in Nigel's mind, flowering in his heart during his years in prison. Unable to find Jean and Monica, he made his way west, working odd jobs, finally crossing over into Mexico with a picture that was more paper than film and a name as common as Smith in the United States.

Still, when he arrived at the small village his father had come from, he was received as a son. His father had died six years earlier in Houston, Texas, but his maternal grandmother remained. Nigel traveled through Veracruz to Yanga to find her, where she'd kissed his face fondly and gone back to making her tortillas. A little woman wearing sandals made of tire treads, Maria Carmen Anna Spiro y Calderón de Salvador. It was her strong eyes that stared blankly out of Elena's face now on the seat next to Nigel, her same strong spirit in Elena that had been choked and almost broken. He could not allow that to happen again.

Elena slid her hand in his. "What are you thinking about? Me? I told you I'm okay."

He laced his long fingers with her shorter ones. "I am thinking of you, of course, but I'm thinking of someone else too. My grandmother Anna. You remind me of her. Very much."

His granddaughter leaned over onto Nigel's shoulder and closed her eyes. "I remind you of her? Really? Tell me about her. Please."

And so he did. Despite the crowd of people around them, Nigel told Elena of the three years he spent with aging Anna in her two-room house in Yanga. He recounted the stories she'd told him of her Jewish father escaping from Austria and her dark *mestiza* mother living through the years of revolution and social change. He shared the stories of his melting-pot heritage—tales of Gaspar Yanga, the slave who'd rebelled and built a free city, and the priest Jose Morelos who fought to do away with the caste system of race and color. He told her about the old woman's tortillas and her constant, piercing prayers.

"I didn't find out until after she died that she was almost a hundred years old. Her hair was white, but her mind was sharp. She laughed when I told her that my mother's family hadn't accepted me. She said that God's people would never find peace about color until they focused on the red blood of

Jesus," he said, suddenly noticing how many people on the train were listening.

Elena sat up again. "So it's just like here? White and black, light and dark? I thought that everyone in Mexico was the same."

He shook his head. "Does everyone anywhere look the same?"

She sat back. "No, I guess not. And I'm glad. I like being different, and I like other people being different too. Does that make sense?"

"It does." The train came to a stop and they stood. Nigel waved nervously as many of the passengers who'd been listening to his stories waved good-bye. He wasn't sure how such a tragic moment had turned into a family history lesson, but he was thankful. Thinking about his grandmother had calmed him down, reminded him of her total confidence in God's providence. It was she who had proclaimed with surety that he would find Jean someday. Little did he know then how much more there'd be to it than just meeting one another again.

As they stepped onto the platform, a swarm of arms enveloped them. Jean took Elena's face into her hands and squeezed it tight. "If I wasn't so happy that you're okay, I think I might put you over my knee. Have you lost your mind?"

Nigel tugged at her sleeve. There'd be time enough for scoldings. "It's still Thanksgiving. Let's just be thankful that we're all safe. And together."

"Amen." Monica's voice surprised him. She'd surged forward when they got off the train; she pulled back just as quickly. He knew from his conversations with Jean about Monica that God was a sore subject, but times like this made everyone thankful.

Jay, who hadn't said a word, nodded his head and walked

to Elena's side. He looked at Nigel with a questioning glance. When Nigel nodded, Jay took Elena's hand and started toward Jean's house.

Jean turned to Nigel with a scowl. "What was that? Don't you see? That's how this all happened in the first place. Boys. She's too young for boys."

Nigel looked at Monica, waiting for her to respond. Instead, she turned and walked into the train station. "Thanks for calling me, Mom. I'm glad everything's okay. I gotta go. Call me when she's ready to come home."

"Monica!" Both Nigel and Jean called her at once.

She kept walking, stopping only to wave a hand over her head. "I just gotta go." She sounded as if she were crying.

Nigel took a deep breath. He'd missed it with Monica, and there was nothing he could do to change it. For Elena, though, he wanted things to be different. Even if it meant fighting with Jean. He tucked her arm under his and talked quickly before she could try to pull away. "Look, this didn't happen because Elena is interested in boys. It happened because she used bad judgment, broke the rules, and went out with the wrong boy. That kid up there is a good kid, and if we're both honest, we'd admit that without him she might have ended up dead today. This whole thing is about him not feeling approved of by you—maybe by both of us—and him telling her that they should put off dating until she's sixteen. That's why she went off with that idiot who tried to . . . to . . . ." He couldn't even say it.

Jean didn't pull away. In fact, she wedged her arm tighter around Nigel's. "I love Jay. He's a great boy. And he obviously has a lot of sense. I think sixteen is a much better idea."

"I agree, but Monica never set that rule. You've told her all her life that at fifteen she'd be a woman and have a big party. Now which is it? Womanhood or just a big party?"

They had been keeping pace with the kids ahead of them, but this last question hit the mark. Jean suddenly stopped. The same hands she'd held to Elena's face a few minutes earlier now pressed into her own cheeks. "Oh, my goodness. What have I done? I've been telling her to act like a woman, but I've been treating her like a child. It *is* more than a party." She shook her head. "That's why she asked for the party again. How could I have missed it?"

Nigel pulled Jean close. "We missed it because we're human. You were a great mother, and you're a wonderful grandmother too. I know I'm new to the game, but I think it's going to work out." He looked back at the train station that Monica had disappeared into. "All of it."

Jean wiped her eyes. "I'm wonderful, all right. I thought maybe once I got older, all this would get easier. It's just getting harder."

He felt like a punch landed in his gut as he reached and wiped her tears. She was right about that, for sure. Every time he was with her, it was getting harder and harder not to push things, not to try to make something grow up out of nothing. Like the first thoughts of his trip to Mexico, this marriage was also a fragile seed, breaking open under hard ground.

Lord, show me what to do. I can't do this by myself.

Jean slid her hand around Nigel's waist as they turned the next corner. "I hope the house is still standing. I don't know if I remembered to turn off the oven or not. Either way, there's probably not much to eat. Sorry if I ruined your Thanksgiving."

He leaned down and kissed her forehead. He thought about his last years in prison, years without Jean's visits, without knowing that she'd press the right button to accept his calls. Thanksgivings that had come and gone like any other day. "Being with my family is all the food I need."

138

12

Elena had played the strong role with Nigel, but by the time he and Jean rounded the corner, Jay was carrying her. She was curled into his chest with her face hidden.

Jean gave Nigel a piercing are-you-sure-about-all-this look. He shrugged and shook his head. "I'm not sure, if that's what you're asking, but we're going to all go in here and act like we have some sense. Promise?"

She sighed. "Promise."

Jean pushed past the young couple to open the door. Jay took Elena to the couch and laid her down and then took a chair near the door. As Nigel entered, the boy pulled his mouth to one side. "Too much?" he asked quietly.

Nigel gave him a stern look. "Definitely. Chill or we're both going to get put out."

The boy threw him an okay sign. "Gotcha."

Though Nigel had said he didn't care about food, Jean headed straight for the kitchen. When she screamed a few seconds later, everyone bolted in behind her.

"It's done! Can you believe it? And—and juicy. For years, I've been basting the stupid thing every thirty minutes. I leave it to burn and it's perfect. Can you believe it?"

Nigel stared at Jean, hair plastered to her forehead and her face free of makeup. Could he believe that something, someone, you left behind could turn out perfect? Yes, he could. "I'm glad we came back when we did so you could turn off the oven, but like I said, it doesn't matter about the food. You don't have to cook."

Elena snorted, then turned and started back into the living room. "I'm coming, *Abuela*. Let me go change my clothes."

Jay went to wash his hands. "I can do the sweet potatoes if you want."

Nigel shook his head and went to the oven to help Jean maneuver the hot bird. "Are you guys serious? It's been a rough day. We can order pizza for all I care."

Both Jean and Jay looked at him as though he'd suggested they commit a criminal act. He shrugged. "Okay, figure out what I'm supposed to be doing until the turkey is cool enough for me to carve it. I'm going to see what's on TV."

Or so he thought. When Nigel reached the living room, he had to squeeze through the influx of neighbor women to get to the couch.

"Where does it hurt, honey, here?" An older Mexican lady from several doors down pressed a raw potato onto Elena's forehead. No doubt, they'd seen Jay carry her in and thought the worst. Although in Nigel's mind, what had really happened was as close to the worst as he wanted to get.

Elena tried to smile but looked to Nigel for help as the next woman stepped up, wielding a tub of butter. "Is that a bump on her head? Yes, it is. Don't you see it? Right here."

Nigel watched in horror as the lady buttered his grand-daughter's forehead. "Uh, ladies? Thanks so much for coming over, but—"

The next-door neighbor, a robust Puerto Rican lady, grabbed Nigel's hand. "A man, that's what we need. I think her leg is hurting. Shake her pants leg."

Nigel grabbed his forehead instead. "Do you smell that? I think something's burning. It smells like—"

"Excuse me," one woman said, taking off for the door.

"And me too," said another.

Not convinced, the other ladies stood their ground. "What'd it smell like?" the Mexican woman said, narrowing her eyes at Nigel.

He swallowed hard, thankful that he really did smell something burning, only from inside their house instead of out. He mumbled the best answer he could think of. "Rice?"

"Oh, dear!" They all ran out one after the other, leaving Nigel and Elena to clean the butter and potato off her head.

"Off you go," he said finally, sending her upstairs. "And not to change and cook either. You rest. I'll deal with your grandmother." Nigel knew that Jean's way of dealing with things that bothered her often involved vigorous, exhausting work. He wasn't going to let Elena participate in it. He was still considering taking the girl to the hospital, despite concerns about any possible retaliation from the boy or his gang. He peeked through the blinds at the neighbor ladies, again congregated on a front stoop nearby, and had second thoughts about bringing trouble here.

Trouble was here long before today, Nigel.

It was probably true, but just the same . . .

"Elena? What's keeping you?" Jean gave a cry from the kitchen. From the sound of it, she was probably pounding, chopping, or kneading something into submission.

He went back to the kitchen, now swirling with the smell of hot olive oil. It was even worse than he thought. The woman was frying something. "I sent Elena upstairs for a nap. She'll be down later. Is something burning?"

Jean looked up from where she was tossing little logs of something that looked like french fries in hot oil. "Not burnt. Just had a problem with the oil. It's a different brand, and this stove is funny. This is frying cheese. Do you remember it?" She handed him a piece that had cooled.

He remembered the taste immediately, but when he'd last had it took him a minute to remember. "Oh, yeah. You made it during the NBA finals, if I recall. Haven't seen that stuff in years."

Jay, who'd been quietly scraping what looked like a ton of sweet potatoes, gave Nigel an encouraging nod.

Nigel rolled his eyes. That kid. Just like his dad. He was about to ask what she wanted him to do when the doorbell rang. And rang. And rang.

She barely looked up. "Aren't you going to get that?"

"Sure," he said. "I just didn't know if—since I don't—"

Jean sighed. "You can open the door here. Okay?"

"Okay," he said with relief, trotting off for the door. He opened it and stared in disbelief. Instead of the returning band of neighbor ladies he thought he'd find, his friends and co-workers from Garments of Praise had come, with all their families. Flex and Raya handed him two stacked pans and a cornucopia before coming inside.

"Ribs," Flex whispered as he passed by. "Don't eat too much though. We're going to have a shootout after dinner. I hope you brought some shoes, old man."

Nigel laughed and waved in the rest of the crowd, including Lily and Doug and several other people he recognized from the firm. He tried to point at Flex, but with his hands full, he couldn't manage. "I'll whoop you in these loafers, son. And on a full stomach."

Everyone booed as he shut the door. Nigel took the food to the kitchen and kissed Jean on the cheek.

She smiled. "I planned for you to be here, though not under these circumstances. Flex was going to come over and drag you here somehow."

Nigel shuddered at the thought of it, though he wished he'd ended up here that way. As if he'd remembered something, he put down the food. "I'll be back in a couple hours. Save some food for me."

Jean turned off the heat and pulled the pan away. "You're kidding, right?"

He grabbed his jacket from the back of a chair in the kitchen. "I wish I was. I'm going to get Monica. She's part of this family too, whether she believes it or not."

Finding his daughter was easy. Convincing her to come home with him was proving impossible.

"Please, Monica. It won't be the same without you. Come to dinner at your mother's and then come over to my house for dinner like I've been asking you. I know you're busy with classes and all, but I really want to spend some time with you."

Monica sat next to him on the lumpy couch in her apartment. She'd been eating a TV dinner when he came over. "I think it's great that you're back. I hope that you and Mom can even work things out somehow. I'm glad that Elena has grandparents. For me, though, it's just a lot to take in. To see you again once is more than I could've hoped for."

Nigel slouched his shoulders. Like her mother, Monica was content to know he was alive, but unwilling to go further.

143

He couldn't blame her. "You're right. It is a lot to take in. I'm sorry I wasn't here to give you the things a father should give his daughter. I'm sorry I couldn't try to answer all your questions or give you advice. I'm sorry that your memories of me are of cold, black snow in a prison-yard visiting center. I'm just sorry."

Monica covered her face. "Why? Why did you stop writing? Why did you stop calling? Did you forget about me? Did you stop loving me because I had a baby?" Her voice cracked as she tried to turn away from Nigel.

He caught her by her shoulders and brought her to him anyway. "Is that what you think? Never, ever will I stop loving you. Your mother didn't accept the calls, and she pretty much let me know that she needed to focus on being a mother. I think she felt like she'd focused so much love on me that you'd gotten your love from someone else. She felt like she had to choose." He paused. "And she chose you."

His daughter lifted her head and stared into his eyes. "But what if I didn't want her to choose me? What if I wanted her to choose us? Our family? I don't know. I guess I was sick of her always giving all the money to that lawyer, going on that bus upstate to that cold, ugly place. I should have gone with her to ride that bus. I should have told her how strong she was . . ."

Nigel swallowed back the bitterness he'd thought long gone concerning his incarceration. For several months after gaining his freedom and not finding his family waiting, he'd asked again and again why he'd been the one falsely accused. There was a small settlement for his emotional duress, money that he spent going to Mexico and getting started with his tailoring. He kept some of it, though, and now he wanted to help his daughter, to try to give her the life she might have had if he'd been at home.

"Just come to dinner with me now. We can talk about the other times later. If you don't feel comfortable coming to my place, then we can go out to a restaurant or a movie. I just want to get to know you again, to hear about your dreams and what you want to do with your life. To see how I can help you."

Monica pushed her hair back out of her eyes and surveyed him closely, as if searching his face for the same truth she thought she'd heard in his words. "You want to help me?"

"Yes," Nigel said. "I want to help you with your education, with your children—"

"I don't see my boy anymore. Not at all," she said, stretching her arm along the back of the couch.

Nigel covered her arm with his. "I know that, and I want to help out with that too. I know there is a lot going on with you, and I won't try to act like I have a clue about any of it. I just want you to tell me what you need—and come back to dinner with me, of course."

Monica dropped her head and began digging into one of her cuticles with her thumbnail. "You're right. I need a lot of things. Big things. The first one is something that I think we both want—save Elena."

Her request caught Nigel off guard. "Save Elena? From what?"

Troubled laughter bubbled from his daughter's mouth. "Save Elena from herself. She's prettier than me. She's smarter than me too. But sometimes I see so much of me in her. She longs after her daddy the same way I longed after you."

Nigel adjusted his weight on the couch cushion he was sinking into. He'd tried to ask both Jean and Elena about Elena's father, only to get a quick change of subject every time. Now Monica had left the subject wide open, and Nigel feared what she might say. Still, he wanted to know. "It's funny that you'd mention Elena's father. I've been wondering about him myself. She's a beautiful girl. Why doesn't he ever come around? Or at least call."

"The same reason you didn't." Monica rubbed her hand around in her thick head of hair, creating a big mess, just like the one Nigel had talked himself into.

He frowned, confused. "He's . . . he's a prisoner? Where? Why?"

She pushed up from the couch. "Upstate just like you. Almost to Canada. Aggravated burglary and a lot of other stuff. Twenty years. He probably could've been out earlier. I don't know. He was young, just eighteen. I tried to go up there, to be strong for him. But after . . ." She picked up the TV dinner and walked it to the kitchen a few feet away. She turned back, but stopped at the counter and leaned on one elbow. "I just couldn't."

Nigel ran his hands down his pants, tugging them at the knees. Not only had his little girl loved him as an inmate, but she'd fallen in love with a man who'd become an inmate too. It'd probably been like losing him all over again. "I'm sorry," he said, staring at the living room wall.

"He still writes. Once a month. To me, though. Not to her. She tried to go up there by herself once. Last summer. He put her name on somehow, but she couldn't get in without ID. We never talked much about it since. We never talk much about anything."

"So I noticed," Nigel said quietly. "Even today it seemed like your mother and I were kind of in your place. I apologize for that. She's your kid. We're not trying to raise her. Well, at least I'm not." He mustered a smile, thinking back to the look on Jean's face when Jay had lifted their granddaughter into his arms. God bless any other guy who tried to come along after they got through this rocky beginning of adolescence.

She started the dishwater for what seemed to be an amazing number of dishes for one person—all glasses and cups. She attacked one heavy glass mug rather savagely with the soap and scrubber. "That's exactly what I want you to do. Raise her. You and Mom both. For now, at least. For starters, I want you to take her down to the police station and file a report."

Nigel rocked to his feet, pressing on the back of the couch to get up. "I wanted to, but Elena said the guy was in a gang. I didn't want to jeopardize her safety, or your mother's."

Monica squeaked around the top of the mug with a dish towel. "Safety? Do you think she's been safe all this time? No. Safety starts tonight when she goes to that police station and tells the truth about what happened today. If she doesn't, then the next time this happens, and the guy deflects the bite and the kick and does what he came to do, she won't tell anybody. Not you. Not me. Not Mom."

A sick feeling wrenched in Nigel's gut. His daughter was right, but that wasn't what bothered him. It was the certainty of her words and the sincerity in her eyes. She wasn't some prophet giving an ill-fated forecast. She was a victim, looking back to recount the sad but true facts. Facts that should have been nightmares, or newspaper headlines about someone else's daughter. If he had been there, it could have been different, but he wasn't there back then. All he had left was now.

He swallowed hard and rounded the kitchen counter, taking the cup from Monica's hand. She shook her head, trying to force back her tears, but he went on hugging her anyway. "I am so sorry, baby girl. I just . . . I can't—"

"Make her do it, Papi. And make sure she has that birthday party. She needs to know that being a woman can be a beautiful thing." She pushed away from her father and took up the mug again. "I need to know it too. That's why I need y'all to take her. I've got to get myself together. It's time."

147

Nigel steadied himself on the counter. What a Thanksgiving.

And yet, Lord. I will praise you. I will trust you. Show me what to say.

"You're doing well, honey. Going back to school and all. You're trying. I'm going to try with you. I'm sure it won't be a problem for your mother and me to take care of Elena for as long as you need. And I'll take her in to file a report. You just tell me what you need, as Monica, not just as Elena's mother or our daughter. What do you need?"

Monica walked over to the pantry and pulled out a small plastic trash can. She pulled off the lid, revealing bottles of every type of alcohol imaginable: beer, wine, rum, vodka, whiskey. There were juice cans and soda bottles too, probably for times when she'd thought enough to mix something in. Slowly, she looked up at her father's eyes from where she was bent over the wastebasket. "As you can see, I am not okay. I thought going to school would be the answer to everything. Everyone promised it would be. It's been good. I'm learning new things, and I feel better about myself. But I've been reading the Bible Mama gave me, especially about the people Jesus made whole. I don't just want a remedy. I want a healing."

Nigel squinted his eyes shut to fight back the tears flooding to his face as he reached for his daughter. She wasn't a preacher. She wasn't even saved, but she'd just preached the best sermon he'd ever heard in his life. "That's what I want too, baby. For you and for me. We're going to get you some help, okay? Now let's go home."

13

It wasn't easy. Though Nigel's return with Monica was a big success, the rest of what he had to do was met with resistance, starting with an unexpected source—Flex.

"I want to talk to you," Flex said as Nigel explained to Jean what Monica wanted them to do, and why.

Nigel stepped aside to talk to his new friend. "I want to talk to you too. Jay is a really great boy, and we're glad to have him around. You already know that he's welcome at my place anytime I'm there. I'm sure the same thing goes for Jean."

Flex didn't smile. "About that. I really appreciate you all reaching out to Jay and all, but I really think he's getting too emotionally attached with Elena. He and I have been praying about this for a couple weeks, and I didn't want to push him in any direction. I just asked him to really seek the Lord on this thing for himself. He came back to me on his own and said he'd rather wait until they were both sixteen next year. Then this whole thing happens with one of his old boys from the block, and he's all caught up in it. I don't like it."

Nigel scratched his head. Until now, he and Flex had gotten along famously despite their basketball rivalry. Now, though, listening to the fatherly concern in his friend's voice, he knew this wasn't going to be easy. They both wanted to protect the people they loved. "I don't like it either, but we've got to go ahead and take her in. It's bad enough that so many hours have passed and some of the evidence is probably destroyed. I should have gone with my first instinct when I found her and gone to the police then, right there in the park. I let her scare me with all that gang talk."

Flex took a firm grip on Nigel's shoulder and blew out a frustrated breath. "That gang talk, as you call it, could become very real very quickly for my son. If they can't get to Elena, who do you think they're going to come after? We've prayed heaven and earth together to get this kid on the right path. As much as I love you and Jean and even Elena, I'm going to have to ask you to use some wisdom in this, especially since she went willingly with the boy alone—"

"Whoa, wait a minute now. What are you trying to say? That she deserved being almost raped because she went and met a guy in the park? She's fourteen. Still a kid. Kids do stupid things." Nigel brushed Flex's hand off his shoulder and took a deep breath of his own, trying to keep his voice down. The women, Raya and Jean, were both focused in their direction and looking concerned. Though they probably couldn't hear the men's words, body language spoke volumes, and right now the two of them looked like two boxers ready to square off for a match.

His muscular arms crossed and biceps bulging through his sweater, Flex spoke in an even lower, more controlled tone. "Exactly. Kids do stupid things. That's why they're not ready to date. My son has already done his share of stupid things. Now we're trying to teach him some wisdom and prepare him for his destiny. And quite frankly, I'm not sure that Elena is part of his future."

Was this guy for real? Nigel threw his hands up. "Part of his future? You mean, like his wife? They're fourteen, for goodness' sake. What do you want them to do, get betrothed or something? I don't think you're being practical. This isn't Jerusalem, man. It's New York."

Flex shrugged. "I don't care where we are. God's Word is his Word. My wife and I met when we were young, but we had that same attitude and thought it didn't mean anything. So, in the meantime, we made a lot of mistakes. We're just trying to teach Jay to seek God in everything and not to despise his youth the way we did. A lot of things can happen that determine your future before the world says you're an adult."

Nigel sucked in his anger and considered his friend's words and the words of his daughter a few hours before. Though Monica was in her thirties, the events of her early teens and girlhood had set the course for the rest of her life. Even he, who had escaped the wrong crowd for the army, had continued to seek out people whom others thought of as bad company. How could he fault the guy for trying to be a good father? It was more than he'd ever had the chance to do.

"All right, Flex. I don't agree with everything you're saying, but I do see your point. The thing is, my daughter has asked me to take Elena to the police. I said that I would. I don't know how to keep my word and do right by you and your family too."

Jean and Raya were approaching cautiously, stopping to chat with neighbors and co-workers along the way.

Flex began to smile, putting on his best husband face, but

151

his voice was still that of a father. "I don't want to get in your business or anything, but if your daughter thinks that Elena needs to go to the police, why doesn't she take the child herself? I know it's been a long time and you want to do right by her, but maybe the best thing you can do is help her be a parent instead of doing the parenting for her. You also need to talk to your wife before you go giving your word on stuff like that. I know it's been a long time, but you'll remember these things if you want to survive. It's just like riding a bike."

"Who's riding a bike?" Raya asked as she and Jean stepped between the two men, melting the tension between them.

Flex's arms swung free to take his wife into his arms. He kissed her gently on the mouth as though they were the only people in the room. "Nobody, baby. Nobody's riding any bikes but beautiful you. You are going to do that ride with me next weekend, right?"

She pursed her lips. "You think you're slick, don't you? Well, you're not. Come on and let these folks talk. Little Ray Ray is over there on Jay's lap about to nod off to sleep."

Allowing himself to be led away, Flex turned back and gave Nigel a wink. Jean's stern look made him turn away just as quickly.

Nigel tried to recall the conversation, knowing he'd need some of his young friend's confidence and wisdom to face his wife. He stood still for a second, waiting for Jean to get going, but she didn't say a word. She only took his hand and tugged him forward as Raya had done with Flex. The difference was their destination. Jean was headed for the stairs.

Nigel pulled back. "What are you doing? There are people here. We can't go up there . . ."

Jean laughed and took a seat on the bottom stair. "This is as far as I was going, silly. All the chairs in the house are taken, and I need to talk to you. I would never try and take

152

you upstairs with a house full of people. For one thing, it'd be supremely rude. For another—"

"Enough, okay!" Nigel waved his hands and burst into laughter. The tops of his ears felt warm. No one but Jean could make him feel shy or embarrassed about much of anything, but somehow she managed to do it every time. It was bad enough that he'd had to look at the neighbor ladies after his last time sleeping over. "Let's talk," he said after another fit of laughter. "And not about that." *At least not yet.*

And so they sat there on the step as he recounted his conversation with Monica and his promises to her. Jean frowned several times but kept listening. A few times, she moved her hands restlessly as though she might have liked to take notes.

"And Flex? What was that about? All that arm waving and man talk you two were carrying on over there?" Jean asked next.

Not knowing quite where to start, Nigel dove in with Flex's opposition to their taking Elena to the police, his opinion of her going with the boy in the first place, and what effects it might have on his son.

Jean bit the inside of her lip and narrowed her eyes as if studying something. It seemed an eternity before she spoke, but Nigel was glad for the silence. Sometimes her words came out in such a rush that it felt like tiny stones pelting his mind.

What she said this time was more like one huge boulder. "He's right, you know. She should *not* have gone. She knows better and has more than her share of common sense. She did it to get Jay's attention and instead almost got herself raped, pregnant, killed . . . God knows what!" The lip she'd been biting started to shake.

Nigel put his hand around her shoulder and thanked God

153

for whoever had turned up the music so that no one had heard Jean's outburst. "Still, Peach. It wasn't her fault. She did not invite that. She went against your rules, which was wrong, but is it even really a rule? From what I see, you think she isn't supposed to do much of anything, and Monica doesn't want to have anything to do with what she does do."

Jean sniffed. "That's a lot of 'do's.'"

He shook his head. "I know, but you see what I mean. Have you ever told her what she *can* do? It seems like she just does things and then you—or we—decide after the fact whether it's right or not. I think Flex is being a little unrealistic about how even Christian teenagers are going to act, but I have to give him credit for setting some boundaries for Jay. I get the feeling that young man might be in some trouble for spending so much time over here today."

She leaned back against the step above her. "From what Raya said, that's right. They are proud of him for calling us and letting us know what was going on, but he was not allowed to get on the train and come over here without their permission. They would have preferred that Jay told them what was going on and allowed them to contact us. To his credit, he left messages with them all the way to let them know where he was and what was going on, but they would rather he stay put in the future until one of them can talk to him directly."

Nigel stretched out his legs in front of him and laced his hands before placing them under his head. He leaned back on the step behind him too. "Wow. It seems like Raya and Flex have really been giving their parenting a lot of thought and prayer. For a couple so young, they have a lot of wisdom."

Jean gave him a funny look as though she was going to disagree, but then her face softened. "Yeah, I guess they really do. Amazing that they're both younger than Monica."

He straightened again. "She's really trying, Jean. Don't act like that, like you're disappointed with her. That's what she thinks already. She's proud of you. Be proud of her."

Jean sat up too. "What do you mean, she's proud of me? She told you that?"

Nigel looked across the room at his daughter, sitting quietly and watching TV. Had he told some secret that shouldn't have been repeated? His mind reeled. What had Flex said, that this was like riding a bike? He'd like to trust his young friend, but so far Nigel found communicating with his wife more like falling off a bicycle than riding one.

No way out but the truth. "Yes, she said that she was proud of you for the way you braved the snow and rode that bus to see me. She said she wished she'd been brave enough to go with you, to tell you how strong you were."

Jean turned her face to the wall. Nigel tried to touch her, but she shook her head. He sat with her in silence for a while. Then he leaned forward to get up, and she grabbed his hand but didn't look at him. She simply shook her head again. *No. Don't go*, the gesture said, reminding him of her stoic demeanor in labor. While the other women had kicked their husbands and screamed profanities, Jean made only low, deep moans and let tears slide down her face. He thought they had hours ahead of them before she'd reach the panic the other women seemed to be in. It turned out that she was ahead of all of them in the process and probably in more pain. The baby came minutes later, to his shock and surprise. When he asked her why she hadn't cried out like the others, she said, "Screaming wasn't going to help me get the job done. It wouldn't make the thing hurt any less either. What's the point?"

He wondered if she felt the same way now, still laboring over the same child in a different way, so many years later.

Finally, she spoke. "I am proud of her. She has survived

and endured. She has dared to love, even when it didn't work out. Tonight she has given me something I didn't even know I needed, and for that, I thank her." She patted Nigel's hand. "And you."

He smiled, thinking it best not to reply. The bike was wobbly, but he was remembering some of the mechanics of a smoother ride. Silence was one of them. Listening came next. Hearing someone's words and actively receiving and understanding those words were not the same thing.

As he thought she would, Jean continued. "I think you're right too about Elena and rules or lack thereof. There's always been confusion because she comes and goes from here as she pleases. It would be very easy at this point for me to take Elena in, even adopt her and set her on the course that I think is best. I do wonder, however, if that's what's best for Monica or Elena. It seems I've been providing a way out of responsibility for both of them."

Nigel stood up and stretched his arms, trying his best to stifle the yawn welling up in his throat. It'd been a long day and an even longer evening. He wasn't sure what Jean meant exactly and how that affected what they would end up doing about Elena's attack, but if he was going to be involved, they needed to make a decision soon. Still, for all his weariness, he tried to concentrate on what Jean was saying, tried to make some sense of it. In a brief moment between falling asleep on his feet and being awake, a small wisp of understanding curled around his tired brain.

"So let me see if I've got this straight. Every time Monica started drinking, she sent Elena over here. Every time Elena wanted to do something her mother might not approve of, she came over here on her own and just did what she wanted to do, like meeting that boy in the park today."

Jean was standing now. "Precisely."

The whole thing seemed anything but precise to Nigel. "So what do we do now? I'm sort of wearing out and need to be getting home regardless of what we decide."

Jean rolled her eyes. "Ridiculous. I'm not sending you out into the cold to catch a train home on Thanksgiving. You'll stay. Don't worry. I'll let you sleep in peace."

He pinched his eyes shut. "Whatever. Now, what are we doing?"

She took his hand. "What we're going to do now is pray. Then we're going over to our daughter and telling her that as much as we love her and Elena, we want to help her be a parent instead of taking her child away from her. Elena can stay here while Monica does rehab, and then Monica can come here too, but if they're ever going to be a family, they both have to start taking some responsibility, starting with today. If she really thinks Elena should file a police report, then she should take her and file that report as her mother. We'd go with her, of course, but I think this is important."

He nodded and took Jean's hand and led her upstairs.

This time it was her turn to blush. "What are you doing? Everybody is looking."

Nigel shrugged. "I'm going to pray with my wife. Those stairs would hurt my knees, and I don't feel comfortable praying in front of a roomful of people."

She laughed as they reached the landing. "But you feel comfortable taking me to bed in front of all of them? Or so they think?"

Laughter rang out on the stairs below them, followed by faint applause.

Nigel blew a breath through his mouth and knelt next to the recliner his clothes had been folded on a few weeks before. He was too tired to care what anybody else thought today. Now it was time to hear what God thought and to try to put his family back together.

He woke up beside her, but not upstairs. They were on opposite sides of the sectional, their feet touching under the blanket. Nigel's thoughts turned back to the exhausting finale of yesterday's events.

Monica hadn't taken their news well at first, but she finally admitted that she'd never really felt like a mother to Elena or felt like her ideas mattered when it came to raising her. Jean apologized for taking over a lot of Monica's authority, while Nigel silently grieved that he hadn't been there to balance things out between all of them. Though they said they'd go with Monica and Elena to the police, when faced with the thought of having to fill out a police report and reveal what had happened on her own, Monica no longer wanted to do it.

It was then that they had realized Jay and Elena were missing from the house. No one could say when they'd seen them last—even Flex, who furiously admitted that, despite keeping a close eye on him all evening, he'd nodded off to sleep himself.

When the two did emerge, they came through the front door with guilty looks, each joining their parents and giving a quick and short explanation.

"We went to the police," they both said.

"It was the right thing to do, Dad," Jay added, pausing to take in his father's hurt expression.

Flex shook his head. "I hope you thought about what this means, Jay. What might happen at school on Monday. To both of you." He rubbed his chin. "Maybe I can pull some strings and get you home lessons in the new year until I can get you placed somewhere else."

It was Elena who spoke up next, this time holding Monica's hand tightly. "We've thought about all that, Mr. Dunham. Jay and I want to stay at our school. We can't let them run us away."

Nigel saw the fatherhood in Flex rising from his toes like mercury in a thermometer. Though his granddaughter had meant well, she'd struck some lava deep inside this man, and he was gonna blow.

He tried to throw a little water on the fire. "Hey, man. What she means is—"

Too late. Flex erupted all over the room, his voice booming so loud that Nigel thought he saw the windows shaking. "Us? Us! There is no US! You are two minor children with no jobs, no money, and obviously no sense. You seem like a nice girl, Elena, but my boy has a thing about people who are in trouble." He shoved Jay toward the door. "He likes to rescue folks. The thing is, he forgets that he was not too long ago rescued himself. Until he's safely on land, there's not much he can do for you, himself, or anyone else. So before y'all start thinking about taking on the world, think about dealing with me. 'Cause as dangerous as those gangs are, I'm ten times worse. Believe that."

Raya tried to interject and smooth things over, but even Flex's loving wife couldn't deter him from getting Jay out of Jean's house and as far away as possible from Elena. Jean nodded for her friend to go on and that they'd talk later. Nigel tried not to think about what might be said when they did talk later.

Monica and Elena had taken the bed upstairs when Nigel and Jean showed no sign of getting up or going to sleep. Though he'd barely been able to keep his eyes open earlier in the evening, the surge of adrenaline after Flex's outburst had given both of them a little wake-up energy. Not to mention that having Jean so close to him made it very hard to think about sleeping.

So they didn't sleep. They talked. More of the blanks from their empty years were filled in, including Jean's hiring a private investigator to find him in California and her being given more-than-candid shots of him and Carmen for her money. She thought then that he'd moved on, that he was happy, and she fully expected to get a divorce summons at any time. It never came, but she never sent one either. She couldn't put her finger on why, beyond the load of Catholic guilt her mother had passed on to her as a child for even mentioning the word *divorce*. There was just always something in the back of her mind, at the bottom of her heart.

Nigel summed it up quickly. "Hope. I had it too." He sat up and touched her hair. "I still do."

At that point they both had laughed and Jean had recommended that they both put their hope to sleep if they intended to wake up at all the next day.

They'd gotten up late the past few mornings, Friday and then Saturday too. They started out at opposite sides of the couch, whispering stories to each other in the darkness. The couch seemed to get smaller each night and more uncomfortable too. At some point in the middle of the night on Saturday, Jean said the words he'd been asking himself since he figured out that part of the sectional was a sleeper as well. "Do you want to pull this couch out? My back is killing me."

He'd almost jumped up and started throwing off the cushions. Once they were in the couch bed, though, he was sorry. Their feet weren't touching anymore, and both of them had turned away from one another out of instinct and longing for a decent night's sleep.

Upstairs, he thought he heard Monica and Elena giggling, but Nigel didn't care. Between the leftovers and all their talking and telling, he was worn out.

Then came today. Sunday. They both should have been in church, but he doubted now that they'd make it. The phone rang, but Jean didn't move. Nigel answered before he really thought about it. "Hello?"

"Heard you had some party over there Thanksgiving, buddy."

He rubbed his eyes with the heel of his hand. "Lyle? Is that you? You're right there. It's a mess. I'd run it down for you, but I'm sure you already know."

He chuckled a little. "Basically. Flex is not one to spare details. Doug left early, I take it, because he seems to know nothing about anything."

Nigel thought about it. "I didn't see much of him. I ran out to get my daughter, and come to think of it, when I came back, he was gone."

"Yeah. Remember that about him. That guy can smell trouble. When he leaves a place, try to follow. If he ditches you, well, go home and pray. I joke with him that he has the gift of discerning craziness . . . and fleeing from it."

Nigel rolled over and looked at Jean, who was still soundly sleeping. "Well, if there is such a gift, old Doug certainly exercised it the other night. I think it's okay though. I think a lot of good came out of it, for me, anyway. I've had a lot to think about since I've been over here."

Another chuckle. "I'll bet."

Nigel rolled back onto his side of the mattress and snorted into the phone. "You guys just never quit, do you?"

"Nope. And we've always got more jokes. Bad ones. We love the Lord, but we have to have fun too, or we'll go crazy. We have to be honest with each other. That's what I'm doing now."

Nigel yawned, then took a tighter grip on the phone. *Here we go, another intervention from these guys.* Though he appreciated their love and prayers, these men were really starting to grate on his nerves. He'd never say it though, especially not to a man who was dying.

"I like that. A good healthy pause. That means I've made you mad, and you're thinking mean things about me and feeling bad about it because I'm dying. Don't you just love that? I get to say anything I want, and you feel bad about not liking it. Well, almost anything. Anyway, what I wanted to say, honestly, is just that I'm so glad you're here and that I think God is going to do something totally amazing in our business and in both your family and Flex's family through this. I hope I get to see it all play out. I love when God does cool stuff."

Nigel smiled. "Me too."

"Right, well, Chenille's coming, so I'm going to have to get going, but since you're up, you might want to go over to the church. They're having a special service for the start of the advent. Something I think you'll really, really like if my information is correct. It usually is. Anyway, check it out."

The line went dead before Nigel could reply.

Jean, who still appeared to be totally asleep, reached out and touched Nigel's shoulder. "How's he doing? Lyle, I mean?"

"He's, uh, good, I guess. He called to tell me that there's some service at their church this morning that I'd really, really like. If his information is correct, anyway. I don't know that I like him having information, but the guy's usually right, it seems, so I guess—"

"We should go." Jean swung her legs over the side of the bed. "To the service, I mean. Monica needs to come too. It's important. I don't go there often, but they send me a calendar in the mail, and Lyle's right. There's something that both you and Monica will be very interested in going on at the church this morning." She quickly stripped the sheets and shooed Nigel off the bed so she could put the couch back in.

Knowing she'd fold the sheets to use again that night, Nigel took the opposite end as she opened it out. "What about you? Is there something there for you too? It sounds great, but I don't know how it's going to work. I don't have anything to wear."

Jean stepped forward to meet her corners of the sheet with his. "Of course you do. Go around the corner and check the back of the hall closet. In the plastic."

He walked slowly to the closet, taking in the fact that she'd kept some of his clothes. It'd been amazing enough when he'd realized on the first night he'd spent here that on the gold chain her beaded strands often camouflaged hung her wedding ring. As he pushed the closet open, he looked down at the matching band on his own finger. It was only after his conviction about sleeping with Carmen and his asking God's forgiveness that he'd put it back on as a reminder that whether or not he knew where Jean was, he was a married man.

He tugged at the plastic for a moment and then stared in astonishment at the winter white Ralph Lauren suit, identical to the one he'd worn the first day he'd come to Jean's office. Though he'd remembered her buying him several suits, he hadn't remembered this one. A chocolate silk suit and wide tie that had gone out of style and come back in again hung next to it.

Without any comment, Jean met him at the closet with a towel, washcloth, soap, and razor. "The other things that you like are in the bathroom. I picked them up in case you ever had to . . . sleep over again." She had several other towels stacked against her, probably for her and the girls.

Nigel put the suit over one arm and took the towel at both ends and rolled it up before swatting Jean's backside with it. "You are something else, you know that, woman?"

She didn't even break her stride, just kept going up the stairs with that smile that drove him crazy. "So they tell me," she said before disappearing above his head.

14

She'd thought it would get to him, but the Lord had taken hold of her instead. Many years ago, as part of their advent celebrations, Nigel had graced their home with a Tree of Jesse, symbolizing the branch from which Christ had sprung. A simple tree cutting in a pot of dirt had made the perfect background for the handmade ornaments they added to the tree every Sunday from Thanksgiving to Christmas and sometimes the days in between as well.

When Jean remembered that they'd be kicking off the advent with a Jesse tree celebration at New Man Fellowship, she was excited to see the reaction on Nigel's face. Nothing could have prepared her, however, for the explosion in her own emotions when the usher, none other than Flex himself, held out a simple clay pot to her.

He looked at her with kind eyes, but he did not smile. He held his hands on hers around the pot and recited Isaiah 11:1: "And there shall come forth a Rod out of the stem of Jesse, and a Branch shall grow out of his roots." He smiled then and released her hands, welcoming Nigel, the next person in line.

Though she'd planned to, Jean did not look back to see what her husband thought of his gift or its giver. Ahead of her, she saw a familiar smile on the face of a friend—Raya. Obviously the service was a family affair today. Jean stepped toward her friend and held out her pot, where she received rich, black dirt as it sifted through Raya's outstretched hands.

"And the Spirit of the Lord shall rest upon Him—the Spirit of wisdom and understanding, the Spirit of counsel and might, the Spirit of knowledge and of the fear of the Lord," Raya said softly, taking time to intone the beauty of the second verse of the same chapter.

As she stepped away, Jean could clearly see Jay's tall form ahead of her, a tree himself in front of a tableful of branches. She approached him slowly, thinking that she saw more and more man in him than boy every time that she saw him. Praying that he would grow up to be the man he had the potential to be. She held her pot close to her while think- ing these things, forgetting until he motioned to her that he needed to put something into it.

With a wide smile, Jay placed the branch deep into the soil and recited the third verse of Isaiah chapter 11 in such a clear voice and with such a sincere heart that Jean felt as if she were hearing it for the first time.

"And shall make Him of quick understanding in the fear of the Lord: and He shall not judge after the sight of His eyes, neither reprove after the hearing of His ears," Jay said in a clear voice, with the same generosity and honesty that he gave to everything.

Flex's mother, whom Jean had seen only a few times over the years, met her in the aisle next, asking the correct number in their family and leading Jean to a row of folding chairs that had been added along the entire back row of the sanctuary. Jean took her seat quickly and took little notice of Nigel or the girls, who also had received their trees and shuffled down the row after her.

Nigel simply held his pot, staring at it. That much Jean had seen out of the corner of her eye. She was grateful he didn't say anything, as no one else seemed to be speaking either. There was something holy in the silence, powerfully quiet. Jean could feel herself opening like a flower, peeling back like a piece of fruit. She'd thought this was for her husband and her daughter, but it had been for her all along.

As the pastor took the podium, she closed her eyes, but not before scoping out the location of the closest box of Kleenex. This was going to be one of those times when she'd need it. She could feel it already.

The pastor's voice filled the church as he told the congregation the story of the trees that they held and of the trees that had meant so much in the Bible: The wood that had made the cross. The wood that had been thrown in the water at Marah to make the bitter waters sweet. The tree spoken of in the book of John, something to be pruned and cut back so that it could bear more fruit.

"Each of us in here will see plenty of trees this season, all of them beautifully decorated and lighted. And that's fine. Though we don't know the exact day of Christ's birth, this is the time that we celebrate it. What I want you to do different this year is to be the tree."

A low murmur went through the church. Jean saw Elena's look of confusion. As she had done with her daughter long ago, Jean pointed to her granddaughter and then at the preacher, telling her to listen and to learn.

"Oh, I got some of y'all then, didn't I? You're saying, 'Now, brother pastor has lost his mind handing us dirt and talking about being trees and such. Doesn't he know they've got a big tree down at Rockefeller Center?' Yes, church, I know about that big, pretty tree, but I also know that come January, it's going to be dead. I'm trying to do the opposite this morning. Some of y'all are dead or dying, and I want to break off the diseased branches, pull off the rotten fruit."

Jean swallowed hard. She tried to look at Nigel but couldn't. Her whole body was focused forward, toward the voice coming through the microphone.

"Some of you planted something so long ago that you forgot where you buried it. Never mind that you didn't water it, ain't prayed for it, don't even know what it's about. You're just mad because it didn't come up when you thought it was supposed to. Well, church, I've got some news. Don't go looking under the tree to see what God is going to give you next until you are willing to dig a hole—y'all ain't hearing me—I said a hole!"

"Yassir!" Someone shot up in front of them. From her previous visits to the church, Jean knew without looking that it was Flex. Or at least she thought she knew. Another glance and she realized that it was Jay, rocking from side to side and nodding his head up and down. She had to smile then, because she felt the same way.

"That's right, son. A hole. And it's got to be deep enough to give your roots room to get to living water. It's got to be dark enough to be sure that frost on the top side don't come in and kill you. It's got to be way down there, people, where none of us wants to go. Why? Because when we get rooted and grounded in love . . ."

The man started speaking Spanish for several seconds, wiping at his face. "See there, y'all done made me forget my English. Come on, now. Work with me. I said love!"

Jay started clapping his hands then. Nigel stood next, adding his own applause. Flex got up next, but his hands were behind his back. His head was down, but bobbing in agreement.

"See, we're all looking for some fruit, but nobody wants to get in the hole. Nobody wants to be watering stuff with the Word every day when the game is on, when you've got email—yeah, I said that. No, we just want Jesus to show up and throw in the branch when things get tough. We want him to make the waters sweet when life starts tasting bitter. But I stopped by to tell you, church, to BE THE TREE!"

"Hallelujah!" someone shouted. "Plant me, Jesus! Put me in the hole."

Jean almost dropped her pot. It was Monica, her atheist daughter, shouting with her hands raised two seats down. Somehow Jean managed to ease her flowerpot to the floor.

One of the deacons chased the pastor with a clip-on mike as he descended the podium and came into the crowd. "He's following me with that mike, but I'm gonna keep preaching because one thing I know God gave me is a big mouth, amen? Now, I don't know about the rest of you, but somebody in here wants to get planted. Somebody in here needs to see some fruit. And the Lord is telling me that this ain't no prayer-line kind of thing. That I need to come down here and see to this thing myself."

And so he did. Winding through what seemed like hundreds of people in the row of added chairs, the pastor came to the corner where Jean and her family stood. He prayed over Monica, over Elena.

And then he stopped.

He said, "I'm sorry to hold up the service, church, but this here is something big. Something like many of you are believing for right now." He turned back to Nigel and put his arm on his shoulder, asking if he could pray for him. The pastor started and then stopped. Eyes closed, he called out for Flex. "Fletcher Dunham, I don't know where you are in the house, but I need you here. Right now. I'm not supposed to pray for this man. You are."

And with that, he didn't turn to leave but stepped around Nigel instead. He took Jean's hand. "Everything that the locust has eaten will be restored tenfold. You just stay in that hole and water yourself with that Word. Don't you worry about my man here or those girls down there. You just stay in that Word. Do you hear me?"

She wiped her eyes. "Yes. I hear."

The pastor smiled as Flex arrived and began praying first for, and then with, Nigel. He turned to Jean and took her hand.

"Well, church, this isn't what I planned, but it's good. I hope you know that. Now there's just one more thing I need to ask this lady, and it goes for everyone in this room. It don't matter how many holes you dig or how much water you put on a tree if it has a disease. If the tree is sick, it won't bear fruit no matter how much love you give it. So before you go out of here, we all have to answer this question." He turned to Jean and said softly, "Will you be made whole?"

As the congregation cried out "yes" in a thunderous roar, the pastor released Jean's hand. He didn't wait for her answer and he didn't look back. Nigel, however, who'd just helped Flex into the aisle, had his eyes fixed on Jean's silent, unmoving mouth. She tried to answer, to agree with everyone else, but it was if her mouth refused to open. Instead, the collective answer rumbling through the church seemed to flow through her as well, as though God was answering for her.

Nigel took Monica's hand and stretched it in the air. "Yes!" they said together, falling together in an endearing hug.

Jean sat still, staring behind them at Elena, who also sat

silent. Her granddaughter reached behind her grandfather and mother, trying to clutch Jean's hand. Jean reached too, grabbing the girl's fingertips for only a second before the two between them sat back in their seats and broke their embrace.

Jean stared down at her pot, amazed that it hadn't been knocked over with all the maneuvering in the row. Nigel's was tucked safely under his seat. Elena was still holding hers. Remembering the Kleenex she'd seen earlier, Jean grabbed the box from under the pew in front of them and took a fistful before passing them down the row.

She shook her head thinking about how certain she'd been this morning that she'd been bringing her family to this service to receive something. And all the while, it had been God drawing her, calling her to dig deep and grow.

Where Sunday had brought unexpected blessings, Monday brought the reality of what had happened over the holiday and how unprepared any of them were to deal with it.

Nigel heard the bullets first, a vicious spray against the apartment building. No one was hurt, but the gunfire, along with the slanderous words whitewashed on Jean's door, had everyone in the neighborhood tense and afraid, despite the timely dispatch of police to the scene.

As the sound of sirens grew closer, Nigel gave Flex a quick call. He'd thought Flex's concern about school safety was over the top, but now Nigel saw the man's point.

Flex didn't seem surprised about what had happened. "I figured as much. I'd already planned to keep him home today. I have an appointment with the principal. That boy doesn't know where we live now, but it probably wouldn't be hard for him to find out."

Nigel felt horrible for putting them in this position. "You're welcome at my place. All of you. There's basically an empty apartment next door. They said it was for me to entertain in, but come on. You guys are about the only people I know here."

Flex respectfully declined the offer. "I hope it won't come to that, but thanks for the invitation. Raya isn't feeling well this morning, so I'm just going to take the boys and run by Heavenly Bodies and see how things are coming along."

"Your new gym. I'm looking forward to coming by sometime. We'll talk soon."

"Probably too soon, I'm afraid."

So true, Nigel thought as he hung up the phone and walked outside toward the policemen, who were getting out of their cars. Photos were snapped and all of them interviewed quickly. Nigel filled the officers in on the probable cause of the attack. Their reaction was swift and sure—everyone should leave the apartment immediately. The police said they'd add an extra detail to the neighborhood. In the meantime, they recommended Jean and the girls go to Nigel's place.

What began as some resistance from Jean about their recommendation then became a full-fledged battle.

"Do you think that's who I am? That my kids start trouble and then I go running when somebody drives by? No, no, Papi. I can't go like that. I have to live here afterward. If everybody is going to be scared around here, I'm going to be here and be scared too."

The police officer shook his head, then nodded at Nigel. "So you staying with them, Pops? We'll still do the detail, but I'd like to know they're not in here alone."

Nigel pounded his fists on his forehead. This was not how things were supposed to go. Why did Jean have to be so stubborn at times?

Because if she wasn't, she'd already be married to someone else by now. His wife's tenaciousness did have its good points.

He blew out a breath. "I'll stay, but I think it's crazy, for the record."

The policeman nodded in agreement.

Monica walked up the stairs and took Elena by the hand to go with her.

Jean, who still stood outside the front door, yelled inside the house to ask her daughter what she was doing.

"Packing," Monica said. "She's got a lot of stuff over here. Elena's coming home. With me. You're both welcome to come with us if you want to."

Convinced he was part of a family of female lunatics, Nigel went back into the house and sat down on the couch, holding his head. He felt Jean run a hand through his hair. "This really is crazy, you know. How am I supposed to protect you over here and them over there? You all are not making this easy."

Jean sat down next to him on the couch. "It's not that. You're just making it hard. There's no way for you to protect us all, even if we are all in the same place. Only God can do that. And he's done well with the job all these years."

Nigel slouched forward, feeling as though he'd been stabbed. "I know I haven't been here, okay? You don't have to go there, to say things like that. I'm here now and I'm trying . . . I'm trying to make it up."

She kissed his cheek. "You're trying too hard. We both are. It's been great having you here the past few days, but like you said the first night you stayed here, us being here together doesn't necessarily make us together. I'm thankful that you're here and you're helping me, but the truth is, I don't know what to do with a husband anymore."

"Hmph. You could have fooled me," Nigel said, making a face at her.

She took his hand and squeezed. "I don't mean like that. I mean like this, trying to protect us and make decisions and all. This was why I was hesitant to mix you up with the kids and get the girls all dependent on you. I mean, did you think that you could just come over here a few times and we'd just become one big, happy family? I don't think—"

Nigel cut her off with a kiss. "Woman, I'm starting to believe that you don't think at all. I don't know what the source of all this foolishness you're saying is, but I think it's fear, plain and simple. I can appreciate that, but I didn't shoot those bullets this morning, so I'd appreciate if you'd not shoot me down with your words. Now if you'll excuse me, I'll be going to leave you alone with your supersafe self."

Jean got up as he did, calling behind him. "And just where do you think you're going?"

He turned back with a tight smile. "To pack. I believe my daughter just requested my presence in her home. See you soon, Peach. Be safe."

15

Tuesday, when Jean opened the conference room door to find Nigel busy at work as usual, she realized the gravity of her decision to stay in her apartment and his decision to go. She saw in his eyes not only that he'd wanted to protect her but that he'd needed to. Why couldn't she just be like other women and play the damsel in distress? She'd sure had enough distress to look the part. When trouble hit, though, it was her own resources, her own punches, learned during her long years as a single parent, that she returned to. Her first jab? Feeding her enemies. She found out through the neighborhood grapevine who Elena's attacker was related to. His mother might be young, so she'd have to dig deeper to make peace—grandmothers, aunties, cousins . . . whoever she could find. There was more than one way to win a fight. Jean's first left hook would be feeding her enemies. Everybody had to eat sometime.

Nigel carefully eyed the contents of a file marked "Mavs." He greeted her without looking up from the pages, stopping to add something else. "I looked up some friends from before, some people with connections to the gang. I have the boy's address and his full name. Some of the guys are going to pass the word to leave Elena alone. Jay too. My last favor in the world, I guess."

Jean tried to hide her surprise. Evidently, Nigel had thrown some punches, doing a little speed-bagging of his own as well. "Okay, that sounds good, although I don't remember you really calling anyone from upstate a friend, but I'll take your word for it. Just make sure you're not making more trouble by trying to stop it. Some people know only one way to pass a word—in blood."

Nigel shifted in his chair. "I hear you."

Did he? Jean wondered. Sometimes their words flowed so clearly between one another that they seemed to beat with one heart. Other times, Nigel seemed to her to be locked away forever in some faraway place she couldn't access. From his expression yesterday morning, she probably made him feel the same way. "I know where he lives too, this boy. Who his people are. I have invited them, his *tias* and *abuela*, to dinner at my house tonight."

The file in Nigel's hand met with the table then. The smile she'd been longing to see since he'd left the day before spread across his mouth. "So let me get this straight. I'm looking up old gangbangers to try and get the word on the street to the kid while you're inviting his grandma to dinner?"

"Basically. What'd you think I was going to do? Drive by his place? Gangs have gun power. Grandmas have grandma power. You've got to work with what you've got." Jean dug into her pocket and pulled out her glasses so she could see what he was going over. Layouts for the Reebok sportswear collection. They'd talked through all the pages and sketched out how they'd present each team's designs, but it was gratifying to see the final result. She looked across the table to the chair where she usually sat and saw a stack of similar manila folders with each team's name.

She rounded the table and grabbed the Spurs file to see how her jacket looked on the page. It had certainly looked great on Nigel. The page didn't quite do it the same justice, but it definitely showed it off. "Very nice. Are we set with the dates for the showing? Is Flex still going to wear the suits?"

Nigel didn't answer. He thumbed the edges of the folders instead, giving her a thoughtful look, a look that Jean had once loved but over the past month had come to dislike. "What. Don't tell me. You've got another idea."

He scratched a spot under his eye. "Believe it or not, I do. After spending one night with our granddaughter and hanging out a few times with Jay, I really do think that our market includes kids their age as well. I'd like to have Jay and Flex, if possible. Especially for the teams with bold designs, like the Heat."

Jean thought for a minute and then agreed. "Sure. Why not? Just keep it simple, okay? It's about the clothes, not the models. Keep the focus on the clothes. Even when you're modeling." She ducked quickly and then inched back up, peering over the edge of the table.

Instead of aiming paper at her head like she thought he might do, Nigel was leaning over the edge of the table, smiling down on her. "So, are we friends again? Can we talk about the craziness that happened yesterday? Did you want me to stay with you, or what?"

She got up and smoothed her skirt, now uncomfortable with the direct line of communication Nigel had chosen. Flirting was so much easier. "Do we really have to talk about this? I just couldn't leave my neighbors, okay? Plus, I really

177

didn't want them to know all the details either, to think bad of Elena. Her party is in a few weeks and—"

"You are unbelievable, you know that? Here I am trying to figure out if you're all going to be killed and you're worried about whether your neighbors are going to come to Elena's birthday party? You're kidding, right? Please tell me that you are, because I don't want to believe that you still care so much more about what other people think than you care about your own family." He dropped into his chair.

Why did everything always have to come back to this? To the two of them? Jean rounded the table, wondering if Lily had come in today like she did some Tuesdays lately. Jean hoped so. All this "communicating" was driving her nuts. "Look, I do care what people think about Elena. A good name means a lot, and sometimes you have to build that name for yourself, showing people by every hour that you work, every meal that you cook, every piece that you design that you are a good person, an honorable person." Halfway to the door, she realized she needed those prototype files and that she and Nigel had planned to consult today on some final placements before sending off for the final round of prototypes.

He sat still, fingers steepled together, staring at her. "So that's it. You're still trying to prove to people that you're more than just some ex-con's wife? Is that it? And Elena needs to let everyone know that she's more than just a prisoner's daughter? That's why you're risking your life in that apartment?" His words were as sharp as before, but not as fast or as loud. It was as if he were asking himself the questions at the same time he was asking Jean.

Her answer, however, made up for his lack of speed and volume. "Yes!" she shouted at the top of her lungs with the same emphasis she had wished for during church on Sunday. "That's it exactly. I didn't come to see you anymore. I didn't send you letters. Instead I tried to keep your name intact, to keep your child in a clean home with decent clothes and her child too. And now, if it'll keep the people in the neighborhood from thinking that my granddaughter is some loose girl who has no better sense than to sneak off with strange boys, then yes, I'm staying at my place. But it's not the only reason. I'm staying because I know how it feels to be left behind to fight alone. I've made a lot of mistakes in my life, but this wasn't going to be one of them."

Breathless, Jean headed for the door, praying that Lily was in her office. Instead, she faced Chenille when she opened the door. Her boss looked pale, and her green eyes were bloodshot from crying.

"I'm glad to find you both here, in one place," Chenille said. "I've got to go now. Someone from the church was sitting with Lyle today, and they had to call an ambulance for him." She buttoned her coat and pulled her purse strap up on her shoulder. "So I've told everyone who has a problem to contact the two of you until I can get back. I don't know when that will be."

Nigel was at Chenille's side, holding out his hand to steady her. "Do you have a cab? Don't worry about a thing. We'll handle things here. Jean and I. Okay?"

She nodded wordlessly, blowing a kiss at Jean. "Thank you. Both of you. I don't know what I would have done—"

He shook his head. "Just go."

And so Chenille started down the hall, staggering under the weight of what she would face at the hospital. Both Nigel and Jean ran after her, helping her out the front of the warehouse and into the waiting cab.

"Thanks," she said, trying not to cry. "He loves both of you very much. He says you have a special love."

The cab pulled away, but Jean and Nigel stood there in

the cold street, watching Chenille drive away, thinking over her words. Then, one at a time, they went back inside the building, both wondering why their special love seemed so hard to hold on to.

The mood around the office was somber. Nigel tried to help as much as he could by sending emails to everyone, updating them on the status of different projects and letting them know they should contact him or Jean if they needed anything. Instead of comforting the workers, this seemed to panic them. "Oh no. Heads are gonna roll," he read in more than one unthinking reply-all response to his initial message.

Jean was as quiet as anyone, and when she did speak, it was usually to give Nigel some background on Lyle and Chenille and the things that had happened to them before he'd come along. "They had a baby. A little boy. She gave birth, but he never did breathe. Just horrible. They made it through somehow. Lyle being Lyle, mainly. He always looks for a way to see God in things. He's wonderful that way."

Then she told him of the cancer and all the scares that had followed. Lyle was declared cancer-free a year ago, and things had seemed so . . . normal. Then the disease came back with a vengeance a few months ago, this time spreading rapidly despite all his treatments. His case was considered a miracle already, since people with internal cancers usually died quickly and Lyle had lived years instead of months. This time it seemed different. Final.

Nigel hadn't been around long, but he had to agree. Everything about Lyle and every one of their interactions had a permanent place in his heart, like something he shouldn't ever forget. That both saddened him and made him glad to have come when he did, in time to get to know Lyle, if even for a short while. When he told Jean this, she laughed, saying that Lyle was wearing off on him. "That was totally something he would say," she said, careful to keep him in the present tense when so many people around the firm were talking as if Lyle were dead and Chenille gone forever.

Jean divided her work hours between making orders for the fall line, checking prototypes for the spring, and overseeing the cutout and beading work on Megan's wedding gown, while Nigel worked on the Reebok project and any handiwork that needed to be done. The two of them weren't making any calls, and Chenille wasn't taking any at the hospital. People went on with their work, but the whispers grew louder and louder until Nigel couldn't take it anymore.

"Why does everyone seem to think they're going to lose their jobs? Have you heard them? They act as if the sky has fallen. I sent out an email saying that they could come to both of us if they needed anything, and now they all act as though I'm some office dictator and they're scared to talk to me."

Jean laughed. "They're probably worried because I've told them all—well, most of them anyway—that if I had the power, I'd fire the whole lazy lot of them. They must think I have the power now, so they're worried. And well they should be."

Nigel shook his head. "You really have no sense of diplomacy, do you? You just see everything in black and white, good or bad, right and wrong. I don't think it's that way at all. I've watched the people around here, and while I agree that some of them could probably be more productive, you all haven't been very proactive in matching people's skills to the jobs either."

Jean looked at Nigel as though he were speaking in some alien language. "Matching their skills to their jobs? Isn't that for the employees to do themselves? They are the ones who applied for the positions. I say just get rid of most of them.

We need that thug LJ's grandmother, that's who we need. She made every stitch of clothes the family wore to dinner last night. Perfect lines, every one of them. How they ended up with that knucklehead in the family, I don't know. But she's a great seamstress. And she's going to deal with that boy and his mother. She was totally ashamed when I told her what had happened."

The boy. Nigel had been so wrapped up in listening to Elena and Monica at night and Jean during the day, not to mention his concerns over Lyle and the employees, that he'd forgotten to check up with his contacts from prison to see if they'd talked to the boy. Jean had it covered though, serving chicken and rice to the boy's grandmother and, from the sound of things, scoping the woman out to offer her a job. He opened his laptop and started his email program, then turned to Jean. "Can you do me a favor?"

"Sure," she said with a smile.

"Clear off this table for me and grab that pot over there. I'll be right back." For once, Jean didn't question him as he took off down the hall and out the front door of the building. He bent over a rather scrawny shrub with a wayward branch pointing out of the top of it like a long, brown finger. Without a second thought, Nigel uprooted it and found a break in the landscaping where he could take some dirt without creating a hole that could be seen from the front of the building.

Satisfied with what he had collected, Nigel bounded back into the building, into the conference room. Inside, Jean had made a quick cleanup of the place. It even smelled better too.

"I lit a candle. Figured you're about to invite in company."

He smiled. "You know it." With a few hasty strokes of the keys on his computer, Nigel drafted an email:

Subject: Tree Party

To: GOP staff

Hello all,

I know we're all having a hard time in Chenille's absence, and our hearts are with her and Lyle. There also seems to be some rumors flying about what's going to happen over the next few months. If I have anything to do with it, this great place that you've all put together will simply become better.

Most of you were at my wife's home for Thanksgiving. Come on down to the conference room for a little afternoon siesta. You might even call it a Tree party!

Thanks,

Nigel, also known as "The Man"

There must have been one person who thought the email was a joke, because people came in slowly at first, like random drops of water. Then came a trickle of women from the pattern department, and finally, the rain. Everyone in the building, including the receptionist, who'd kept her headphone on just in case, wandered into the room. Jean had found some food somewhere and made tuna and crackers. Raya offered her secret stash of Coke.

While everyone snacked, Nigel shared with them all his past experiences with a Jesse tree growing up in Detroit, then later with his wife and child, and finally, the Sunday before at Lyle's church. Though it was primarily an Advent symbol, Nigel talked about Jesus being the Tree of Life and how Lyle had spoken life to everyone he met, except himself. For himself, he willingly accepted death, knowing he was going into the hands of the Father. It was not his own end that concerned him but rather what would happen to Garments of Praise, and for that reason, he'd asked Nigel to stay on and to ensure that the business endured and his wife and her employees could continue to reach for their dreams.

There wasn't a dry eye in the room as people pulled out things that Lyle had given them: crosses, bracelets, Scripture memory cards. They talked about other, more intangible things, like money he'd lent and never asked back, or the way he'd urged Chenille to hire some of them even when they didn't have all the experience for the job. One by one, people put something on the crooked branches, sharing a story of how this couple had touched them, how much this job had meant to them. They laughed, recounting one man's use of his creative hour to color in coloring books. Jean rolled her eyes at the mention of it, but Nigel grabbed his chin, thinking again.

"That coloring book. Do you still have it? I'd like to see it."

"Sure," the man said, his embarrassment giving way to intrigue. "But why?"

Nigel tried to pull his thoughts together and give a simple explanation, but his ideas refused to neatly fold together. So he let them tumble out instead. "Here's the thing. I have a theory that everyone has something that's their thing. They might be good at something else. Even great. But there's something out there that each of you were wired to do within this company. I'd like to find out what that thing is. I'd love it if each of you would submit some of the things you've worked on or are working on during the creative hour. I'm not looking to appraise you or anything, I just want to see more of who you are. Each of you.

"And since I'll have to evaluate these things on weekends

184

or evenings since I'm still on Reebok's dime until January, don't look for some shocking revelation before the end of the year. Just keep doing what you're doing and doing it well."

The receptionist, who'd long since turned on the company answering machine, raised her hand. "So heads aren't going to roll?"

Jean doubled over in laughter. "If I had my way, honey, but not you. You're good. Some of the rest of you? Eh . . ." She scooped a cracker into the dish of tuna.

"She's kidding, people. You all know that better than I do. Besides, like she said, it's not up to her. Chenille is still in charge. I'll just be acting in her interests in her absence. I'm hoping not to shake things up too much. So, no, we won't be rolling heads. Instead, we're going to roll up our sleeves and get to work so that when Chenille comes back, she doesn't have to worry about getting things back in order, because we'll already be in order. Sound good?"

Everyone seemed to agree, but Jean gave him a funny look. Raya stayed after the meeting to apologize for not being able to help more.

"I've just been so sick lately. Some kind of virus, I guess. I don't know when I'm going to get over it."

Jean hooked her thumb in Raya's direction, but turned her body to Nigel. "She's about as dreamy as you, isn't she?" She gave Raya a kiss on her cheek. "You'll probably be feeling better in about two months, sweetie. The second trimester was pretty good to you last time, if I recall."

Raya's eyes widened. "Trimester? Are you kidding? I'm not pregnant. I have a—" She covered her mouth and ran for the bathroom.

"Tell that to the baby, honey," Jean said, waving at her back.

Nigel stared at his wife in disbelief. "You know, if I didn't know you like I do, you'd scare me. How on earth did you know she was pregnant?" He was truly amazed.

Jean wasn't. "If you've seen it once, you've seen it a million times. Not too hard to tell. You just have to know what to look for." She picked up some files and headed for the door, pausing to look over her shoulder. "I'm going to my office for a while."

Nigel didn't say anything more, lest he get some information he'd really rather not know. What this did mean was that, except for Lily coming in a few days a week, he and Jean really might end up running things come the New Year. He tried not to consider the irony that they might be able to run someone else's business but they couldn't seem to run their own home. Or even create a home for that matter.

Home meant family, and Nigel's thoughts shifted to his family with its share of problems. Monica had met with the pastor about going to their Christian rehab center over the holidays. He tried to figure the dates and deadlines, but both his brain and body were tired. Leaving his desk to find a quiet place to pray, he could only think that it would all work out somehow. It had to.

16

"I'm just calling to see if you'll be attending the party on Christmas Eve . . . Yes, we realize it was late notice, but we'd be honored and pleased if you can make it . . . No? All right. Well, thank you."

Jean tried not to slam the phone down into the receiver. She failed. Over a hundred phone calls to those who hadn't responded, and nearly everyone said the same thing—"Sorry, we can't make it." She'd known this was a possibility with so many people going out of town for the holidays and with things being thrown together at the last minute. But how many of these same party invitations had arrived at her door late, sometimes even asking Elena to be one of the female court, leaving Jean sewing long into the night to make a dress in some ridiculous color she could never use again.

And yet these same people left her to their answering machines, ignoring her messages until she caught them at home. And then, the same reply: they were unable to make it. More than anything she'd wanted to

187

make this happen, to give Elena this party despite the chaos churning through her life. Jean didn't want her granddaughter's virtue to go uncelebrated, even if it meant allowing her to date and changing the rigid limits that Jean had set in her mind and the nonexistent rules that Monica never discussed, much less imposed. With the Reebok project almost done and the possible threat against them somewhat diminished, Jean tried to focus as much time as she could on getting the party together. Now, though, she was wondering if her community had cast a dark spot on her granddaughter despite all Jean's best efforts to let them see that they were good people.

Was that what the people were doing, she wondered? Were they freezing her out? Would all her invitations from now on be ignored? When the smell of her food escaped the windows and the sound of music escaped under the door, would they no longer come to see what was going on? She remembered those years, those times after Nigel left, when she had become invisible. Monica's baby, the granddaughter she sought to celebrate now, had brought the cooing women back around again, but Jean had wished the circumstances had been different, with no shame curdling the joy. This time, she'd thought that she could make it different, especially with Nigel here.

Nigel. Jean walked to the couch they'd shared for several nights the week before. She'd been so sure she wouldn't need him when she sent him away, but she hadn't counted on how much she'd miss him. In the short time he'd been back, she let herself get comfortable again. Without realizing it, they both walked away with each other's hearts. What they would do with those feelings now, she had no idea.

At least not until the doorbell rang. It was dark outside and she wasn't expecting anyone, so Jean took her time getting to the door. Then she heard his voice.

"It's us, Peach. Let us in," Nigel said in a tired voice.

She moved across the room with purpose and opened the door to Nigel and Elena, pulling them both in out of the December wind. She almost started with questions first, like where Monica was or why they'd come back. Instead, she just hugged them, knowing that the answers would come.

Nigel had what looked like a box of kindergarten papers under his arm and two duffels in his other hand. He put everything down and walked over to the couch and started flinging off pillows. "Monica was having a hard time. I wanted to call you, but she didn't want me to. Tonight it got really bad. She asked me to call the pastor—"

"Oh, so she could call the pastor but not her mother? That's something."

By this time, Nigel was pulling out the couch. "You're not going to get to me tonight, Peach. Too tired. I called the pastor because he's been through this and because the church has a treatment program. Seriously, what were you going to do, lecture her?"

Jean took Elena by the hand and gave her another hug as though she'd just realized the girl was in the room. "Of course not. I would've listened to her. And made her dinner maybe. She doesn't eat well. That's part of the problem."

Nigel stopped what he was doing and just stared at Jean. Elena did too.

"What? Is there something wrong with dinner? So I'm no licensed counselor or anything, but I do think a mother's love counts for something."

Nigel slipped off his shoes and pulled off his jacket. "Sure it does. That's what's gotten her this far, Peach. Anyway, she wanted to go to rehab tonight, so we took her. I'll go back later with more clothes." He tumbled into bed in his shirt and jeans.

"You took her tonight? With the clothes on her back? Are you sure? I don't know that she really needs that. She really seemed to enjoy church last Sunday. Maybe—"

"I love you, *Abuela*," Elena said, heading up the stairs. "I know now that you truly do think the best. Of all of us. This is really what Mom needs right now. Trust me. Trust her too. I don't know where you're sleeping, so I'll set both alarms." The girl continued upstairs.

"I'll be up in a minute," Jean said, standing over Nigel, already fast asleep. She went to the kitchen to take down a pack of turkey bacon for breakfast and emptied Nigel's bag into a clothes basket, sorting it quickly into two loads and throwing one in the wash. Then she poked him a few times to be sure that he was sleeping and pulled off his clothes to toss them in with the next load. She covered him with a blanket before setting off to the hall closet to find him another suit for the next day. She hadn't thought he'd be able to fit in them, but he did. Still the same. Forty regular.

If only their marriage had stayed the same.

She turned that thought around in her head as she stopped to put the first load of clothes in the dryer and the second in the washer. Did she really want what they'd had before? Or something totally new? Apart from Nigel's waist size, so much about them had changed. She stared into the box of foolishness he'd collected from the employees to help assess their gifts, and shook her head. So much had changed, and yet so much had stayed the same. Nigel was still looking to save people, to hear their stories, to see what made them tick. He was interested in everyone that way, it seemed, except her.

As she emptied his pockets, she saw glimpses of his care and concern. A copy of the police report Elena had given and a card for some detective. Someone had written "Not evidence for a case against him anyway" on the back of the policeman's card. Jean had thought as much about the incident, but it was another thing altogether to have her hunch validated. There was the intake sheet where he'd signed Monica into the New Man Freedom from Addiction program and some scribbled notes about caterers and DJs for Elena's party. And of course, there was that box full of paintings and papier-mâché, journals and sketches. On the top was the famous coloring book.

Jean couldn't help but smile as she turned off the lights and leaned down to kiss Nigel's forehead.

She almost screamed when Nigel's hairy arm reached out and pulled her to his mouth instead.

"G'night, Peach. You'd better get up there. You told that girl you'd be up in a minute."

Still a little breathless from the kiss, Jean laughed softly. "For a woman, that is a minute. You know we can't just fall into bed. There's always something to do."

He stroked her hair before sleep claimed him again. She stood, slowly unwinding from his arm. She climbed the stairs slowly. Things could have been different. They could be different now. She just didn't want to be one of those women in church trying to resurrect a dead marriage, trying to get fruit from something so diseased that it could never produce anything. If anything was going to happen for her and Nigel, they'd both have to come whole and healthy, ready to be planted in something new. For now, she'd have to start there, digging deep and trying to get whole.

They weren't taking visitors at the hospital when Nigel arrived to visit Lyle and Chenille, and there were a lot of doctors and nurses coming in and out of the room, but the waiting room was full of friends and family and people from the church. People were playing board games or catching up on each other's lives as card after card crossed the room to be signed and left when the visiting hours were over.

Nigel saw some people from work there and sat down to talk with them. When Flex arrived, he excused himself and walked over to greet him. Eager to know if Jean's prediction was true, Nigel threw out a general question, right on the border between being concerned and nosy. "So is Raya okay? She's been sick quite a bit lately. She mentioned something about a stomach virus."

Flex made a funny face of exasperation that Nigel had only seen once before, when he'd done a behind-the-back pass to himself on the basketball court and cut around Flex to the basket. Like then, Flex looked as though he simply couldn't understand how such things could happen. "Come on, man. You know and I know that's no stomach virus. She knows it too. That's why she won't take a test. That girl is gone, I tell you. Just as pregnant as the day is long." Though he made it sound like Raya was unwilling to believe it, Flex was the one who looked dazed.

Nigel laughed. "You are really funny. You can't keep your hands off that woman, and then you have the nerve to stand here acting confused like you don't know how she got pregnant. As much praying and studying and loving as y'all are doing over there, you might be having twins."

Flex was laughing until the last comment brought him up short. "Man, don't even play like that. Those kids already have me huffing to keep up with them now. And if this one is a girl. My goodness. A daughter in this world? I might have to hurt somebody. Anyway, you're right. I have no business acting surprised. I guess we're doing good to have gotten the space that we got, huh?"

Nigel and a few eavesdroppers agreed. With the subject of pregnancy out of the way, the conversation turned to other things like the previous Sunday's sermon, Elena's party, and the untouchable subject—Nigel's marriage. Though he'd dealt out the funny remarks about Raya's pregnancy, Nigel had little to say as Flex joked about his "sleepovers" and the white wedding suit he'd worn to church the week before. Nigel endured the jeers and signed all the cards, but when he left the hospital, he decided to go to his own house instead of Jean's. Pullout couches weren't made to be slept on regularly, and he was starting to get a permanent imprint in his back where the bar was in that bed.

He hadn't told Jean what he planned to do for the evening while they were at work, so he didn't think she'd be waiting up for him. He'd get the clothes he had there over the weekend, but tonight he just needed one night of uninterrupted rest on a decent bed. Having everyone suddenly look to him for answers was great, but it was stressful too. His apartment had seemed cold and lonely when he'd first come back to New York, but tonight it'd be just what he needed. Quiet.

Preoccupied with thoughts about his day, Nigel ignored the blustery snow on his walk from the subway to his apartment. Laughing a little at some of Flex's jokes, he put the key in, then paused. Had he heard the buzz of a television inside? He pressed his ear to the door. Nothing. Probably his own heartbeat.

Nigel turned the key and pushed inside, not bothering at first to turn on the lights as he swung the door closed behind him. Then he stepped on it. Something soft.

Someone soft.

He dived for the light.

"I knew you'd come home sometime, sugar. Everybody does," Carmen said, sprawled out on his floor wearing little more than her own skin. She was drunk and Nigel was furious. Had she copied a key when he moved in, or what?

Nigel threw his coat across her. "Come on, Carmen. Get

dressed. You can't stay here. I don't know where you want to go, but I'm calling you a cab."

She waved him off, putting both arms in his jacket and trying to zip herself up. "Not that cab thing again. That didn't work, remember? There's only one thing that works for us. I tried all the other stuff, trying to get married, trying to be good. I'm just going to stick to what works."

Nigel closed his eyes for a few seconds, praying that this was some kind of bad dream. When he opened them, Carmen was still there, smiling. He went through the house, flicking on lights and finding her clothes. He wadded them into a ball and returned to the front of the apartment. "Where are you staying? The Ritz?"

She wagged a finger in front of her. "Ah, ah, ah. A lady never tells."

He felt a stab of pity. She was a lady, even if she didn't know it. He felt again the remorse he'd felt so many times before for not being a better friend to Carmen. There was just so much going on with work, his family, his new friends. He could at least do better than throwing her out into the street half-dressed.

He called around to her usual hotels until he found the place she was staying. Next he called a cab and asked the driver to call when he was down front and escort the lady inside the hotel when he dropped her off. He found her clutch purse wedged under the couch and marveled that she'd been able to maneuver his stairs in her condition.

He wondered how many nights she'd been waiting. The hotel didn't say how long her reservation was for, only that she wasn't in her room. As much as he wanted to help her, he wished she wasn't in his place either.

"Come on, girl. Get up." He pulled her up onto the couch and tried to pull her clothes on without looking at her.

Carmen obviously took it as something else, because she swung one leg over his and slid onto his lap.

He jumped up, but not fast enough. The door was open and there stood Jean, staring. He winced when he saw the casserole dish in her hand tilt, expecting it to drop. But she pulled it back up, walked into the kitchen, and came back empty-handed. "I thought you might be hungry here alone, but I see you've got quite a dish."

Nigel pushed Carmen back gently. "Wait! No. She was here when I got home. I don't even know how she got in. I was just trying to dress her and send her back to her hotel in a cab. I just didn't want to send her out into the street like that—somebody might get the wrong idea. I don't want anybody to hurt her. I guess I'm sensitive after Elena."

To his surprise, Jean turned back and came to the couch. "Move," she said firmly.

He obeyed, watching as she started to put on Carmen's clothes and wondering whether Jean was doing it for him or for Carmen.

A still, small voice whispered in Nigel's heart. *Neither of you. She's doing it for me.*

He grabbed a sweater from the closet near the door. "I'm going to go downstairs and pay the driver." Nigel didn't look back now as he heard the sound of his jacket zipper. Definitely time to go.

Jean agreed. "You do that. We'll be down. Take your phone. I'll call if I can't manage her, but I think I can get her down."

As he opened the door, Nigel felt relief rush in with the wind. Having Jean show up was the last thing he would have wanted to happen, but it was probably for the best for all of them. Though he got mad at Jean for always caring about appearances, he had to admit that him dragging a half dressed woman out of his apartment and tossing her into a cab wouldn't look too good either.

He paused before closing the door. "Peach?"

"Yeah," she said, obviously tugging on something.

"I owe you."

She made a grunting sound. "Boy, do you. Now get going. We're right behind you, and I mean it this time."

He shut the door without responding and hustled down the steps. If this winter was for pruning, then Nigel couldn't wait to see what God was going to let spring up through the soil of his life next year. He just hoped it was something good, as everything seemed to be going bad.

"Don't you think you're overreacting?" Lily Chau spoke softly so as not to wake her mother.

Jean tried to be mindful of her volume, but she was so angry that it was difficult. "I'm not overreacting. I'm simply reacting in a realistic way. Nigel and I will always be connected through our children and grandchildren, but I cannot go back and undo the past. I should have stayed and waited for him. I didn't. I was trying to survive. I've got to survive now too." She palmed a handful of almonds from a bowl on the table in front of her, hoping the protein would help her scattered thoughts come together.

Lily eased back onto the couch, allowing the generous folds of her kimono-style robe to open like butterfly wings. "It sounds like he's telling the truth. It sounds like you think he's telling the truth. So what's the big deal? Sure, nobody wants to put underclothes on a woman who's got the hots for her husband, but you did it. You gave grace to her and to Nigel. Why not give grace to yourself?"

Jean's cheeks swelled and then flattened as the air hissed

out between her teeth. "You just don't get it, do you? This is my grace. I'm going to find a new job in my old world. A place where I can really do what I do best, be who I am best. I've never really fit in at our place. You know that and I know it too. Every day that I work with Nigel, I see it more and more. He has taught me one thing—there's good, there's better, and there's best. I came to work with Chenille to heal, I think. I didn't know it then, but God knew."

Lily sandwiched a piece of provolone cheese between two green apple slices. "I'm not going to fight with you. If you think that this is what you want and you're sure that this is what God wants, then you do it. What bothers me is that you haven't mentioned God in this decision at all. It's all about you."

Jean rubbed a hand through her hair. She was too tired to explain anymore. God was in this, all of it. God had steadied her hands to dress Carmen and lead her down the steps, to help the woman who'd been in those pictures so long ago with her husband. In that moment, that long trip down the stairs, Carmen had sobered up enough to know who was helping her. Though all she said was thanks, Jean could hear the plea for forgiveness in her tone, the same plea that she heard in her own voice sometimes when talking to Nigel.

"You're welcome," Jean had said before hailing a cab of her own and heading for Lily's. During the ride, she realized that it was time for her to move forward, in every area of her life.

Lily got up, her robe flowing behind her. "Okay, so no more fighting. No more explaining. I was going to do some work, but you can use my laptop if you want. I get the feeling you'd like to be alone, and my husband would be more than happy to actually see me before midnight this week, so have at it. Use anything you need."

Jean crunched more almonds, resolved that she'd come to the right place. She and Lily might not always agree, but they tried to give each other space to see the other's view, to work out their own salvation. .

She checked the time and decided to go home and work on her résumé instead, since Elena would be home from her youth group outing soon. She left Lily a short note thanking her for listening and started out the door, almost setting off the alarm when she couldn't remember the correct code until the last second.

On the train home, she sketched out the additions to her old résumé, including her current project with Reebok. The contrast between her previous jobs at high fashion menswear houses and her current job clashed like a denim lapel on a silk suit. Still, for all her wonderful experiences years before in the fashion world, the past few years had been some of Jean's best in regard to her personal life. Spiritually, she'd gone from resenting God to trusting him.

She stopped writing. Was it really time to move on?

She could definitely do the work on the high-powered side of the aisle, but was her faith strong enough to withstand the hard, cold world she'd face? Or would she become the woman she'd once been if she went back to menswear? Could anyone ever develop a faith too strong to fail? Or was that God's job anyway?

Again and again she wrote out the pros and cons of staying, but one thing weighted down the cons column like a pile of lead—Nigel. She could see him at holidays, birthdays, even church, but the tangle of work and home was too much for her to bear. She'd gone to his house with dinner, hoping he'd see that she wanted to share much more than a meal with him—but he'd made no commitment to staying at her place. Even though Carmen was drunk and nothing seemed to have happened, Jean saw how easily he could go home at any time and do what he wanted. Jean had been the one opposed to commitment, but now she longed to lay claim to her wedding vows. She realized how Nigel had felt that first time he stayed over. It hurt. She wondered if maybe her love had come too late. Things were confusing now, and any middle ground that might have existed had long since disappeared.

Sticking around Garments of Praise had always been about helping Chenille, and now it was about being with and helping Nigel. It was time for Jean to accept that bringing her own family back together might not work out, that sometimes the only way to go is straight ahead, even if it means leaving what you know. What you love.

You've done this before. Think about it.

She was tired of thinking, tired of hoping, even tired of praying, about Nigel anyway. Some things were just too confusing to figure out. As it was, she could barely put a birthday party together. That should tell her something.

17

Jean tried to sift her thoughts through Elena's blaring music. A deafening mix of soca, rap, dance hall, worship, and some other styles that Jean couldn't identify, the girl's playlist was a wild ride. Jean endured the tunes to try to keep up with Elena. Just as she was closing her door to shut out some of the noise, she noticed Elena in the bathroom applying way too much of that dark lipstick Jean hated. True enough, it had moved up from black to burgundy, but it still made Jean think of some bad punk rock video from the eighties.

"Hey, you. Going somewhere?"

Elena turned around from the mirror, where she was trying to insert the earring at the top of her ear. "Now that you mention it, I am. Jay and I were going to go with his mom to the Creole church and help with the English as a Second Language class."

Jay and I. There it was again.

Jean tried to keep calm. "Wow. Sounds like a good cause, but I hope Jay has talked to his dad about it. You certainly didn't talk to me about going. And you don't know Creole, so I'm not sure how much help you might be anyway."

Elena whipped out the hairspray next. Jean took two steps back. It seemed like Elena sprayed the entire can of that stuff every time she used it. "Go easy with that. A little goes a long way."

Her granddaughter put the can down. "Right. Don't want it to be too stiff. Sorry that I didn't ask you. You've been so busy that I didn't want to bother you. I didn't think it was a big deal since Miss Ray is going and all. But I guess since Jay is going, it's a big drama."

Jean frowned, more because the girl had a point than anything. "Look, everything that you do is important to me. Whether or not Jay was going, I'd want to know what you're doing and who you're doing it with."

"Do you mean it? Because it just meets at the Creole church. There's lots of Dominicans there. Puerto Ricans and Mexicans too. Lots of cute kids." She checked her teeth for lipstick in the mirror.

"So you've been to the class before?" Every conversation with Elena was full of surprises.

"Sure. A few times. Mom didn't care."

I'll bet. "Did your mother even know?"

The girl shrugged her shoulders. "I don't know. I told her, but she didn't always quite hear what I was saying. She didn't care as long as I was with someone she knew anyway."

This is going to be a long school year.

Jean started back to her room. "You can go this time, but I do care. Remember that. I want to know where you're going and who you're going with. And when you're coming back, of course."

Elena smirked. "Well, you know what, Grandma? I've got an idea. Since you're so concerned, why don't you come with

201

me. I'll go and call Miss Raya right now, and I'm sure that she and her grammie would love to have you."

"No—wait . . . I—" Jean couldn't even think up an excuse that made sense to herself, let alone to someone else. "Forget it. I'll come. Give me a minute to get dressed."

And so they'd gone, Jean, Raya and her grandmother, Jay and Elena. Though Elena had mentioned the children, Jean was unprepared for so many of them, all so beautiful, with shining eyes. After the orientation, she picked up the first little girl she saw and began reading to her, pulling both their fingers along under the words on the page. Soon there was a line in front of her, and she arranged the children around her in a circle.

When a little Haitian boy asked why none of the children in the books looked like him, Jean suggested that they make up their own story, each person adding on as they went around the circle. The room became quiet as the children spoke softly, using their English, along with their hands, feet, and faces. A familiar-looking man picked up paper and quickly sketched out each person's piece of the tale, making bright rainbows and round, full suns.

After the fourth or fifth group, the program director sent the children to the playground for snacks, hoping to give Jean and her artist a break. He shook both their hands. "You two work great together. Most of those children you had today haven't said more than their names in all the times they've come here. That story concept is a whole program in itself."

The artist smiled. "We work together on our regular jobs. That's probably why things went so smoothly."

Jean dug into her pocket for her glasses. It was him. The coloring book guy from Garments of Praise. "You really are an artist. I mean, you're good. Amazing."

He smiled. "Thanks. It was because of your husband that I started trying to draw again. Let's do this story thing again. It was really fun."

The mother of the Haitian boy came to Jean and hugged her, nodding many times her approval for what she'd done with her son. Then the woman stopped and let go of Jean's hand. She started speaking quickly in Creole and pointing frantically at the cross.

Raya ran over to them and tried to get the woman to calm down. After a few minutes, Raya seemed to understand and must have convinced the woman that she would pass on what she had said.

Now curious, Jean rocked from side to side, waiting to hear the translation. "What? What did she say?"

Raya took Jean's hand and held it tight. "She asked me why you are still fighting, why you refuse to be made whole?"

Nigel almost went back home after church, but after seeing Monica's smile as she sat with the other people in the program, he was encouraged. Jean had smiled at him too, but said nothing. It was Elena, as usual, who crossed the bridge between them.

"Are you coming over? She cooked already. You should come."

Jean's eyebrows knit together, but she didn't say anything.

Nigel laughed, drinking in her antics like fresh rain. Jean hadn't said much to him at all since the night she'd helped him get Carmen out of the house. It'd only been a few days ago, but it seemed like an eternity. He'd played the scenario over and over in his mind, trying to figure what he could have done differently, but in the end, he decided to let it go. Family was family, and he wanted to see them.

"I'll come, Elena, but only if your grandmother wants me to."

Jean turned away quickly, but not fast enough for her smile to escape him. "It's fine, Nigel. You still have things at the house anyway. I guess it'd be good for you to come and get them before I start wrapping them in plastic and storing them in the closet."

He shoved his hands into his pockets. "I guess that would be a good idea. For me to get my stuff, I mean."

And so they walked along, Elena hugging his arm and Jean keeping pace with a few feet between them. Once they got back to Jean's house, everyone changed into comfortable clothes and gathered at the table to eat. They discussed the sermon and the significance of them spending another advent Sunday together. Elena told them about things at school, never mentioning Jay but always mentioning him at the same time. They were reviewing the preparations for Elena's party when suddenly the girl went quiet.

Nigel looked at Jean and asked the question that she must have been thinking as well. "What is it?"

Elena took a drink of tea. "It's nothing. Well, something really, but it would make both of you really mad, so I'm going to forget about it."

The two grandparents grabbed hands under the table.

This time, Nigel spoke first. "What is it, hon? You can tell us anything. You should know that by now."

The teen took another gulp from her glass. "Yeah, but this is different. It's like really, really bad, and *Abuela* is going to lose it totally, so let's just forget it."

Jean grabbed Nigel's hand with a tighter grip. "No, I won't lose it. I'm fine. Now go ahead."

Elena locked her hands behind her head and blew out a breath. "Okay. Here goes. I said I didn't want the party in the first place because, well, I really didn't want it. Then, some of those girls *Abuela* tries to make me hang out with told me that after your quince party you can date. That you'd be like a woman and all that. Well, I knew that Grandma was sort of crazy about the dating thing, so I went for the party . . ."

Both Nigel and Jean had been leaning forward as far as they could, still holding hands under the table.

Jean broke their grip to push forward on the table. "And? What else, sweetheart?"

Elena tossed back her head. "Well . . . now I want the party and the church service and everything, but I don't really want to date. Not like me and Jay alone in the dark at a movie date. He asked me to pray about it and I have been, and he's right. We're not ready. I like to be with him when one of you or somebody in his family is around, but that whole thing in Central Park was really stupid and caused a lot of trouble. I see now what a lot of guys are looking for, and I don't want to deal with it yet. So I want to wait a year. There. Done. That's it."

Nigel waited for Jean to speak her piece, but he was actually relieved. He didn't like the thought of throwing together the party at the last minute, and Elena waiting another year to date would do them all good. He watched as Jean got up from the table and hugged Elena, kissing her on both cheeks.

"I'm really proud of you. It took a lot of guts to say that, especially to me, knowing how I can be about these things. I think that you've made a great decision, and I'll take care of everything. We can still have a Christmas Eve dinner at the church or something. I'll work it out."

Elena relaxed, the tension draining from her like a deflating balloon. "Oh, my goodness. I feel so much better. I thought you were totally going to freak, both of you. I'm still excited about it though, and I'm looking forward to doing it next year." She got up and walked around the table to hug both of them. "I know I've really been putting you through it lately, Grandma. Thank you for everything. And, Grandpa, I thought you were cool from the first time you came to my blog, but now I know you are. I'm really glad you're here with us."

Nigel just smiled. He was glad to be here with her too, even if it was only for a few hours. He could see now why Flex had been so intense with him about Jay. Raising a teen was almost like going back to the toddler stuff again, only teens' accidents could be a lot worse than spilling juice or falling down. The mistakes during these years could determine the rest of Elena's life. He watched his granddaughter walk away in her low-rider jeans and black nail polish, and a shudder went through him. How could Jean try to raise this girl alone? What she'd been through with Monica was too much to ask already.

As they gathered for the Advent reading listed in the church bulletin, Nigel reached into his pocket for a piece of cloth with a hook in it. He attached it to the branch. "It's to represent the sign of prophecy. Not quite Joseph's Technicolor coat or anything, but it's a piece of the rebozo blanket that my grandmother carried my father in as a child."

During the afternoon, Jean had only touched him during their dinner panic, but now she came to him easily, reaching up to plant a kiss on his cheek. She took his hand as they recited the Advent prayer together, asking the Wonderful Counselor and Mighty God to heal their hearts and their family, to give them a fresh start.

As they let go of each other's hands and Elena disappeared into the kitchen, Nigel knew what he needed to do. He pulled Jean close and whispered into her ear. "Will you let me come back here and live with you? To help you raise her? There doesn't have to be anything between us. We can work that out later. I just don't want you to have to do this alone again. You don't have to."

Jean took a deep breath before answering. "Do I want you here? Oh my, yes—"

"Thank God." He held her close.

She pulled closer to him and lingered a long time before pushing herself away. "But can you really be here without there being anything between us? No. I think you know that. You tried to tell me, but I wouldn't listen. We're going to have to decide what we want to do, who we want to be—Nigel and Jean or Mr. and Mrs. Salvador. You were right—having something on paper isn't enough." She stared at him the way she had when he was wounded in Vietnam and unable to speak. Then, like now, he understood every word.

I'm afraid, her eyes said.

Nigel tried to still his racing heart, his runaway thoughts. He was scared too. Scared of wasting any more time. He'd lost enough. But what about her? Was Jean really ready to let him love her again for good? Or would they always be playing sleepover games? Was he enough for her? Was anyone? Or would his hurt end up on the cutting-room floor like one of Jean's discarded designs? Nigel didn't have all the answers, but he did know the right question. He whispered into Jean's ear before putting on his coat.

"Will you marry me?"

She had hesitated. That was all the answer Nigel needed.

"Wait," she'd said as he slipped out the door. "You caught me off guard."

You caught me off guard too, he thought now, back at work and back to business. When he first met Jean, he'd been covered in blood and sandwiched between two other men, writhing in agony. Jean had reached out to him then without hesitation, caring for his wounds with tenderness and concern. When he'd proposed to her the first time, she'd said yes almost before he finished his question, despite having been engaged to Doug just a few days before. He learned later that she called off the engagement soon after he'd arrived at the hospital. Whether or not she knew Nigel would propose, he never asked, but he figured it was just her fading feelings for Doug that had sparked her decision.

There was no hospital to go to now, to tend his wounds. He'd have to trust the Lord to do it, to wash away the hurt he was feeling, so that he could concentrate on the project and supporting Chenille and Lyle. Still, when Jean swept into the conference room, this time smelling of jasmine and pears, Nigel felt breathless, as though he'd climbed the roof of the building and scaled down the wall. He hoped his face didn't show it. "Good morning."

"Hi," she said, pulling a wool shawl around her shoulders.

She wore a salmon-colored suit. Her shoes were green, with a burst of colorful flowers in the center. It was more a spring outfit than winter, but it suited Jean well. Not quite as slim as she'd been when he'd first arrived, some of the hips Nigel remembered filled out the skirt nicely. He smiled against his will. "Ready for the big day? The Reebok team should be here around ten."

Jean nodded, taking a deep breath. "I guess I'm as ready as I can get. Thanks for everything you've done. This is a really great collection. That jacket looks even better on you today than it did the first time, if that's possible. Are you still modeling today?"

Nigel looked down, admiring the argyle inset jacket that

Jean had designed. He'd come to love all the pieces in the Suiting Up collection, but this jacket really held first place in the lineup, in his opinion. It had a great look that could be dressed up or dressed down, it fit well, and Jean had made it. Hard not to like it. "I suppose I will be modeling. Flex and Jay should be here in about thirty minutes so we can run through everything. You've got all the cards, right?"

Jean shuffled through the stack of mocked-up cards on the desk. "I've got them, although a few of the ideas that we discarded ended up in there too. The blue and burgundy suit with the gold piping? Did you put that back in?"

Nigel scrambled to check his notes. "I think the last thing we said was to take another look at it before the final presentation. Or at least that's what I have written down here." He scrolled through his computer files also, just to be sure.

"Well, I can't speak for you, honey, but I've seen enough." She held up the card with the picture of the outfit. "It looks like a couch to me."

Honey? What was she trying to do, kill him? "I agree. Toss it. Less is more anyway. I'd rather not overwhelm them. With two of everything, we've got quite a few pieces already."

The half hour passed quickly as they rechecked all the pieces and lined them up in order. Flex and Jay arrived on time, and Nigel invited all the staff into the conference room for the run-through of their presentation. Some of the male employees helped him remove several leaves from the conference table so that they could get it out the door. They lined the room with chairs and checked the sturdiness of the mock stage they'd ordered and assembled. It bobbed a bit under Flex's muscle at first, but a few adjustments held everything in place. Several staff workers trickled in to watch the run-through.

Though he and Jean had decided against the usual Power-

Point presentation to explain each piece in the collection, Nigel had moved a screen into the room just in case. With things like this, it was hard to know what you might need until you needed it. Love, unfortunately, was like that too. He knew now that those years with Jean had been casual for him. His marriage had been something like air or water, something necessary but taken for granted. Jean was the more affectionate one then, often proclaiming her love, while he chose to show it in quiet ways, ways that she hadn't always heard or even understood. He watched her as they prepared, moving between all of them like a tree in full flower, a ripe fruit in the middle of winter. No longer was this his peach, juicy but bruised in places, sweet but stained. She was something altogether new. And despite all that had happened, he wanted a taste.

All things are possible, but not all things are profitable.

Nigel sighed as the music started, and he stepped out onto the runway. Jean bared her teeth at him, reminding him to smile. He might have laughed under other circumstances, but it took all he had in him just to smile. His mind replayed that moment of hesitation after he'd offered her all he had, all he could, and she'd stared at him—with the same look of pain he remembered when the judge pronounced him guilty so many years ago. When he put himself out there, her true feelings showed on her face. He had to accept it. They were Jean and Nigel, not Mr. and Mrs. Salvador. That part of their relationship was over.

The presentation ended to a standing ovation crowd, including, to Nigel and Jean's horror, the entire Reebok team!

"Bravo!" the team leader said, clapping his hands. "Very nice."

Nigel jumped down from the stage, but Jean had already reached them and explained that this was the run-through, not the final presentation.

"If you could just wait a few minutes, we can do it again," she said, nodding to Nigel for his approval.

He quickly gave it. "Yes, do sit down. We have folders for you, and a light lunch is coming in . . ."

Several of the Reebok people laughed. "We like what we've seen so far. We'll take the folders and get back to you on specifics. As for the lunch, we were going to take the two of you out, actually. It's the least we can do. We'll talk more details on the pieces and launch dates then. What do you say?"

Jean nodded to Nigel again, reaching for his arm.

"We'd be honored," he said, bristling at her touch. He'd have to get over that. Somehow. "We'll meet you out front." He pulled away from Jean, his hand extended toward their guests.

They shook hands with everyone and watched them go before the employees let out a collective cheer. Flex and Jay joined in the hugs as they descended the stage.

Nigel didn't know how to thank them enough. "You two really sold it. That father and son thing you did, sort of trying to outshine one another during that last run, that was great. Jay, you make a great model too. You didn't even fall off the stage." He shook both their hands firmly before Jean reached out and hugged them again. Nigel tried not to be jealous.

Love keeps no record of wrongs.

Nigel's thoughts skittered through all the praying and studying he'd done over the last twenty-four hours. First Corinthians 13 had quickly reminded him of how far his own weak emotions were from true godly love, the kind that he wanted to have not only for Jean but for everyone around him. He couldn't keep focusing on his past experiences with people, good or bad, in determining how to treat them now. Today, and every day after it, was the day of salvation for

211

whoever chose to receive it. He wanted to start loving people in their mess, the way God—and Jean—had loved him.

Lily, who'd showed up to support them, gave a quick critique before running off to close on a new house big enough for her mother and a full-time caregiver along with their budding home business. She made some good comments about her favorite pieces and said she couldn't wait to get Doug into some of the designs. Nigel agreed. His friend would look great in them.

"I should have asked him to model too, but with you two being so big-time and all . . ."

"He would have eaten it up." Lily laughed and hugged both of them, thanking them for inviting her.

Nigel smiled but didn't say more. He had considered asking Doug to model but decided against it. Though the two of them were friends, he was still mindful of Doug's place in the fashion industry. He wouldn't make the request any more than he'd ask Ralph Lauren to grace their makeshift runway. His army years might be long behind him, but Nigel still had a good sense of rank and file. And in the world of fashion, Doug was a four-star general. The question was, what would Nigel become, and would Jean be there with him? Though they'd worked on the Reebok project with success, he didn't know how things would play out once he took over the firm in January. He decided he didn't need to know. Today had enough excitement of its own.

Raya congratulated them too, before announcing she was going home for the day and running off for the bathroom. Both Nigel and Jean shook their heads and gave Flex a grin as the room emptied, leaving them alone.

"I guess this is it, huh?" Nigel said as he gathered the remaining folders and his laptop and turned out the light.

Jean paused as if trying to figure out what he was really

saying. Nigel didn't explain further. He couldn't. He wasn't sure himself. She draped her shawl around her as they stepped into the hall. "Is this it? For this project maybe, but—"

"Congratulations."

The voice stopped both Nigel and Jean midstride as they stepped out into the hall. Carmen stood awkwardly against the wall in a black pantsuit and leather trench coat.

"Thanks," Nigel said. "Were you in there too?" Considering how things had gone the last time he'd seen Carmen, he didn't really know what to say. Still, it was nice of her to have come to support him. She'd always been good that way.

She smiled. "I was. For a few minutes at least. I knew after the third set that it was a sell. I went to the front to wait for the team and get a feel for what they thought. I also wanted to thank you, both of you, for helping me out that night. I'm sorry for going in your place, Nigel. And Jean, I'm just sorry. You taught me a lot that night."

Jean shrugged it off. "It's okay. We all need help sometimes. Now, what did they say up front?"

Nigel stiffened as Jean took his hand in anticipation of Carmen's news. He was still trying to process Carmen's apology, to come up with something honest but positive to say, while Jean had brushed the whole thing off as though it was nothing. Maybe it had been nothing to her. Maybe he was nothing too. She seemed shut down to everything that had anything to do with him. He, on the other hand, continued to make a fool of himself, again and again. As gently as he could, Nigel pulled his hand away. He didn't dare look at Jean. "Do tell, Carmen. What'd they say?"

Carmen paused as if trying to gauge the meaning of the exchange she'd just seen. Then she caught herself and responded to their questions. "The line? Well, they loved it, but not exactly as you put it together. Their vision put a lot of the jackets with different bottoms for a mix and match sort of feel. They loved that loud, fiery one for the Heat. They think that'll be a big seller. That argyle jacket too."

Mix and match? Jackets with bottoms? Nigel released the laughter that had been brewing in him on the runway. So he and Jean would end up together after all, on store mannequins. "I never would have thought they'd go that way in a million years." He took Carmen's hand. "Thanks for coming."

She closed her eyes at his touch, then opened them. Carmen looked over at Jean next and replaced her hands at her sides. "I wouldn't have missed it. I've been doing a lot of thinking since I saw you last. Praying even. The kindness that you two showed me was probably the best sermon I've ever heard. And I thank you. Now you'd both better get up front and into that limo. Don't want to keep the bigwigs waiting."

Nigel agreed and rushed to the lobby with Jean. As they turned the corner, he looked back and saw Carmen still watching him, still following. It occurred to him then that she loved him the way he loved Jean. He turned back, jogging to catch up with Jean and saying a prayer for Carmen . . . and himself. Loving someone who didn't love you back was a heavy burden.

18

She got the job. With all that Jean had been going through after Nigel had proposed, she pretty much forgot about the frenzied night at Lily's and her resolve to leave the firm, to get away from Nigel any way she could. And now, now that the courier had come and delivered the offers—two of them, in fact—Jean didn't know what to do. Now she wanted to be near Nigel more than ever, only he seemed to do everything he could to be as far away from her as possible. And what else could she expect after how she'd responded to his marriage proposal? Maybe this really was how things were supposed to be. As she'd done on that night after dressing Carmen in Nigel's apartment, Jean went to Lily for help.

Lily smoothed the two pages out in front of her, then picked them up, one at a time. "Wow, and wow again. When you came in here, I was furious with you and ready to give you a speech about your motivations in this, but reading both of these offers . . . They seem totally perfect for you in every way. And the money sure doesn't hurt either. Have you prayed about it?

I just don't know what to say. I know Chenille would miss you, but I also know that she wants for each of us to reach our potential and to be in the places God has for us."

Jean pulled a hand through her hair, now much longer than it'd been back in November when Nigel had first arrived. She'd picked up a few pounds too, though most of it seemed to be muscle as she'd dropped some of her cardio time but kept her strength training regimen going. Although some of her clothes didn't fit, she almost preferred this version of herself. Nigel seemed to also, or at least he had. Now it was as if she wasn't there at all. If she did leave, he'd probably hardly notice.

Jean buried her face in her hands and leaned over in her chair, her forehead touching Lily's desk. Several seconds passed before she lifted her head. "I did pray about it when I did this. I really did. I felt so sure, like when you just know something is right. Now, here it is, this thing that I thought that I wanted, and all I can think about is him. He asked me to marry him, can you believe that?"

Lily stood and leaned over the desk. "What? What did you say? And aren't you already married? You two drive me crazy."

Me too, Jean thought. The whole thing was crazy. Things between them had always been that way, it seemed. This was too much, though. "It's complicated. We were, uh, together once. He stayed over and things got out of hand—"

"Raya was right! I knew it too. Man, you're just so wrong. We tell you everything, woman. And here you are holding out on stuff like that? I mean, seriously. So how was it? Oh, man. I'm going to have to call Chenille at the hospital."

Jean shook her head. They were lunatics. All of them. "Will you shut up? I'm dying here and you're trying to get details."

"Hey, details are important. You've gotta admit." She shuffled in her drawers, though most of them were empty. "I just knew I brought that camera with me. I must have taken it home after your presentation the other day. Yep. I did. I remember now because I showed Doug that jacket. He loved it too."

Jean ground her teeth together. "Why in the world are you looking for a camera? I'm having a crisis. Can't you see that? What are you going to do—put up a website like Chenille and chronicle my breakdown for the world to see?" Every day in her email, Jean got a link from Chenille to her web journal about Lyle's progress. She'd read it a few times, but for the most part, it was too painful to think of strangers reading such personal information. Elena did the same thing, but Jean did check that page from time to time to make sure that she wasn't disclosing any personal information. Since the incident, though, she hadn't spent much time on the computer at all. Basketball practice had started now, so she probably wouldn't be back on it anytime soon either.

Lily took a handful of pistachios from a dish on her desk and began to shell them. "Hey, I know you're losing it, and believe me, I'm here for you, but history is history. You've got man face, woman, and that sort of thing must be recorded. It's just a fact."

She threw her head back and groaned. *Man face*. But Jean made no effort to deny it as she would have before. "That should tell you how critical this is. Take your dumb pictures or whatever, but listen to me. Seriously. After he stayed that night, he said he wanted us to renew our vows and move back in together. You know, be husband and wife. I just didn't know how to take that. I tried to be a good wife. Really I did. It just didn't work out."

No longer joking, Lily came around the desk and sat down next to Jean. She gave her a quick hug. "You were just scared. You still are. Being married is hard, and that's without all the other things that you two have had to deal with. Stop freaking out and think it through, all of it, like why you didn't

217

immediately say yes and call me after. Not that I think it's even necessary, but I'll let that go for now."

She nudged Jean with her elbow. "And about Chenille, that's a blog, not a website exactly."

"Whatever." Jean stood and stretched her arms over her head. She'd lingered in bed this morning and ended up rushing her workout and cutting short her final stretch. "I'm sorry. This whole thing has me snippy I started it, actually. With us going to church and Monica going to rehab, I realized that Nigel was right. We couldn't just go back and forth in some undefined limbo. My parents did that. When they got older, my mother went back to Puerto Rico and my father stayed in the Dominican Republic. He wasn't leaving the DR for anything."

Lily nodded. "I know a lot of Asian couples like that too. Must be a non-American thing. Still, I don't think it's what God intended for marriage or for you. It sounds like you know that, so why didn't you accept the proposal?"

Jean stood and rotated her head from left to right. The tension she'd felt in her arms seemed to have moved to her shoulders and neck. "I choked. Froze. It happened to me in church too. Remember how good I told you that sermon was, the Sunday after Thanksgiving? Well, when the pastor asked if I'd be made whole, I didn't answer. I couldn't. It's like something in me has been so hurt that it's just broken. I wanted more than anything to say yes to him, but instead, I just stood there like a deer in the headlights."

"Oh no." Lily made a face.

"Oh yes," Jean said, pacing around the room. "I could see the hurt in his eyes."

Lily followed Jean around the small space. "So what did he say?"

"Nothing. He just grabbed his coat and left. He hasn't been back to the house since. I'm hoping he'll come by this weekend for church so we can pray around the Jesse tree, but I don't know. The way he's acting . . ." Jean stopped moving and leaned over on the desk.

"Can you maybe just talk to him? Tell him what you just told me? Sometimes it's that simple, saying how you feel. You don't always have to have a solution or a plan for what comes next. When Doug and I were getting together, it seemed impossible, remember? Him wanting to go back to Nigeria, me having to stay here with Mom, the design show. It was a mess, but here we are. You guys can renew vows anywhere or move in together anytime, but maybe for now, you just both need to be secure in your love for each other and God's love for both of you."

Jean sighed. The love of God. How steady and persistent it was, and how she needed it. Her love paled in comparison. Whether she could ever be the wife Nigel needed she wasn't sure, but she definitely wanted to try. More than that, she wanted him to know that she really did love him, even if sometimes she didn't know how to show it. "He finds a way to disappear every time I come near him now, but I think you're right. I'm going to have to find some way to talk to him and at least let him know how I feel. I'll leave the rest to God to work out."

Lily shook her head. "God has worked it out. He brought Nigel here, didn't he? No, I think it's time for you to step up and really show him your commitment. He took a risk, and you let him fall on his face. This time you're going to have to throw your heart in the air and pray that he catches it."

As the shofar horn blew in the hall signaling the end of their creative hour, Jean gathered up her job offers from Lily's desk, more confused than ever about what to do about anything. "What are you suggesting, Mrs. Marriage Expert?"

"Well, if it were me—and it's not, so take this the way you want to—I think I'd propose to him. I'd probably make a pretty grand gesture of it too, if you know what I mean." She eyed Jean up and down. "But that's just me. You pray about it and do what seems right to you. Same goes with those jobs. Whatever happens, I miss you and I hate that it takes trouble to bring us together."

"Me too," Jean said, kissing Lily's cheek before leaving. "Thanks for listening and for talking too. I'm surprised that you actually gave me some advice, but I'm glad you did. I think I just might take you up on it. And I'm going to work on us getting together and talking during peacetime, if you know what I mean."

"I do," Lily said, walking Jean to the door. "But if we only have time for trouble, then that's okay too. That's what real friends are for. By the time this is all over, I'll probably have a mess to bend your ear with too." She smiled and pushed down the doorstop on her door.

"I hope not," Jean said as she started back to her office. "I wouldn't wish this on anyone."

"So do you think he's coming?" Elena asked for what seemed like the hundredth time.

As before, Jean gave the same answer. "No, honey, I don't." It was snowing outside, fast and hard. Jean watched it mournfully, sympathizing with the desperation of the pelting cold. Jean felt the same urgency within herself to get some time with Nigel, to try to at least tell him how she felt. On a few brave mornings, she'd even considered proposing to him. Each time he wheeled around her, preparing for their final presentation to Reebok, mumbling a staid response before she even said anything.

Was that how he felt she'd treated him? She hoped not. She tried to show him she cared, even if she'd failed in all the ways

220

that mattered. "Come away from the window, Elena. And change your clothes. You are going to church, after all."

The girl pouted, ignoring Jean's comment about her clothes. "You gave him my invitation, didn't you? I don't understand. I just knew he'd come this weekend. I was so sure of it."

I wasn't.

Jean tried to change the subject. "Seriously, put on something else, okay? You're going to see your mother today. I don't want her to think I'm not taking good care of you. And don't worry about your grandfather if he doesn't show. It's not about you, it's about me. Sometimes grown-ups just—"

"Oh yeah, I know the speech. Sometimes grown-ups just don't love each other anymore. Sometimes they make bad decisions. Sometimes they wreck your life! I'm sick of that, *Abuela*. You all get to tell me what to do and what's right and what's wrong, but then you never have to follow any of it. That's not fair, and don't tell me that there's no such thing as fair. It's not just, either, and you know it." Elena slammed down her jacket and her Bible on the couch.

Normally Jean would have given her granddaughter a sharp rebuke for an outburst like that, but the truth in the girl's words silenced her for a second. When she found her voice, she thought about love, God's love, and how much they all needed it. "You're right. The adults in your life have all made some pretty bad decisions. And you're right that it's not fair or just that you have to suffer for them. For my part, I apologize." She opened her arms to Elena.

Elena ran into her arms. "I'm sorry too, Grandma. I shouldn't have said that. You've always been here for me. I thank you for that. It's just that I thought . . . I thought that things were going to be different, that he was going to stay."

Jean blew out a breath. She didn't have the heart to tell

the girl that he would have stayed. Forever. "Come on, let's just go to church."

"Wait, don't you want me to change my clothes?"

Jean looked at her granddaughter again. Her sweater was too short and her jeans too tight for church, even a church as casual as New Man, but at this point, she just wanted to get there. Fighting her own feelings and the snow outside would be hard enough. "If you feel like what you've got on is appropriate, Elena, then you wear it." Jean tried not to think of what people might see if the girl raised her hands during praise time or if she bent down to pick something up. Still, Elena had accepted Christ now, and she'd have to start working through her faith on her own. Jean had enough to do just to keep herself straight.

Elena didn't answer but went up the stairs instead, returning a few minutes later in a sweater set Jean had bought her last Christmas and her favorite pair of kitten-heeled boots. Jean wondered how the shoes would fare in the snow, but she didn't bring it up. There'd been enough criticism on all sides for one Sunday morning. If she had to, she'd pick Elena up a more sensible pair of shoes on the way home. Right now, she just wanted to get to the church.

Nigel must have been thinking the same thing, because when they arrived, several minutes early, he was there too, waiting in the foyer.

"Good morning, sweetheart," he said to Elena, kissing her cheek. "Thanks for your invitation, but I don't think I'm going to make it today. It's good to see you though. I'm going to go out to the hospital after church and see Lyle, and then Doug and I are going to hang out for a while. Things have been so busy since I've gotten here that we've never really had a chance to catch up."

Elena smiled as though she understood, but Jean knew she

didn't. When Nigel nodded hello to her, Jean gave him a little wave, knowing better than to step toward him lest he flee the church at top speed. Still a little thick for her most recent wardrobe, Jean had to go to her old clothes this morning, most of them in the same front closet with Nigel's suits. As his eyes fastened on her outfit, a black velvet skirt set, she remembered that she had worn it once in a picture she'd sent him.

From the look on his face, he remembered too. "You look nice this morning," he said quietly before taking Elena's hand and walking away with her.

"You too," Jean said, admiring his suit, a pin-striped double-breasted one she'd never seen. Though Jay had done their pieces justice during the demonstration, Jean still had a preference for designs intended for grown men. There was just something about a broad back in a well-made suit that fit. She had chills as he walked away until it hit her—he'd walked away with their granddaughter. If Monica was allowed, she'd probably sit with him too. Though she'd been the one loving all of them for longer than she could remember, Jean suddenly felt alone. Shut out.

She wanted to plow through the crowd and jump on Nigel's back, wrap her arms around his neck. She wanted to make him stop moving away, make him hear that she loved him and that he was right about Elena too. The job of raising her, even for a little while, was bigger than Jean had imagined. If things were going to be different for that girl, for Monica, things needed to be different between them too. She wanted to shout into the church microphone how much she needed him. How much she wanted for him to come home with them and never leave.

Jean wanted to do all those things, but instead, she took a bulletin from an usher and disappeared into one of a thousand faces in a back row by the door. She had a feeling she might need to run, both from Nigel and from God.

19

The waiting room wasn't crowded this time, but Nigel recognized a few faces from work and from church. After exchanging hellos, he approached Lyle's room with caution, not wanting to disturb his friend's time with his wife. Instead of the closed door he expected, he found it wide open and the room exploding with flowers.

Lyle's eyes opened slightly. At the sight of Nigel, he smiled. "These flowers are ridiculous, huh? They all seem to think I'm dead already. Either that or they're trying to kill me off with an asthma attack. Come on in."

Nigel looked around for Chenille, but she was nowhere to be found. Her computer was hooked up and her purse shoved under a chair, so he knew she hadn't gone far. She was often protective of her husband, and the more Nigel got to know Lyle, the more he was inclined to agree with her. Lyle was a rare breed, the kind of person the world needed. The kind of friend he needed. "Sorry I haven't been around the past few days. Some stuff going on."

"So I hear."

Nigel adjusted the sheet around him.

"Chenille's been getting faxes and calls from all over, asking which job Jean is going to take."

Nigel felt the blood drain from his face. She was leaving? Did being around him bother Jean that much? He sank into the chair next to Lyle's bed. "I didn't know anything about that. I was just talking about getting the final choices ready for Reebok."

Lyle made a smacking sound with his lips. "So you didn't know? Look at me, home wrecking on my deathbed. Oh, well, I've got to go out with a bang, I guess. You'll remember me at least, right?" He managed a chuckle. "I do hope she stays around New York though. There've been calls from Paris, Milan, LA, everywhere."

Nigel wasn't laughing. He'd spent the past week trying to force himself to accept the truth—that his marriage was over and probably always had been despite both his and Jean's attempts to resurrect it. As much as he respected Lyle, Nigel suddenly regretted his agreement to stay on and help Chenille run Garments of Praise. Though he'd fallen in love with the place, painful reminders of Jean were everywhere. "Like I said, I don't know anything about it. I'd hate to see her go far with our granddaughter so close to her and all, but I guess it's her decision."

Chenille stepped around the curtain that separated the room's beds. Evidently, that was Chenille's new bedroom. "Hey, Nigel. How are you? Hope you're not paying too much attention to my husband and his ramblings."

"I am, in fact," Nigel said before standing up to give her a hug. "You scared me a little coming from over there. I thought there was another patient in the room."

She laughed. "Nope. Just me. And the rest of the flowers, of course."

"Are you kidding? There's more?" It didn't seem possible.

To prove it, Chenille pushed back the curtain. It looked like a garden had come to visit. "We think they're robbing graves at this point," she said with the same morbid humor as her husband.

Lyle chuckled. "Isn't she funny?"

Not really. Nigel shook his head. "You both have an interesting sense of humor, to say the least." He took his chair again after Chenille chose another one. Even if the two of them said something genuinely funny, he doubted he'd laugh. Everything that had happened in the past few weeks, besides connecting with Monica and Elena, seemed like a joke. Instead of hanging around trying to work things out with Jean, he should have been leaving too, on assignment somewhere else for Reebok or on his way back to Los Angeles. Why God would let Nigel get so close to getting Jean back and then let things fall apart he didn't know. He wasn't even sure he wanted to know. What did it matter, anyway? In a few weeks, Jean might be halfway across the world.

Lyle looked as though he was dozing off. Nigel got up to leave. Chenille, who was on the computer and had her back to them, held up her hand. "He's just resting. Feel free to stay."

Unsure, Nigel kept standing.

"Really, it's okay. He's doing a lot better, and he usually has a good day after one of your visits. So, be my guest and his too."

Nigel took his seat. Lyle opened one eye. "Tricked you, didn't I? Had to get a little shut-eye real quick there. I saw you over there doing all that deep introspection, and I figured I might need to sleep in for the rest of this visit. It's dangerous looking that deep inside yourself, you do know that, don't ya?"

Chenille crunched Cheetos in the background, but she managed to agree. "Uh-huh. Dangerous."

Nigel did laugh then. "It wasn't anything all that deep really. I was just trying to figure out why things are going the way they are. Why I'm even here."

It was the Rizzos' turn to laugh. Lyle spoke first. "Why? No need stumbling with the little questions—you just like to get things stirred up from the beginning, huh? Why'd you end up in that jail cell when you didn't do anything? Why am I here dying when all I want to do is serve God? Well, why not you? Why not me? Are we above struggle? Above pain? Christ wasn't. It's not the pain that matters so much, friend. It's the love. Don't let the pain kill your love."

The tears came slow at first, some for Lyle and Chenille, and others for himself, for Jean and Monica, Elena, even Carmen. He knew that what Lyle was saying was right, but he was just tired. Just human. "I hear you, man. I guess I just need for something to go my way, you know?"

Lyle closed his eyes again, but Chenille took up his slack. "Something to go your way? You've just designed an entire line of suits based on one of the most popular professional leagues for one of the biggest companies in sports. Your daughter is getting treatment, and you probably saved your granddaughter's life. Your wife is alive and healthy, and regardless of what happens from here, you know she never stopped caring about you. I'd say that some pretty good things have come your way lately. You just seem to have a hard time seeing them when they show up."

Nigel sat back in his chair, stunned and feeling more than a little stupid. Here these people were losing everything and still ministering truth to him about his life and the small things he'd been making into giant problems. Was life all about having some perfect love? Was any love really perfect anyway? What else had he been missing that was right in front of his eyes? "Well, he said I was digging deep, but I think you pretty much scratched the bottom of the barrel on that one."

"Sorry if I was harsh," Chenille said. "I didn't mean to be. It's just that I have to talk myself out of my pity parties every day. It's so easy to get caught up in what comes next that I have to force myself to deal with now, today. Today my husband is alive. That's enough. It has to be."

Lyle's eyes stayed closed, so Nigel talked to Chenille, thanking her for the way that she and Lyle had received him despite his broken past. "When a lot of church people find out that I've been to jail, everything changes. Not that I blame them or anything, but I just appreciate both of you. I know you're really Jean's friends, and you could have just left it at that. You've made me feel part of your family."

"You've really brought a lot of joy to us and to Jean, whether you know it or not. I know it's hard to hear from a dying man and his wife, but listen—God delights in resurrection. Some things have to die before they can truly live. See all these plants? Some of them started that way, a seed that had to die in order to be planted and to grow. People are that way too sometimes."

Nigel took the words to heart, but if he was honest with himself, he didn't think his marriage was going to come back to life. It was Lyle's resurrection and the hope of it that made him smile as he got up to leave.

Doug was late and Nigel was too. There weren't any messages on the machine, but Nigel wondered if he'd missed him and Doug hadn't thought to leave a note. Just as he was about to shoot off an email, the doorbell rang.

Nigel ran for the door and swung it open. "There you are, you old—"

"Expecting someone else, I hope," Carmen said with a smile. She was wearing a red dress with a conservative neckline and matching boots. She held a picnic basket and a sack of groceries from the market a few blocks down from him. "Should I come back another time?"

He rubbed his hands together and then held out one palm to guide her in. "No, no, it's fine. I was just expecting a buddy of mine, but it looks like he's been held up. Are you on your way to a picnic? Sounds fun, except it's a little cold for that, I'd think."

"I hope it sounds fun. It's for you, after all. Come on." She went straight to the kitchen. He followed, helping as she unloaded her goods from the market bag. Three steaks of good cut were marinating in something. There were baking potatoes too, sour cream, butter, a pumpkin-smelling something in a tub, spinach, and red vinegar. At the bottom of the bag, in a baker's box, was a chocolate cake that looked so good Nigel wanted to dig right into it.

Carmen reached into the picnic basket and took out an apron before asking the location of his seasonings, pots, and pans. Nigel watched in amazement as she pulled out a tablecloth, two china settings, and a set of candlesticks in silver holders. The silverware came next, along with a poinsettia wrapped in plastic, which she took out and set in the middle of the table. She put a Peabo Bryson CD on the table. "This is for you. I remembered I borrowed yours and left it in a hotel somewhere."

Feeling relaxed all of a sudden, Nigel stretched and let out a yawn. "Yeah, you did. Left Peabo all up in the hotel. Seattle, I think. Give me that. I'm going to put it on right now." He went into the living room and turned on the CD, letting the sounds flow through him, allowing himself to really be grateful and content with everything that God had brought into his life—even Carmen.

All things are possible, but not all things are profitable.

He brushed the thought away, reminding himself to be careful. Still, he needed to relax, to talk . . . He sighed, knowing he was fooling himself. In truth, he liked to see the love in Carmen's eyes, to know that he was still worth loving. They'd have dinner and that'd be it. Nothing more. He'd make sure of that.

The smell of rosemary and the sizzle of meat drew him back to the kitchen. "Pan searing, huh? So maybe you don't ignore everything I say. Smells good. Looks good too."

Carmen's face lit up at his approval. "I remember everything you've taught me, Nigel. About cooking, about love, about life . . . even about God."

He'd wanted to stop her at the love thing, but she'd been talking too fast. He was definitely stumped on the God deal. What had he taught her about God but how to go against him? "I don't think I've been a very good mentor in the spiritual department, but my steaks are pretty good."

She punched his arm playfully before pulling the pan off the burner and turning it off. "You taught me that commitment means something, both to people and to God. I came here today to thank you for that. I came to thank both of you, actually. Even though you weren't sitting together in church this morning, I expected her to be here. Or for you to be there. I was just going to keep going until I found both of you."

Nigel stared at Carmen, trying to process what she'd said. He thought so hard he couldn't even hear Peabo singing. "Did you say 'church'? You were at New Man today?"

Carmen bent over to put the steak in with the potatoes. Nigel tried not to look but turned away a little too late.

Flee immorality.

Couldn't a guy just get some dinner and a little conversation? Did everything have to be something sexual? Probably not, but if he was honest, what else did he and Carmen really have between them? Would throwing her out really be showing the love of God though? What if this was some of the good things that had been in front of him all the time but he hadn't been able to see?

His shoulders slumped as he tried to reason it out; then an itch broke out on his hands. Nigel started scratching like crazy.

Carmen looked concerned. "Are you all right? What's wrong? You found some poison ivy somewhere? Hard to do in this city."

Nigel shook his head. "No poison ivy. I spent some time at the hospital this afternoon, and something there must be getting to me. I have sensitive skin—"

"I remember." She was rinsing the salad now and tossing in some grapes he'd had in his refrigerator.

This was definitely starting to look like a bad idea. "Yeah, well, something's itching me."

She sighed. "You're always supposed to take off your clothes and shower immediately after coming home from a hospital visit. Didn't anyone ever teach you that?"

"Can't say that I've heard it before. I don't go to hospitals much if I can help it." He'd also tried to avoid romantic dinners with old girlfriends while he was still married. Up until now, at least.

Carmen told him to step back while she ground a little pepper into the salad. "Look, go and get cleaned up. I'll be cooking anyway. And don't worry, I won't peek or jump in there with you or anything. It's not like that."

Nigel pressed his lips together. Firmly. He didn't want his

mouth to say something that his soul would regret. "Okay, I'm going to go clean up. If someone comes to the door, that's my friend Doug. Let him in and tell him I'll be out to razz him about being late in a minute."

"Are you sure? I just don't want to give anyone the wrong impression. We do have three steaks though." Carmen looked excited about the prospect of another guest.

Nigel prayed that Doug would show up, even though other thoughts were going through his mind too. He needed to get showered and through this meal and send Carmen home. Quick, before Nigel discovered just how human—and how sinful—he really was.

It was time and Jean knew it. From the moment she got home from church, she'd stayed in her room in prayer, trying to make sense of what was going on, trying to figure out what to do. All that kept coming to mind was what Lily had suggested, that Jean throw her heart at Nigel and pray that he catch it. And so she decided that she'd do just that. She'd spent hours making a vanilla cake before slipping back into her black velvet outfit and applying her makeup to perfection.

Elena had stayed out of the way, acting as though she didn't know what was going on, but Jean had heard her on the phone with Jay, asking him to pray that this would "do the trick." Jean wasn't sure what that meant, but she hoped it would change things too. After deciding on her jasmine perfume, she set out against the cold, against her fears, pointed in the direction of her husband. Her future.

On the train, however, every man seemed to think that she was on her way to him. They called to her in Spanish, Creole, French, and even some African dialects she'd never heard. Though the words weren't always clear to her, the body language filled in the blanks. It was like she'd always said: when you set your mind on a man, it's as if all the rest of them can smell it on you. It makes the rest of them want you too.

But she didn't want them. Not a one of them. Jean smiled and tried to be as polite as possible so that she could make it off each train without any trouble, but those men and their strange words were the farthest thing from her mind. She'd called the hospital and talked to Chenille earlier, just after Nigel had left. By the time she got to Nigel's, he and Doug should be back, if they'd even gone anywhere at all. She'd considered calling Lily to be sure, but she wanted to own this moment, to let it be hers. Her friends had done enough to help her get here; it was her turn to finish it once and for all. She'd even practiced getting on one knee. She'd done it easily and thanked God for all the lunges she'd performed over the past two years.

With the way things had been going, it had seemed impossible for Jean to think of her and Nigel together and happy. But she was finally able to look at their relationship with the eyes of faith—and forgiveness. Like an orange with a rotten spot, their love had gone bad in places, but it was nothing that God couldn't cut out to save the rest of the fruit. Nigel had said himself that God could use their weaknesses to make them strong. Now Jean knew it was true. Something in her wanted everything that God had for her. All of it, including her husband. On the way to Nigel's, Jean felt more sure than ever that Christ not only came to save her from hell but that he could save her marriage too. What she'd say to Nigel she wasn't sure, but whatever it was, he'd hear her. He'd have to.

If it weren't for the cake holder, she'd have climbed the stairs to Nigel's two at a time, but she didn't want all that work to fall on the ground. So she went slowly, thinking and rethinking her words, praying and praying again that he'd say yes and the coldness between them would end. Either way, he'd know how she felt, and right now that seemed more important than anything.

At the top of the landing, she squared her shoulders and walked to his door. She pressed hard on the bell, putting her weight behind it.

"Com-ing!" a woman's voice rang out. "Just a minute."

Jean stared at the house number first and then at the door. Was she at the right house? When the door opened a second later and she saw Carmen standing in Nigel's door in an apron and red boots, Jean knew she had the right house, just the wrong man.

Carmen looked surprised to see her but recovered quickly. "Jean! Do come in. Nigel is just getting cleaned up from his trip to the hospital. I stopped by hoping to find the two of you. I'm so glad you came. Do come in."

Was she insane? "I don't think so."

Nigel's guest looked scared. "No, really. He didn't invite me. It's nothing like that. I even have three steaks to prove it. Three place settings too. See?" She pushed back the door to give Jean a better view.

It wasn't the steak or the third place setting that caught Jean's attention but the two flickering candles and the soft music, Peabo Bryson from the sound of it. One of Nigel's favorites. And not just for dinner music either. Oh, and the cake. Double chocolate it looked like from here. Nigel loved that too. Jean wanted to run all the way home without stopping and stay there forever. "It's beautiful. You two have a good time. Please don't tell him that I was here." Her voice was trailing off, and she was trying to turn around, to get her bearings.

Carmen tried to reach for her, but she was already too far

away, moving toward the stairs. She shouted out the door anyway. "Wait! Please! I'll get him. It isn't what you think. Not anymore."

Jean was running now, taking the steps like a tiger. She was trying with everything in her to get away from those candles, that woman, that music. She was trying to get away from a truth that she hadn't been willing to face—Nigel was a good man, but he was still a man. No man could wait a lifetime for a woman to pull herself together, and her husband was obviously tired of trying. How could she blame him when he had a beautiful woman who loved him enough to chase him all over the country? That had to be enticing when your own wife couldn't make a bus ride upstate to visit you when you needed her.

It meant something to Jean too. There would be no second chances. Her failure was complete.

Lord, just help me to make it home.

A cold shower had done wonders for Nigel. He'd called Doug from his room and asked him to come over. Flex too. Stringing Carmen along wasn't right, and he knew it. There just wasn't really any way for them to be friends, at least not here, alone with Peabo playing and candles burning. He'd have to pay her for the groceries and her trouble, and rude as it might seem, ask her to leave. Even if Jean didn't want him, he wanted her, and he'd waited too long for her to give up now.

Dressed in a fresh jogging suit and running shoes that Reebok had given him, Nigel came into the kitchen, determined to say what he had to say without trying to be logical. Some things just required obedience. "Look, Carmen. I need to tell you something."

She turned to face him with red-rimmed eyes. "Me first. Jean was just here. She had this cake with—with meringue on it and that dress she wore to church this morning and jasmine perfume . . . I don't know what I'm doing here. I ruined everything again. I'm so sorry."

"Meringue?" He could hardly breathe. She'd made vanilla cake for him? And brought it way up here?

And I was in the shower.

He looked around at the scene: Carmen, the candles, the music . . . "I'll pay you for the food later, but I'm going to have to ask you to go now. I'm sorry too. For everything."

She nodded. "I know. I was planning to leave before you came out, but I wanted you to know what happened. She told me not to tell you she was here, but I had to. Everything's all messed up."

Tell me about it.

He was snatching on a parka now and going out the door. "Lock up when you leave, okay?"

Carmen nodded. "What are you going to do?"

Nigel shook his head. "I'm going to find her. After that, I have no idea."

20

He found her, but not in any place he wanted to go, not under the circumstances. The call had come from Chenille saying that Lyle had slipped into a coma. Could Nigel come, she'd asked in a small, detached voice like some operator trying to get a survey. With the same vigor and dread that had moved him through the cold, wet night look-ing for Jean, Nigel made it to the hospital. Along with the others—Flex, Raya, Jay, Lily, Doug, Elena, and what seemed to be the entire congregation and pastor of New Man Fellowship—Jean was there, staring straight ahead.

Nigel slipped into the seat next to her, not even attempting words. Language had once seemed so efficient, so provocative, allowing him to say all the things to people that he felt, that he thought. Now, though, the syllables seemed to dance around his head, with nothing suitable for the moment or the person coming to mind. Instead, he mustered the courage to look at his wife, taking his time and thanking God for ev-erything about her as he'd done in prison staring at her picture. Her picture in the black velvet, the same outfit she wore now. Or what was left of it. There was a rip at the hem, and a handful of loose threads poked out at her shoulder. She'd run hard to get away from him, away from them, and yet here they were together for all the wrong reasons.

Jean didn't move away from Nigel's glances, but she didn't return them either. She rocked forward and back on the waiting room chair, ignoring the creaking sound. The seat wasn't made for movement but for steady, still waiting, something Jean really had never known how to do. Nigel loved that about her. Even when the letters had stopped coming, he'd felt it—her restless longing for him. And his for her.

Chenille came out of a door a few feet away. She walked unsteadily and looked a bit dazed, but her smile, the infectious one that she and Lyle had in common, was fixed on her face. Red curls fell in damp ringlets around her shoulders, which shrugged upward and back down. "No change," she said softly, turning around slowly in every direction as though she wanted to make sure that everyone heard.

She's worried about us.

Nigel couldn't believe it, but it was true. Chenille wanted to get away, to go somewhere and scream, he could tell, but she felt an obligation to her friends, to her work family, to let them know what was going on.

His wife's touch, a feeling he longed for, warmed his wrist. When Jean didn't move closer to him, he leaned in to her.

She looked at him this time, taking one side of his face into her hand. "Go to her. She won't take any of us back there. Just go to her and hold her up, hold her hand. Don't let her come back out here. If there's news, you bring it. Good or bad, you come and tell us."

Nigel looked around at the crowd of people. "Me? Why

would she want me? Her pastor is here. And . . . and all of you. She doesn't really know me."

A weary, burdened smile came to Jean, one similar to the one Chenille had just worn. "God knows you. And somehow, Lyle knows you too. Even better than I do, I guess. He wanted you to be here for her, to be the man. So do it. Do what he would have done for me."

Nigel's jaw tightened as tears started to burn at the corners of his eyes. He wasn't the man, and he couldn't hold anybody up, not his wife or even himself. He wanted to run from the hospital the way Jean had run from his house, to get away from the dread pressing down on him. And then he thought of Lyle, with his crazy jokes and open heart. He thought of the guys who had fallen beside him in Vietnam and never gotten up, men whose last wishes had been for him to tell their wives and mothers that they loved them, that they had died as strong as they'd lived. That was what Lyle needed from him now, Nigel knew, and so he reached inside himself and found the soldier within, despite how out of place he felt in his mind.

He stood, and paced across the room, and held the door open for Chenille. On the other side of the door, a nurse moved toward them quickly, wanting to know who Nigel was.

"Family," he said, moving past the woman like a blur. "The family of God."

The nurse stopped pursuing them, and Chenille moved forward. Nigel could hear footsteps behind them. Nigel held his breath for a moment, thinking that someone had seen that he shouldn't be here, that he didn't belong. He exhaled at the sight of someone familiar, someone qualified to deal with all this—Chenille's pastor. The man stopped in a smaller waiting room. Nigel could hear him praying in Spanish.

239

Nigel could only form a few pleading words in his mind.
Have mercy. Have mercy. Have mercy.

His plea had come just in time, as nothing could have prepared him for the bloated, motionless body of his friend. Though the monitors still recorded life, without them, Nigel wouldn't have suspected it.

Chenille laced her hands in Nigel's. "Nigel's here, babe. He brought me back in here. I got a little wobbly out there. Confused. I know I've been asking you to fight for a long time, baby, but—" she stopped to wipe her eyes—"I know that I can't ask that of you anymore. You've been so good to me, giving me this time. And God too. So you go on and go to him, to Jesus. Kiss his face for me, and you take care of our little boy."

Lyle's eyelids blinked frantically and then went still again. Nigel strained through his tears to see the monitors. The red numbers blurred against his vision. Chenille squeezed his hand. He knew without looking at her that she was telling him to say something to her husband, but he didn't know how to find the words. He already felt as though he'd heard something he shouldn't, that he should go and leave them alone.

Tell him you'll take care of it.

Take care of what? Nigel wondered. The business? His own marriage? What? Still not sure, he opened his mouth and forced himself to speak. "It's me, Lyle. The man, as you call me. I just wanted to come back here and tell you that I'm going to take care of it." He paused as he began to think the phrase through. "All of it. The business, Chenille, things between me and Jean, the prayer group, everything. Okay? I've got it." He wanted to be as strong as Chenille and tell Lyle that he could go, but Nigel couldn't make himself say those words. He hadn't known this man long and he hadn't

240

known him well, but Nigel knew that Lyle was a man of God. A servant.

Chenille squeezed his hand again. Her grip was hard this time and steady. Nigel blew out a breath, knowing what she wanted him to say.

God, help me.

"So that's it, friend. I've got it and God's got me. You can go now."

And he did. The numbers on the monitors didn't go down gradually, they just stopped. Something beeped, but Nigel couldn't see where it was coming from. He was too focused on holding Chenille up as her legs gave out beneath her. Nigel was fixed on that and on Lyle's face. His brows relaxed, and his lips seemed to part as if he was saying something. His fingers relaxed, leaving his hands open. Something peaceful, joyful, wonderful, seemed to pass through him in the bed and through Nigel and Chenille looking on. He stared at the ceiling with a delighted look. Nigel followed his gaze, but saw nothing. He smiled, wondering what his friend was seeing now. Chenille clutched his hand. He put an arm around her shoulder and cried with her, both with joy that Lyle was no longer in pain, and sorrow that they'd lost his kindness, that his wife had lost the love of her life.

After what seemed like a long time, but was probably only a minute or two, the pastor joined them in the room. The man took a deep breath and turned to Nigel. "Take her out with the others please. She's been here a long time. He's gone to the Lord now. He's at peace."

Despite the truth of the pastor's words, Nigel couldn't help feeling their sting. He'd thought he lost Jean forever on more than one occasion, but there was always the hope that he'd find her again. This was different, wasn't it? Or was it? These two would find one another again as well, only not in this life.

From the grip Chenille had on his elbow, Nigel doubted that she would find much comfort in that knowledge right now.

Chenille was tugging on Nigel's jacket. When she turned toward him, he found her cheeks red, her eyes demanding. "Is he really gone?" she asked, looking at Nigel carefully as though she would believe whatever answer he provided.

He put his hand on hers, trying again to sort out the right words, to give her some comfort. "He's gone from that bed, from all the pain, but he's still alive . . . He's still with us. He always will be."

She nodded her head and collapsed into a chair near the waiting room door. Though she didn't ask, Nigel nodded. "I will tell them."

The door creaked open with a sound he hadn't remembered hearing earlier. The crowd of people, who'd all been buzzing in a low murmur as if scared to speak at normal volume, quieted. Nigel blew out a breath, thinking of the beauty of Lyle's passing. He'd told the man he would take care of it, and so he must. He thought of Lyle's smile and managed one of his own. "He's gone, everybody. He's gone."

She'd known it was coming. They all had. Lyle had joked about his impending death for months. So much, perhaps, that Jean had begun to think it really was a joke. After sitting through Lyle's funeral with Chenille, she knew it was real. As real as it gets. As real as the decision she had to make now, this minute, whether to stay or to go. Most of the senior staff were crowded into Jean's office to talk through what would happen in the company next. Nigel had his head down, scribbling notes, but several times during the morning, he'd given her a weary smile. Each time, she'd returned it.

Chenille, who should have been at home instead of the

office, reached out and took Jean's hands. "Whatever you decide, I want you to know that it's okay. Don't think about Lyle. Don't think about me. Just do what you think God wants you to do."

Jean didn't have to think hard. Thinking about others was what Jesus was all about. He hadn't had to come to earth and be hammered to a tree. No, he could have stayed in heaven, the place where he truly belonged, the place where he was purposed to be. Instead, he'd allowed himself to be out of place, to live with people who didn't understand him, to love people who didn't know how to love him back. Jean was one of those people. And she was tired of running out on people when they needed her. The jobs she'd been offered were all perfect for her, all places where her talents could have been used better, where her design style could have flourished. And yet her place was here.

"I'm staying," Jean said, daring to look across the room at Nigel, who'd been silent throughout the discussion.

He jerked forward at her response, then rested back in his chair. She watched as relief flooded through him. And then something more . . . love. They hadn't spoken about Carmen and her candlesticks and chocolate cake. Lyle's death had drowned out all the little questions and even some of the big ones.

Raya clapped her hands before slumping back in her chair in exhaustion. Chenille leaned back on the desk and closed her eyes.

"Okay," Chenille said. "So I guess that's it. We're all staying. That's the good news. Now there's a few announcements that aren't so great, but nothing we can't work around."

Everyone nodded. Most of them had been at the hospital the night when Lyle died and then at the wake and funeral afterward. They'd all done their share of crying, of trying to get

Chenille to take more than a week off, but now they were all willing and wanting to get moving again. To get to work.

Jean wasn't sure what she wanted to do. She was still calling Chenille's phone once a day to hear Lyle's voice on the answering machine. Some had suggested Chenille change it, but Jean was thankful she hadn't. The sound of his voice, the way his laughter trailed off the tape as though he'd been too tickled to hang up, it gave Jean an eerie comfort.

Some of the employees tensed at Chenille's comment. Their boss shook her head. "Gosh, you guys, lighten up, okay? No firings. How many times do I have to say it? That's not what I have to tell you at all. Just some changes of plans for a few of us." She turned to Jean. "First off, you did a really great job in cutting out Megan's wedding dress. I guess she was too scared to bother you the way she did the rest of us, so she came in yesterday for a fitting with me."

Jean didn't like where this was going. "And?"

Chenille moved from the desk where she'd been talking to Jean about her decision, and slipped back into her office chair. "Believe it or not—and Raya, I know you'll believe it—she doesn't want the dress."

A pencil sailed across the room and into the trash can. It was the coloring book guy who'd been at the church with the children. Jean had remembered his name then, but now she couldn't think of it for anything. She agreed with his sentiment, though.

"She's totally out of her mind, you do realize this, don't you?" someone else asked.

Chenille laughed. "Well, I'd usually be inclined to agree, only when she put it on, it didn't look right to me either. It fit and everything, but it just didn't look the way it had before. I don't know if she's changed or I'm just out of it or what, but when she said she didn't want it, I really wasn't surprised."

Jean was surprised. Though she hadn't thought she would like anything that a young socialite would wear, while cutting out the dress and looking over the design sketches again, she'd fallen in love with its simplicity. It was more like an evening gown in some ways, which made Jean think she would hate it, but there was still something bigger about it, something bridal.

If I'd known she was going to pull this, I might have kept that thing for myself.

The thought both shocked Jean and surprised her. She'd been married in a dress from a thrift shop, along with a hundred other army brides who'd joined in the group ceremony. She'd never given too much thought to not having had a beautiful gown or diamond ring, but their lack of honeymoon still haunted her.

She smiled across the room at Nigel. Maybe it wasn't too late for that too. She swallowed hard, trying to listen to what else Chenille had to say. Planning Elena's party on such short notice had started her losing her mind, and now losing Lyle like this had loosened up the rest of it.

At the thought of Elena's party, Jean sat straight up in her chair. The guests. Most of the initial hundred she'd invited had declined, but she hadn't told her church friends, her neighbors, and the Garments of Praise staff that the party was canceled. And the food. Had she canceled the caterer? The cake . . . She felt herself start to slide down into her chair like a limp piece of spaghetti.

It was Nigel who pulled her up. "Are you okay?"

She started to tell him that she wasn't, that she needed to get to the phone before their mess got messier, but she decided against it. "I'm okay. Just tired. So sorry, everybody. Go ahead, Chenille."

Chenille gave her a funny look. "You sure? You're acting

the way I should be acting if I had any sense. Nigel, you feeling all right over there? She's acting like her husband is dead."

The room went silent. No talking. No rustling of papers. This happened at least once a day now, one of these comments that cut them all to the bone, especially Jean. Chenille meant to be funny, the way Lyle had always been, but that type of humor didn't come to her easily. It just left them all feeling guilty, feeling sad. This time was no exception.

Like a basketball player diving for a rebound, Nigel started to laugh, draining some of the irony from Chenille's words. "I'm feeling fine over here, Chenille, but if it'll make you feel better, I'm pretty good at that chair-sliding thing too." Sporadic laughter hiccuped around the room. "Just so you know, though, you don't have to make us laugh. You don't have to be him, to fill his space. Just be you. It's okay to be sad."

Chenille lowered her head, then curled in to herself. A fit of sobbing racked her body. A woman from accounting reached out and grabbed her hand. Several others came to her side, as a murmur of support flowed through the room.

After a moment, Chenille motioned for everyone to take their seats. She took a deep breath and gathered herself. "I may do that now and again. Let's move on. The wedding dress, right? I'm okay. Really."

No one responded, so Chenille shuffled through her notes. "Okay, here it is. Megan paid for the dress, but she wants to start over—"

A collective groan went around the conference table. Raya began to laugh hysterically for a few seconds, then put her head down on the table.

Nigel shrugged his shoulders. "This wedding dress thing is really a sore spot with you people, isn't it?"

"Oh yeah," Raya said, without lifting her head. "A big-time sore spot."

Chenille waved her arms. "Listen up before you freak out, everyone. I'm still going to take off in January the way I'd planned. I'll be going through Lyle's things over the holiday—" She paused and put a hand to her face.

Jean reached for Chenille, but her boss shrugged away her touch. She sniffed in deeply. "Then after Christmas, I'm going to design Megan's dress, at home. She and I together."

Raya sat up straight. "You're kidding, right? Chenille . . . you can't do this now."

Chenille laughed. "Neither can you. No, it will be good for me. I can think about weddings, about love. I'm still in love with him. I always will be."

Nigel's eyes met Jean's. They held each other with their eyes, saying more in that moment than they had in the last several days. Someone produced a box of Kleenex and started passing it. Jean pulled some out as the box came by and then took a few extra. For later.

"So that's that about the dress. The other thing is that Reebok isn't too happy about Nigel staying on with us after this project is complete. In fact, they're a bit angry. You guys are all so good I have to fight for you, see? Anyway, they're trying to cite some clauses in his contract with them as to why he needs to stay on with them. I have our lawyer going over the contract now, and we'll see what happens. Just be praying. That's all, really."

That's all? That's ALL?

Nigel didn't look surprised by anything Chenille had said, so he'd obviously known about it and hadn't thought to share any of it with her. Not that they'd shared much of anything besides holding hands at the funeral or a bit of chitchat in the conference room about the kids and the weather. Though she'd gone to his house that night to throw her heart and let him catch it, like Lily said, Jean still hadn't moved from her corner. He didn't know much more about how she felt about things, and she wasn't sure now what might happen in the next few weeks. She'd wrestled with her decision to stay, but now would he be going? It didn't seem possible.

He's still here now.

It was true. Her husband was here, alive and well. Lyle had been the love of Chenille's life, a good and godly man. Now he was gone. And yet Jean's husband was here, separated from her by only a few chairs.

As the meeting broke up, Jean grabbed a piece of scratch paper from the table and scribbled a note on the back of it. She didn't know what would happen or if he'd even accept, but it was what she wanted now, what she needed.

With people filing past them, she reached Nigel and forced the paper into his hand, thinking over the contents in her mind as she walked away.

Come home to me. Eight o'clock.

21

She didn't make vanilla cake. She didn't make the food at all. After the meeting, she'd called one of their neighbors and asked her to use her emergency key and go into Jean's kitchen and cook some dinner. "Nigel is coming over," she said, and no other explanation had been needed. With the rest of her time, she'd gone to Flex's new gym for a much-needed workout and some time in the sauna, praying over what to do and where to go.

Go home and love your husband.

Be made whole.

"Yes," Jean whispered into the steam, thankful that she was the only person in the room. "I'm willing. Heal me, Jesus. Give me something to give. Help me so I can let him love me."

When she got home, he was already there, talking with Jean's neighbor, who was furiously setting the table.

"You're early!" Jean tried to run upstairs to put on her makeup, to put on the dress she'd planned to wear, but he caught her and kissed her sweetly.

"Do you think I could wait? I've been here for hours. You look beautiful. Sit down."

Jean wiped her eyes. This wasn't how it was supposed to be. She was supposed to sweep him off his feet, to do something special for him, not the other way around. As her neighbor slipped out the door with a wink and a knowing smile, Jean remembered what she'd prayed for in the sauna, that she'd be able to accept love as well as give it.

Though there were no candles on the table or romantic music playing, Jean's prayers were more than answered. They'd eaten a fraction of the feast the woman had cooked before retiring to the couch. Jean had scrambled to find a movie for them to watch on TV, but Nigel turned it off.

"I just want to look at you," he said. "Talk to you. I want to be with you like this is the last day of both of our lives. Like tomorrow might not come. I want you to tell me everything. To show me." He took her fingers to his lips and kissed them one by one. Then he opened her hand and kissed her palm.

She fought back her tears at first, but finally let them flow, pressing her hand against his. They lay on the couch that way for hours, talking and listening, touching and hoping.

Nigel kissed the space between her eyebrows and traced a path with his finger along the inside of her arm. "I'm sorry that I never asked you for your story. About the war, I mean. So many things had happened that I think I needed to know that I hadn't had some kind of nightmare. I needed to hear those guys say that they saw it too."

Jean kissed his ear and pressed her face to his cheek. They'd talked around the war but never really about it. It had brought them together in one way and torn them apart in another. "I think I was the opposite. I knew it was real. It had to be. I think I wanted to forget it, even though I knew I couldn't.

You were forgetting it, but you wanted to remember." She pulled back and rested her head on the cushion.

Nigel propped himself up on one elbow. In the dim light from the kitchen, Jean could see his stunned expression as though she'd told a secret he hadn't known he was keeping. He held a fist to his mouth, then moved it away. "That's exactly right. It was the way people feel when somebody dies and they begin to forget what the person looked like, how their voice sounded. It's like you owe them to remember." He scratched his ear. "I felt like that. I guess I still do. The thing is, I forgot what I owed you, what I owed God—to keep living, to keep loving. To be whole again even though my world had been riddled with bullets."

Jean nodded, and their long night began, the night of her story, one she'd thought long forgotten and folded away. But as she spoke, the story unfolded and shook itself out, draping over the corners of Jean's mind. Her life in Vietnam before she met him came first: her deployment, the different hospitals she worked, the things she'd heard and seen.

She told him about the nights when she was one of the only women in a jungle full of maimed and homesick boys. Nights when what had been respect became desire. Times when things were taken without asking, things above the call of duty. Nights when Jean had stopped believing in God. "When you came through, I was in the process of giving up on men as well. Something in you, about you, gave me hope. Made me want to believe that somehow we'd get through."

Nigel's arms pressed tight against Jean as she told her story, sometimes so tight that she knew he was holding himself as well. Other times, his arms went slack and he buried his face in her shoulder. When she went silent, he prodded her on with kisses and back rubs. And so she went on, somehow finding the words to explain how she'd summoned the courage to love Nigel, to believe in him. She and Doug hadn't loved each other exactly, but they'd understood each other. The choice had been safe.

But when she'd seen Nigel there on that table, bleeding and smiling and calling her Peach in the middle of a mess of death, she'd decided to do something crazy and let him try and save her with his love.

"I failed at that, of course." He had his hands in her hair now.

She put her hands in his. "You had to fail. You couldn't save me. Only Christ could do that. Only he could make me whole. I know that now. We both do."

The room was finally silent as though there was nothing more to be said. A million things ran through Jean's mind, like if Elena took everything she needed to spend the night at Chenille's, or why she still hadn't checked to be sure that she'd canceled the caterer. And had she called the church?

Her husband silenced her questions, pressing his lips against hers. Jean opened her lips to him, her heart to him. Just as she thought she'd be lost in the moment forever, Nigel stopped and pulled her onto his chest. "When I left here the last time, I asked you something—"

Jean pressed a finger to his mouth. "And when I left your house last time, I'd come to ask you something." She pulled her hand away.

Nigel closed his eyes. "I'm listening." His voice sounded strangled.

Hers did too, but that didn't stop her. "Will you marry me?"

"In a heartbeat," Nigel said, scooping her into his arms and heading for the stairs.

Jean punched at his chest, laughing into his shirt. "So it's like that, huh? I propose to you, and you carry me off to bed?"

He kissed her nose. "What can I say? It's honeymoon practice."

When Jean woke up, she felt a second of panic before opening her eyes. Had last night been a dream? Was Nigel gone? Still not quite awake, she reached out for him and smiled when her hands slid over his skin.

"I'm here," he said, kissing her fingers. "I'm here, watching you sleep."

That got Jean's eyes open. Was he crazy? She reached behind her for the pillow and bopped him on the head with it. "Don't do that! I might drool or something."

He laughed. "You did. Just like a puppy. It was really cute."

Jean sighed, but she was smiling too as the night rushed back to her, its love even sweeter than the last time. "You'd better be glad you're cute, or you might be outside with somebody's puppy."

Nigel didn't laugh at that. Like Chenille's death jokes, the humor of being closed off from Jean must not have been funny to him. "You do remember what you asked me last night, don't you? Not that it matters, really. I guess we're married already, but you know what I mean."

She did, and gave him a kiss of her own to prove it. "I do remember. I remember everything about last night."

"You and me both," Nigel said, lacing his fingers under his head. "I woke up and thought I'd dreamed that I was a kid again and we were back in that first apartment. Before Monica. We were crazy then."

Jean took a deep breath. She remembered it well. "Um,

253

yeah. I think that's how we got Monica, if I recall. Now we're old and—"

"Hey, now, speak for yourself. I was twenty-five last night. At the most."

Twenty-three. Easy.

She shook her head as Nigel took her into his arms. "Yeah, well, I think I was twenty-eight last night, but it's wearing off. I'm rapidly approaching the fifties. Especially my back."

Nigel snorted. "Me too. Got any Advil?"

They both collapsed in laughter and picked numbers to see who would go downstairs to start breakfast. Nigel lost but took his time about leaving Jean. "It's weird, though. I do feel young again when I'm with you. Maybe just because you knew me then, and not many people I hang out with now have known me that long. Except Doug, of course."

Jean agreed and watched him wrap up in her floral robe to go downstairs. After she was finished laughing at that, she tried not to think about how long or how well Carmen had known him. None of that mattered now. It couldn't.

Still, I'm going to have to get some of those candlesticks. Gold though. And that CD too . . .

She heard a happy but disgusted scream and a fit of laughter downstairs and knew that Elena had come home. Jean grimaced, imagining what Nigel must have looked like in front of the stove in her robe. She held her sore stomach with one hand and wiped her tears with the other. She'd missed this, the funny but embarrassing moments. The silly good times.

Nigel was laughing too and coming back upstairs from the sound of it. "Hey, quit laughing, little girl, or you can forget about breakfast. I mean it, now."

Jean could hear Elena laughing harder.

"It's a good thing I spent the night over at Auntie Chenille's, huh? I probably should have stayed over there. You guys

254

are scaring me. How long are you staying this time anyway, Grandpa?"

Nigel was back upstairs now and heading for the bed. He dived in headfirst, then shouted back downstairs. "I'm staying as long as your grandmother is comfortable with me being here. Through the holidays at least, I guess."

Jean lay there, smelling him, listening to the rumble of his voice. Would she ever get used to him being here, being a part of her life again? She never wanted to take their relationship for granted again. She hoped that every day she'd remind herself how much they had lost and how much God had restored. She hoped she wouldn't forget the things they'd talked about last night and all the other nights before that. She pinched his elbow. "You stay as long as you want. I know that there's still the possibility that you may have to go, so any time you can be here is great."

He rolled onto his stomach and stared at the headboard. "I'm hoping we can work all that out, but you're right. We'll just take it as it comes. It's a shame we canceled the church service and Elena's party and everything. We probably could have renewed our vows right then, after her ceremony."

Jean slapped her leg. "About that—"

"Hey, I'm coming up, old naked people. My eyes are covered, don't worry." Elena paused at the top of the stairs with both hands over her eyes. "And in case you're thinking about it, Grandma, don't throw anything at me."

"There aren't any old people in here, little girl, but if you know what's good for you, you'll stay out until we invite you in. Your grandmother is balling up things to throw at you." Nigel laughed as Jean put down the sock she was wadding into a ball.

"Okay, okay. I'll stay out here. I just came up to tell you to call Auntie Chenille. I was going to stay and look at wedding dresses with her, but I needed to come home for some clothes. She said that you two had some big thing with Reebok at your job this morning. I told her it was Saturday, but—"

"Oh no! The meeting. We forgot about the presentation." Nigel sat up straight, ignoring the protests of his back, still strained from last night's wed-in-bed sleepover. While fumbling for his clothes, he heard Jean yelling for Elena to get her some things from the dryer and to call Chenille and tell her they were on their way. While Jean scraped hangers across her closet's clothes rod, Nigel managed a quick shower and a change.

When he emerged, Jean just about dived into the bathroom, only to come out twelve minutes later looking amazing. How she did that, he wasn't sure, but on days like this Nigel was thankful for it.

Jean came out with a bottle of pain reliever. "Our granddaughter called us old, but she'd have thought different if she saw us last night." She kissed him tenderly on the mouth. Nigel took a deep breath, drinking in the scent of her perfume. He'd made love to his wife the night before like a man in his twenties, but this morning all his muscles shouted his real age. By the way Jean was counting out pain relievers, he wasn't alone.

"Have some," she said, handing two capsules to Nigel. "We've got thirty minutes to make that meeting and we might have to run for the train, a cab, everything."

Nigel took the pills from her and pulled her close. His body may have been protesting this morning, but he didn't regret one minute of last night. He hoped he would be able to say the same for today as well. "Give me some water and let's go. We'll make it."

He wasn't sure if he meant the meeting or their marriage, but either way, he meant every word.

22

They didn't make it on time, but Flex and Jay had been at the office with Raya and saved the day by unlocking the doors and welcoming everyone in. They made quick apologies and then pulled out the mannequins with the suggested changes from the first showing.

Everyone seemed impressed, including Carmen, whom Jean tried very hard to ignore, despite how the woman was smiling at her.

Maybe later, Lord, but let me focus on this now. One thing at a time.

Nigel looked as though he was thinking the same thing, only about Jean instead of their work. Though things had been jovial at the house, here in the conference room, the grief that had surrounded them for the past two weeks clouded them again. Jean's thoughts strayed to Lyle, and she wondered if they shouldn't put up a picture of him somewhere, so that they'd always remember. The end of Nigel's presentation cut through her thoughts, and after a moment's pause, she added a few comments of her own.

When they were done, the team leader, a man named Frank, gave his appraisal. "It's brilliant. Now that we got the right pieces together, anyway. Those elbow patches for the Mavericks are right on. And that argyle inset is sweet. You had all the right ingredients, but it was like you were afraid to put them where they belonged."

Tell me about it. Jean took Nigel's hand.

"We're really pleased with how things came out, though we came prepared to draw some lines this morning on letting you come to work here. We'd hoped to retain both of you to work on this for us, if possible, but there seems to be something about this little warehouse that keeps people around."

Nigel nodded. "You could say that."

They spent a few hours more talking over marketing strategies and product placement, but Jean had been in enough meetings to know that it was a sure sale. With her heart in her throat, she went for the brass ring. "Frank, it's been great working on these designs. We really think that this is going to go big. And because of that, we'd both like to stay on the project—"

"What she means is—" Nigel's eyes widened. He tried to focus on relaxing his face, his mind . . .

"What I mean is that we at Garments of Praise would like to produce these coordinates as well. Instead of trying to contract this out, just let us do the whole thing."

Frank looked skeptical, but he didn't shoot the idea down. Instead, he huddled with his team. He waved Carmen over too. Then, he asked Jean and Nigel to step outside.

Both of them smiled until they were on the other side of the door, and Nigel erupted. "What was that? You totally blindsided me. It was a great idea, true enough, but I didn't know where you were going."

Jean wrapped her arms around his waist. "You're just mad that you didn't think of it."

Nigel shrugged. "Basically, but still, you can give a guy some warning. I was about to start tap dancing to cut you off."

Raised voices echoed from the other side of the door. Jean rocked up on her toes, leaning toward the door in a feeble attempt to make out any of the words. It was no use, and she wasn't sure she wanted to hear anyway. Asking to manufacture the suits was something that had jumped into her mind at the last minute. With Lyle passing and Chenille talking about making Megan another dress, she wasn't sure if they could pull off that kind of production here. They were contracting out a lot of their things too. Still, it seemed like the right thing at the time.

Just like being with Nigel was the right thing. Right now and forever. She inspected his tie. "You couldn't have tap danced in there if you'd wanted to, mister. That Advil only lasts so long. After last night and that run for the train, we'll both need a week of sleep to recover."

Nigel doubled over in laughter and coughed a few times. He hadn't mentioned Carmen at all, and Jean was glad of it. He reached out and mussed Jean's hair a little. "Don't be so fresh, Miss Twenty-eight-Year-Old. I don't think you'll be two-stepping any time soon yourself. I don't know about you, but regardless of what they decide, I'm taking a nap when we get back home."

"A nap. That sounds innocent. Elena is probably still there, you know."

He shook his head. "You really must be twenty-eight. Or crazy. I mean a real nap. On the pullout. By myself. I love you and all, but my back is killing me," he whispered as the door opened and they were ushered back into the room.

Frank tugged at his lapels. "We really don't think this is the ideal site for manufacture, but we're willing to work with the owner here to expand the facility and bring in some new people with experience making these types of pieces. We do feel that it'd be best to keep both of you involved in the process with this collection and many more to come."

Nigel pumped his arm in the air, but Jean stood quiet for a moment, trying to process what she'd heard. It sounded like she'd come out of this with everything she could have dreamed of. "So, can Mr. Salvador stay on with us?"

Frank nodded. "Yes. Carmen told us a little of the history between the two of you, and we agree that you need to stay together. Not to mention that it's a great publicity story as well. So, yes, he's staying, even though we hate to lose him."

Jean looked over at Carmen, who was still smiling. The woman lowered her eyes and gave Jean a little salute. In her eyes, Jean had seen regret. She recognized it easily, after seeing it enough times staring back at her from the mirror.

She could feel Nigel's hand gripping her shoulder, and she knew that he was praying. Jean paused to give her own prayer of thanks and added one of forgiveness regarding Carmen. She too needed to be made whole. As the two women's eyes met, Jean knew that God was working things out in both of them.

Nigel shook Frank's hand as the Reebok team exited. As soon as Frank walked out, Nigel ran down the hall to tell Flex and Raya. With shaking hands, Jean called Chenille and told her the good news. Chenille couldn't speak, but Jean held the phone anyway, listening to her friend cry. She'd heard it a lot lately, that sound. But this time, it sounded to Jean like Lyle's laughter on the answering machine. Painfully beautiful.

When Jean got out her planning lists to see what was left of her reservations, she sighed. A few of the places had offered her deposit back, but none seemed available on the day she wanted. It was too late and she knew it, but God sometimes made a way for things to happen. Jean hoped this was one of those times. She had the papers spread out across Lily's floor and didn't know where to start.

"The only place still available is the church. I'd reserved that for the blessing part of Elena's ceremony. I was really looking forward to that, to seeing a new promise, a new blessing. Oh well. I'll call them again and try to cancel."

Lily sat Indian style on the carpet beside her, spooning chocolate sauce and strawberries into her mouth. "Why cancel? Weren't you and Nigel going to renew your vows anyway? Just call everybody from work and tell them the changes and take it from there."

Jean stared at her friend. "I used to be the smart one who came up with stuff like that. When'd you go and get all diva like this? And get me some of those strawberries, please. You know I want some."

"You've got a man now. That fresh love addles your brain for a while. And as for the strawberries, I haven't seen you eat chocolate in two years. How was I supposed to know?"

"You just said yourself that I'm in love. That automatically means chocolate. You're a wedding planner, you should know these things."

Lily stuck her spoon in the air and left her mouth hanging open. "Oh no, don't even think about it. I'll be doing good if I can show up to the thing. Besides, you don't need anything planned. You already have everything done. Look at all this madness." She motioned to the stacks of paper littering the floor.

"I don't have a dress though. That's where I need your help, Vera," Jean batted her eyes.

On her feet now, Lily laughed. "No Vera Wang here, honey. I'm totally not going for this bait no matter how you try and pull me in. This one's easy anyway. Use Megan's dress. She left it there. It's just hanging there, and you two are about the same size now."

Jean jumped up and slipped on some of her guest list. "Did I say diva? You're a genius, girl. I'll have to ask Chenille about it, though. You don't think she'll tell, do you? I was thinking of trying to surprise him."

Lily paused, then shook her head. "No, not for something this big. It'll be hard, but she'll hold it. We're the last thing on her mind these days. I don't think you have to worry about ruining the surprise."

Doug padded through the kitchen and to the refrigerator. "As loud as you two are talking, good luck with surprising anybody." He craned his neck over at Lily. "Is that chocolate? And strawberries? Maybe you should surprise Nigel, Jean. At home. My wife is eating love food without me." He moved his eyebrows up and down.

Jean shook her head side to side. "I give up. All married people are goofy. Myself included. It's just part of the package. But I get the message. I'm going."

Doug shook his head. "Ha. Stay. I'm totally all talk and she knows it. I'm going to bed. Good to see you. Tell that man of yours we're looking for him at prayer meeting in the New Year. We'll give him a few weeks off for this little romance phase you two are going through."

Jean tapped her papers against the edge of the table and slipped them back into her folder. "That phase you're talking about seems to be still going pretty strong over here too, Mr. LaCroix, but I'll pass the message along to my husband." She packed up her things and grabbed her coat as Doug disappeared down the hall.

The night nurse for Lily's mother came out for a drink of water and waved to Jean, who waved back but didn't initiate their usual Spanish small talk. Despite Doug saying he was kidding, she knew better and turned to Lily to confirm it. "He's in there fuming, isn't he?"

Lily nodded, grabbing a quart of strawberries from the refrigerator. "Not fuming, exactly. More like waiting purposefully. The furniture will probably be rearranged if I don't get in there soon."

Jean started for the door, knowing how hard it was for the two of them to agree on furniture placement. They'd had arguments about their nightstand that she couldn't even comprehend. "I'd better get out of here, then. That furniture thing is dangerous."

"Don't I know it," Lily said, tugging the scrunchie out of her hair and heading down the hall. "Hate to run you off, but you understand. Lock up on your way out. Come back anytime."

I think I've been doing quite enough of that.

Jean pulled out her phone to retrieve the code to Lily's alarm as she stepped outside. It wasn't a hard one or anything; she was just so frazzled lately that she couldn't think. When she flipped the phone open, she remembered that she'd turned it to vibrate a few hours before. She found the code and entered it, then checked her voicemail. Three messages, the first one from her home line.

She smiled and curled the phone to her face, thinking about what kind of silly message Nigel had probably left. When she pressed the button, though, it was Elena's voice that she heard, and what she said cut Jean in two.

"*Abuela*? This is Elena. You need to come home. Some guys came here for me again, writing something bad on the door. I tried to tell Grandpa to wait for the police, but he went out there. There was a big fight and he tried to break it up. I think he's hurt."

With the same strength Jean had used to run from her husband before, she ran to him now, leaving a trail of fluttering paper behind her.

"You're going to need a lot more than Advil for that," Jean said, leaning over the rail of Nigel's hospital bed to kiss the spot on his face that wasn't swollen.

"I guess so, huh?" His smile faded to a frown. "Sorry they had to call you. I'm okay, really."

The doctor came in and said that things looked worse than they were and that perhaps Nigel might want to be a little less gallant. Jean definitely agreed.

Nigel wasn't so sure. "I'm banged up, I'll admit, but I got a chance to talk to some of those kids. I even prayed with a couple of 'em after the fight. I don't think they'll be back, except for Elena's party. I invited them."

Jean put a hand to her head in response to a sudden headache. "You're kidding, right? We canceled Elena's party, remember? And even if we didn't, why would you invite a bunch of people who wanted to say bad things about our granddaughter into my—our house?"

The doctor tiptoed to the door.

"So I can keep an eye on them, I guess. They're still kids, Jean. Stupid, but kids just the same. Some of them shouldn't have even been there. You could just tell. The real bad ones were taken to jail anyway." He sat up a little and read the discharge papers that the doctor had left on the table. "And for the birthday party. I didn't mean that big shindig thing, just something at the house on the day. You still do that, right? Dinner on the day."

She did still do that, but she hadn't been planning to do it this time. This Christmas Eve they were supposed to be renewing their vows and eating a big cake, not making beans and rice for a bunch of thugs. But did it really matter? An hour ago, she'd thought Nigel might have been badly hurt or worse. It's times like those that lend a lot of perspective on things.

So instead of having her big, fancy, surprise ceremony, she told Nigel what she'd planned to do and how she would have wanted it to be. "But we can always do that later. Being with you is what matters. We'll just do something nice for the kids in the neighborhood."

Elena, who'd been asleep in a chair at the back of the room, or so they believed, lifted her head. "I say we do both: something for you, something for me. A party's a party, right?"

Nigel forced his bruised face to smile. "Right, little girl. I knew you'd come in handy."

23

Everything fell into place. The swelling on Nigel's face even went down totally by the next weekend, leaving him looking as handsome as ever. Chenille talked to Megan about the dress, and she was more than happy to let Jean have it. The caterers didn't mind about coming to an apartment as long as they got paid. And so there were two parties: one for Elena at Jean's apartment and one for the couple at Nigel's apartment.

Not wanting a traditional wedding dress, Jean opted for a tea-length Vera Wang dress in a shade somwhere between salmon and sun-kissed orange. Raya and Lily spent most of the night adding silk roses to the skirt and sequins down the back. Raya loaned Jean a pair of shoes from her grandmother's just-in-case bridal collection. Peach roses and white orchids made a simple bouquet and a statement of quiet elegance in the room. Nigel wore a black Lauren tuxedo . . . and a pair of cowboy boots. They both looked regal and anything but regular.

The "old people's party," as Elena referred to it, was to take place in the afternoon, with the teen gathering at night. Everything had gone smoothly until Jean started across Nigel's living room in front of all their friends.

In front of Nigel.

Though she desperately tried not to, she started to cry. Lily and Raya had done the last-minute decorating, stringing beads and flowers on the walls and chairs and hanging Asian lanterns overhead. Tangerines and baby's breath filled glass bowls all over the room. It seemed too beautiful, especially when she saw Nigel's Jesse tree on the ground at his feet, each branch covered with something from their life: Jean's dog tags, Elena's baby picture, the piece of baby blanket from Nigel's grandmother, scraps of letters and Christmas cards that he'd kept. Jean tried to keep walking, but her crying made it nearly impossible.

The pastor from New Man Fellowship, who'd agreed the morning before to do the ceremony, motioned for Jean to come. "Now, you two have been crying for long enough. I know they're tears of joy, but get on up here and let us pray for you."

Lily got up from her seat and helped Jean to her place beside Nigel, who wore the winter white wool suit Jean had saved for him. Jean's hand shook as her husband reached out and took it. They stood still as the pastor talked about marriage, what it meant and how much it could cost at times, how sweet its rewards could be. Minutes later, when their friends and co-workers stretched their hands out toward them in prayer, Jean found herself crying again, remembering that generous fall morning when God had kissed her on the mouth.

Lord, you had this planned all along.

They lit a unity candle next. After that, Nigel leaned over

and kissed Jean's hair, despite the flowers and veil pinned to it.

The pastor shook his head. "You have to watch these renewing folks. They get ahead of you. Let me hurry and let him kiss this woman."

Everyone laughed, including Jean and Nigel.

"Before I close, though, Brother has some things he'd like to say."

Jean looked around. What was this now? As Nigel took her hands, she didn't know what to think.

"Don't be scared, babe. I just wanted to say some things to you, things I've been thinking for the past few weeks. For years, I prayed to get you back, my wife, the woman I married. Instead, I got something better, God's woman, the fresh fruit of a new tree. Someone gentler, sweeter, and if possible, even more beautiful." He choked up but started again. "Someone whole."

He kissed her fingers one by one, and when he got to Jean's ring finger, he slipped a round, sparkling diamond ring on her finger. Jean gasped, but he kept going. "You've always been my peach, bruised and thin-skinned but always sweet. While I've been gone, God took that and grew something else. Someone else. The sweet and juicy is still in there, and I think I've figured out how to peel back the skin."

The pastor held up both hands. "Keep the skin on, brother. At least until we're done."

Nigel nodded. "I am done."

"And what about you? Are you going to call him some kind of tree? This is getting real deep and biblical. I might have to preach if you don't watch it."

Jean smiled and kissed the top of Nigel's hand. "What I have to say is neither deep nor scriptural. I love you, Nigel Salvador. I always will. I'm so thankful that the Lord brought you back to me, and I'm looking forward to practicing for our honeymoon."

Everyone clapped as the preacher directed them to kiss and wiped his brow when they did. "These two were feisty, weren't they? I didn't think they were going to make it to the end."

Neither did I. Jean smiled, silently thanking God for the grace that brought them there.

As their friends approached, Nigel held on to Jean, whispering in her ear. "I don't know why you waited for me, but I'm really glad you did."

Jean rubbed his back. "Once you've had real love, nothing else will do."

Nigel relaxed his grip and reached out to shake Doug's hand, leaning back and whispering in Jean's ear one last time. "Meet you on the practice field after the party."

Jean smiled. "Midnight. See you there."

Acknowledgments

Each book I write is a journey, and trips are no fun without friends (especially creative, hardworking ones). So I'd like to thank everyone who keeps buckling up and hitting the road to New York City with me: Jennifer Leep, my editor, thank you for your patience and understanding throughout this series. You're a blessing to work with. Barb Barnes, Kelley Meyne, and everyone on the copyediting/proofreading team, God bless you! Thanks for all your hard work. Karen Steele, Cat Hoort, Audrey Leach, and everyone in marketing, thanks for your hard work to promote this series and for answering all my questions and emails. Cheryl Van Andel and everyone in the art department, once again, you rock! Thank you for another beautiful cover. Erin Bartels and everyone in catalog and copy, thank you so much for making my books look and sound great. You guys are unbelievable. Lonnie Hull DuPont, thanks for just being you. You inspire me.

To my family: Fill, Ashlie, Michelle, Fill Jr., Ben, James, John, and Isaiah. Thank you for putting up with me while I played with men's suits and stacks of books. You all are a gift to me.

To my mother Donna McElrath, my cousin Mike Swain, my brother Mauice McElrath, and all the Freeman Clan and friends. You all are the best street team ever! Thanks so much for getting the word out in Atlanta and Dayton, Ohio, about every book I write.

To Linda Dwinell, Maureen Crystal, Joan Berault, Laura Arnold, and the Calvary Chapel Tallahassee family. Thanks for the tea party, the scrapbook, and the book signing. Thanks for understanding the times when I disappear for a while or show up looking dazed and confused.

To my writer friends: Claudia Mair Burney, Jennifer Keithley, Amy Wallace, and Staci Wilder. Thank you for always taking time to read this story, even on short notice. You all are the Threshing Floor indeed!

Lisa Samson, Claudia Mair Burney, Kendra Norman Bellamy, Norma Jarrett, Laura Jensen Walker, and Sharon Ewell Foster, thanks for giving me some great reads when I should have been writing.

Dr. Gail M. Hayes, thanks for reminding me that hot flashes are just "power surges"!

Barbara Joe Williams, thanks for putting up with me when I kept canceling on events because I was writing. Thanks for giving me a ride all over the country to promote these books.

To the owners of the Pescado's restaurant in Tallahassee, Florida, thanks for showing me what a *quinceañara* party looks like.

To Linda Mae Baldwin, Rachel Hauck, Pam Meyers, Peg Phifer, and Lisa Tuttle, my fellow board members of American Christian Fiction Writers. Thanks for putting up with me and my disappearances.

To bloggers and readers of the Rhythms of Grace community and folks on the Word Praize email list. Forgive my long silences. I hope this makes it up to you.

And last but never least, to He Who Keeps Me from Falling (and picks me up when I fall anyway). Jesus, whew. You did it again!

marilynn griffith
words with heart... and sole

Dear Reader,

Thanks so much for taking the time to enjoy Jean and Nigel's story. The writing of this book took me to many unexpected places in my heart as I listened and learned about the way incarceration affects families. I also had a chance to explore the depth and breadth of married love, even when stretched, strained, and abandoned. Taking this journey with an older couple was especially fun. I hope that you enjoyed this family's tale and will join me in praying for the thousands of children and families with a parent in the prison system. For more information on how to help, please visit Prison Fellowship Ministries (http://www.pfm.org). My family and I have participated in the Angel Tree program many times, and it is truly a blessing to families.

Again, thanks for reading and for all the emails you send about this series. My publisher and I appreciate it. See you next time for Chenille's story!

Blessings,

PS. Please email and let me know what you thought of the story at marilynngriffith@gmail.com. Thanks!

Marilynn

Discussion Questions

The questions below are intended to enhance your personal or group reading of this book. We hope you have enjoyed this story of strength in weakness, power in forgiveness, family, love, and faith.

1. Though Jean has no problems giving advice to Lily or other co-workers at Garments of Praise, she has a hard time receiving counsel from them.

   - Do you think this is a trap many friends fall into, especially if one is older than the other?
   - Did Jean grow in this area as the book went on? If so, how did receiving input from friends affect her life?

2. Jean lived a long time with a big secret—she had a husband that no one knew about. She probably kept her marriage to Nigel from her friends because she was ashamed about his having been in prison.

- Do you have a secret from your past or family that people you love don't know about? If so, what stops you from sharing? Fear or rejection? Pride?
- Pray and ask God how he might give you an opportunity to tell your story to someone.

3. Though Nigel has been out of Jean's life for many years, when he joins the Garments of Praise team it's like he's been there all along. Lyle feels immediately that this is the person God has sent to help his wife with her business in her absence. Yet Nigel himself isn't sure.

- Has this ever happened to you?
- Have you ever gone into a situation that you thought would be temporary only to find that God planned for it to be permanent? Or the other way around?
- Did you make the right choice?
- How has your life been changed as a result?

4. When the book opens, puppy love is brewing between Jean's granddaughter, Elena, and Raya and Flex's son, Jay. As the book goes on, however, both young people realize that relationships can take a lot of time and energy and, if not led by God, can actually be harmful at an early age. Though they both made wise decisions regarding dating, the adults had a very hard time with the situation.

- How would you have handled the growing attraction between the two teens?
- If you have raised children, how did you deal with this time in their lives?
- If you are a teen, do you agree with how the two young people worked things out?

5. Nigel and Jean had a long, complicated history together. They came together during wartime, and their relationship was characterized by dramatic high points and low points. It was only when both husband and wife sought Jesus for themselves that they were able to come together and try to make some of their ups and downs level off. Even then, it wasn't easy, but they were willing to allow God to heal them.

   • Do you have a relationship like this in your life?
   • Have you gone to God and asked him to make it whole? To make *you* whole? If so, what happened?

6. Each designer at Garments of Praise seems to have her own gift in a certain area. Jean's specialty is men's design, though she was afraid to return to it because she couldn't see how it was going to fit into her new life and work with God. She saw using her gift as a choice between returning to the wild world of high fashion and remaining with the friends, family, and God she'd grown to love. But God brought Jean an opportunity that let her use her gift and hold on to her faith and family.

   • Do you have a dream that seems impossible? Take a moment and write it down.
   • What can you do to cultivate this gift so that if God brings an unexpected opportunity you'll be ready to accept it?

Marilynn Griffith is a freelance writer who lives in Florida with her husband and seven children. When not chasing toddlers, helping with homework, or trying to find her husband a clean shirt, she writes novels and scribbles in her blog. She also speaks to women at conferences and prayer gatherings. To book speaking engagements or just say hello, drop her a note at marilynngriffith@gmail.com.

marilynn griffith

Shades of Style

jAde

Woven with humor, heartache, and hip friendships, the first two books of the Shades of Style series have a lot of colorful threads. Join Raya, Lily, Jean, and Chenille as they search for the pattern for success— in life and love!

...for a group of fresh, funky designers